the long home

william gay

ff

faber and faber

First published in the United Kingdom in 2002
by Faber and Faber Limited
3 Queen Square London WC1N 3AU

First published in the USA in 1999 by MacMurray & Beck

Printed in England by Clays Ltd, St Ives plc

A CIP record for this book is
available from the British Library

ISBN 0–571–21090–2

2 4 6 8 10 9 7 5 3 1

Like flies, the minute-winning days buzz home to death, and every moment is a window on all time.

—Thomas Wolfe, *Look Homeward, Angel* (1929)

Also when they shall be afraid of that which is high, and fears shall be in the way, and the almond tree shall flourish, and the grasshopper shall be a burden, and desire shall fail; because man goeth to his long home, and the mourners go about the streets.

—Ecclesiastes 12:5

by the same author

PROVINCES OF NIGHT

Acknowledgments

The author would like to acknowledge a debt to his editor, Greg Michalson, and to thank him for his skill and patience. He would also like to thank Renee Leonard for her help in the preparation of this manuscript.

This first novel is for my first daughter,
LEE GAY WARREN, in love and gratitude, and with
the knowledge that her belief never faltered.

Prologue: 1933

Thomas Hovington was walking across his backyard when he heard a sound that caused him to drop the bag of feed he was carrying and stand transfixed. It was a curious kind of sound that seemed to come from the bowels of the earth, from somewhere beneath his feet, a dull, muffled boom that he could feel in his teeth and hear rattle the glass in the unglazed windows behind him. While he stood motionless it came again, somewhere beneath the branch-run, like great round stones rolling down chambered corridors in the earth or some great internal storm flaring in the hollows of the world, lightning quaking unseen in sepulchres dark and sleek and damp, the surfaces of the earth trembling at the thunder's repercussions.

He went back to the edge of the porch and sat uncertainly and stared at the solid earth he'd taken so for granted. Hovington was in his twenties then and his back not yet bent. He had just recently commenced bootlegging and some vague childhood remnant of religion troubled him, made him look about for signs of retribution. It might be a sign. A warning.

If so, it wanted no misunderstanding. When it came this time it sounded as if a truckload of dynamite had exploded and almost immediately the branch began to rise and the air filled with water and flying stones. "They Goddamn," Hovington cried. He threw his arms about his head and leapt up wildly while rocks were falling on the roof in a rising tintinnabulation and below the spring a veritable floor of limestone rose in a solid sheet and subsided in slabs half the size of automobiles. A sluice of water shot upward.

Hovington cowered on the porch alternately praying and swearing in a desperate attempt to cover all the bases. A cloud of rock dust shifted and dissipated in the water and the spring branch had deepened perceptibly. After awhile it began to fall again and everything was very quiet.

When he had his courage built up sufficiently he eased through the stones to the spring. About fifty yards from his house the earth had opened up in a shaft eight or ten feet across. A haze of powdered rock still hung over it. He could smell something like cordite.

Brimstone, he breathed. He peered down the sides of the shaft. Smooth stone fell away dizzy and plumb and all there was below was darkness. He dropped a stone and heard it go skittering away down the sides of the aperture to ultimate blackness but he never heard it strike bottom.

He cut chestnut poles and built a fence around the hole four feet high. At first there was no sound at all out of the shaft but in a few days he began to hear a murmur from deep in the earth: you had to strain to hear it but there was an indefinable far-off sound. Some folks likened it to a swarm of bees, others reckoned it was just subterranean waters. Hovington called it voices. They bespoke him with languorous foreboding and if he listened long enough he could separate the sound into different voices, point and counterpoint, query and reply. He wondered what such curious folk as these might have to talk about, what language they expressed themselves in.

Nathan Winer was a native of the county and by trade he was a carpenter who farmed a little on the side. He had a wife and a seven-year-old son who was named Nathan as well and was already much like him.

"Go through life mindin your own business and everybody will mind theirs," he used to tell the boy.

But in spite of minding his own business, he was forced in the spring of 1932 to go down to Hovington's looking for Dallas Hardin, a man who had simply moved in on Hovington, taken over his bootlegging business and, folks said, his wife Pearl, as well.

In the past year Hovington's health had so deteriorated that he stayed abed. His spine was bent like some metal God Almighty had heated to pliable temperature and laid hands on and bent to his liking. He could not even turn over by himself. Already the disease that would kill him incubated within him. He lay curled by the window where, by day he could see across the yard to whatever traffic accomplished itself on the road. By night his own lamplit reflection, the room its weary backdrop.

The house had four rooms. The long front room where Hovington slept—lived, actually—and where Hovington's black-haired daughter slept on a foldup army cot that doubled as a couch in the daytime. A kitchen. A bedroom where Hardin and Hovington's wife Pearl, slept. A room that was used to store oddments of junk and as a repository for the cases of beer and wine Hardin had taken to stocking.

Hardin came through the kitchen door carrying a coaloil lamp just as a rap sounded on the door. He set the lamp on the sewing-machine cabinet and opened the door a crack. Wind from the rainy night guttered the flame, it dished and wavered in the globe, steadied.

"I need to talk to you, Hardin," Winer said. Lamplight glinted on two goldcapped teeth.

"Then come on in out of the rain."

"I want to talk to you out here."

Hardin took down his hat from a nail beside the door and stepped into the muddy yard and closed the door behind him. He stood coatless in the rain.

"What was it you wanted that had to be said in the rain?" he asked.

"I wanted to tell you somethin," Winer said. He stood with his feet apart, hands shoved deep in his coat pockets, his head cocked back a little, his face flinty and arrogant beneath the ruined hat.

"I found your whiskey still on my land and this is what I come to say. Now, I don't care if you make whiskey till you're ass deep in it but don't make it on my land. If the law found that still they'd come down on me, not you."

"That's about the way I figured it too," Hardin said. "Did you bust it up?"

"You damn right I did. I broke that whiskey too."

"Now, you ortnt done that."

"Why, Goddamn you. If the son of a bitch hadn't been so heavy I'd've dumped it in your front yard. I don't know who you are or where you come from. Nor what kind of deal you run on Hovington here. But I'll tell you one thing. Don't mess with me. If piece one of that thing goes up on my ground again, me and you goin around and around."

Hardin's face looked as if the skin had suddenly been drawn taut. "I never took a order in my life from a tenant-farmin redneck and I'm too old to start now."

Winer grasped him by the front of the shirt and jerked and slapped him hard openhanded then slung him backward into the mud. Hardin looked like a drunken bird falling, legs askew as if they were too fragile to maintain his weight: he lit sitting and fumbling out a pistol. Winer saw what he was about and advanced rapidly on him, his knife out and his left hand on the blade opening it when Hardin shot him in the left eye. He fell straight forward like something suspended from a rope suddenly cut and landed across Hardin's body, a leaden weight that pinned the other man for a moment where he lay. Hardin shoved at him, cursing, he could feel Winer's blood seeping down his side. He came scrambling from beneath the body, tearing his bloody shirt off as he arose.

He stood leaning into the rain, hands on knees, his sides heaving. The door opened a crack and yellow light spilled into the yard and in this light the rain fell plumb and silver.

"Dallas?" Pearl said.

He could hear the rain beating on the tin. The knife lay gleaming in the mud beneath his feet, halfopen. "Shut the fuckin door," he said. The light disappeared. He picked up the knife and wiped it on his trousers. He closed and pocketed it, stood trying to think what to do.

Pale light from the weeping heavens. By this light Winer's face upturned, right eye staring up unblinking, left a black hole, long hair fanned out sliding through the mud, head leaving a weallike track in the slick yard. Mouth open a little, a glint of spare light off the gold teeth.

Hardin had him by the feet, a leg under each arm, walking backward through the yard toward the spring. Winer was a big man and every few minutes Hardin had to stop and rest and catch his breath. He rested hunkered over the dead man's feet and scanning the road for car lights. Then rising and taking up the legs again and hurrying until they were out of sight in the brush and he could breathe a little easier. The going was rough until they reached the limestone lip of the pit and he moved faster here, Winer's head bouncing a little across the uneven stone floor. He dragged him through the honeysuckle to the lip of the pit and paused to go through his pockets, storing in his own such miserable chattel as he found. A handful of linty change, a cheap pocketwatch from which his ear could detect no ticking. Little it seemed to him to show for a life as long as Winer's.

"Get your last look at this world," he told Winer. "It shore looks dark in the next one."

The depths of the abyss looked beyond blackness. Like a pit cleft to a stygian world leaking off blackness to fill this world as well. He rolled the body with a booted foot, the legs swinging over the precipice, the body overbalancing on the edge in illusory erectness and the startled face fixing Hardin with a fierce and impotent eye and then vanishing.

BOOK ONE
1943

William Tell Oliver came out of the woods into a field the Mormons used to tend but which was now grown over in sassafras and cedar, the slim saplings of sassafras thick as his arm, but not as thick as his arms had once been, he reminded himself, he was old and his flesh had fallen away some. He didn't dwell on that though, reckoned himself lucky to still be around.

Oliver was carrying a floursack weighted with ginseng across his shoulder. His blue shirt was darkened in the back and plastered to his shoulders with sweat. It had been still in the thick summer woods and no breeze stirred there, but here where the field ran downhill in a stumbling landscape of brush and stone a wind blew out of the west and tilted the saplings and ran through the leaves bright as quicksilver.

He halted in the shade of a cottonwood and unslung the bag and dropped it and looked up, shading his eyes. The sky was a hot cobalt blue but westward darkened in indelible increments to a lusterless metallic gray, the color he imagined the seas might turn before a storm. A few birds passed beneath him with shrill, broken cries as if they divined some threat implicit in the weather and he thought it might blow up a rain.

Standing so with his upper face in shadow, the full weight of the sun fell on his chin and throat, skin so weathered and browned by the sun and aged by the ceaseless traffic of the years that it had taken on the texture of some material finally immutable to the changes of the weather, as if it had been evolving all his life and ultimately become a kind of whang leather impervious to time or elements, corded, seamed, and scarred, pulled tight over the cheekbones and blade of nose that gave his face an Indian cast.

He hunkered in a shady spot to rest. He had been smoking his pipe in the woods to keep the gnats away from his eyes and now he took the pipe from his mouth and knocked the fire from it against a stone, taking care that each spark was extinguished, for the woods and fields had been dry since spring and he was a man of a thousand small cautions.

Below him Hovington's tin roof baking in the sun, the bright stream passing beneath the road, the road itself a meandering red slash bleeding through a world of green. He sat quietly, getting his breath back, an old man watching with infinite patience, no more of hurry about him than you would find in a tree or a stone. The place was changing. A new structure had been built of concrete blocks and its whitewash gleamed harshly. Newlooking light poles followed the road now, electrical wires strung to the end of the house.

Yet some old strain of second sight from Celtic forebears saw in the lineaments of house and barn, the gradations of hill and slope and road, something more profound, some subtle aberration of each line, some infinitesimal deviation from the norm that separated this place from any other, made it sacred, or cursed: the Mormons had proclaimed it sacred, built their church there. The whitecaps had cursed it with their annihilation, with the rows of graves their descendants would just as soon the woods grew over.

All his life he'd heard folks say they saw lights here at night, they called them mineral lights, corpse candles. Eerie balls of phosphorescence rising over money the Mormons had buried. Oliver doubted there was any money buried or ever had been, but he smiled when he remembered Lyle Hodges. Hodges had owned the place before Hovington bought it for the back taxes and Oliver guessed that Hodges had dug up every square foot of the place malleable with pick and shovel. It had been his vocation, his trade, he went out with his tools every morning the weather permitted, working at it the way a man might work a farm or a job in a factory, studying by night his queer homemade maps and obscure markings, digging like a demented archaeologist searching for the regimen and order of elder times while his wife and son tried to coax crops from soil that would ultimately produce only untaxed whiskey. Even now Oliver could have found the old man's brush-covered mounds of earth, pockmarked craters like halffinished graves abandoned in hasty flight. Hodges worked on until his death, his dreams sustaining him. Oliver reckoned there was nothing much wrong with that though his own dreams had not weathered as well.

In the upper left quadrant of his vision a car appeared towing a rising wake of white dust along the drybaked road. As it drew nearer he recognized it as a police car and some intimation of drama touched him, the prelude to some story, and he seated himself to watch.

It was a silent tableau that unfolded below him: the car stopped in Hovington's (Hardin's, he thought) frontyard and a deputy named Cooper got out, stood for a moment in the timeless way cops stand, sauntered to the porch with an air halfarrogant and halfdeferential. Hardin came out. They stood talking for a minute while the deputy gestured excitedly with his hands, apparently conveying some information of importance though no word of it reached the old man's ears.

He didn't need it anyway. Hardin took out his wallet and counted money onto Cooper's waiting palm. Well, well, Oliver thought, we just might see a show here. Oliver was never surprised anymore and sometimes thought he'd seen all there was to see, but onetheless he remained beneath the cottonwood watching. He took a flat pint bottle out of his pocket and rinsed his mouth with the tepid water, spat, drank. He thought vaguely of the cold spring behind his house but he was loath to leave.

The police car left. Almost immediately the hollow was vibratory with activity, a hornet's nest slammed with a stone: Hardin loped across the yard to the sleek black Packard and cranked it and backed it to the porch's edge, got out with the motor running, all four doors standing open, and unlocked the turtledeck and raised it. Pearl came through the door of the house with a case of half-pints, stowed it in the car. Hovington's daughter, her long dark hair swinging with her motion, hurried out with a cardboard carton. Above the throaty idling of the Packard he could hear the almost constant slap of the screendoor and occasional voices, Hardin giving orders.

The back door sprang open and two uniformed soldiers and a woman staggered into the yard and across it toward the thickening greenery around the abyss. One of the soldiers stumbled and fell into the branch and arose swearing and bright shards of the woman's laughter fell on Oliver's ears like a gift from a dubious source.

When the car was loaded Hardin and the girl got in and the car pulled away, going east, away from town.

After awhile the breeze tilted the sedge toward him and dried the sweat on his face to a salty glaze he could feel drawing and tightening on his skin. Swift clouds chased shadows across the field. Where a bottleneck of sky showed between the hills, dark and light clouds lay in alternating layers like varicolored liquid that would not mix. The air had chilled and he got up stiffly and took up his homecarved walking stick. As he arose he saw like some by-product of imminent storm three cars pacing themselves along the roadbed, the sheriff and two cars of the Tennessee state troopers. As they wheeled into the yard there was a brief squall from the siren and they got out and started walking rapidly toward the house. Thunder rumbled, faint and far off. Pearl came out and stood lean-

ing against a porch support with her arms crossed, just waiting with
an air of stoic forbearance. The old man shook his head and
grinned to himself before he turned back toward the woods.

The trees were in motion, the wind murmuring baleful in the
clashing branches. Past their waving green tops what he could see of
the sky was lowering, the air taking on a quality of depth, of weight,
a world under roiled water. He moved through a heightened reality
now, imbued with the urgency the air conveyed. Lightning flared
silent and sourceless, eerily phosphorescent in the unreal green of
the woods, and he quickened his steps, his movement stiff and jerky,
a comic figure resurrected from an oldtime film.

He turned down a footpath, slowing his descent tree to tree,
and warily crossed a barbed-wire fence into a flat bottom tangled
with weeds and went up a path past his corncrib. As he came out
into the barnlot he could see beyond the worn gray of his house the
rain begin, past the pale dust of the road where a pastel field
stretched to a darker border of woods he saw the horizon dissolve
in a slanting wash of rain and the jerk of weeds advancing toward
him portentous with motion.

He went hastily in the back door just as the first drops were
singing on the tin. The room was dark and cluttered, shapes softly
emergent like benign familiars from the cool ectoplasm of shadow.
He emptied the floursack of ginseng into an enamel washpan and
turned to the stove, took from the warming closet a pan of beans.
He dipped some onto a plate and took bread left from breakfast and
set the plate atop the stove reservoir and filled an earthenware mug
with cold coffee. He took up the plate again and with it and the coffee crossed from the long kitchen to the living room, stepping
down where the level changed, through a room almost as dark as
the kitchen, mismatched oddments of furniture, random debris
beached by time.

He kicked open the latchless screen door and crossed onto the
porch. The noise intensified, the porch was unceiled and the drumming on the tin precluded any other sound, even the wind whipping the trees seemed to do so in silence.

He ate in a swing hung by lengths of chain from the porch rafters and set the plate by his foot on the board floor when he had finished and slowly drank the coffee, staring past the earth yard where the road had already gone to mud. The rain fell in sheets, sluicing off the unguttered tin, dissipated to spray the wind took. Thunder boomed almost directly above him, a few scattered pellets of hail fell and lay gleaming white as pearls in the mud. The trees were in constant motion, all the world he could see was animate. The chaff-filled air seemed electric, unreal.

For a time he sat and listened to the soporific rain and when he had drunk the coffee he set the cup atop the plate. The end of the swing nearest the yard darkened with moisture and drops of spray dampened the old man's clothes but he did not move. The frenzy of the storm subsided and the intensity of the rain leveled off, the woods across the fields gained clarity like a scene viewed through clearing glass or turmoil constrained to stillness. He grew drowsy. Finally he slept, scarred big-knuckled hands resting on his knees, head leaning against a length of taut chain. From time to time his eyelids quivered with the progression of bits of dreams, dreams of when he was young, fiery dreams of iron furnaces and trains, dreams of walls and bars and time built as carefully as a mason might erect a structure in stone.

He awoke late in the afternoon, a dull drizzle leaden on the roof and the air smelling fresher and cooler. He took out a pouch of roughcut tobacco and began to pack his pipe. He lit it with a kitchen match and sat bemusedly smoking and letting the balance of the afternoon wear itself away. He had the air of someone used to waiting.

All there was to show he had ever farmed was a motley collection of old equipment about the yard, castoff discs and haymowers and archaic looking scratchers like something abandoned by early man, all slowly dissolving into rust. It had been years but still he felt some affinity for the earth and the clocking of its seasons. There was something reassuring about the rain, what grass there was in his yard had been dying in circular patches and even the trees had begun to look stunned and wilted. He'd secretly suspected some turning away of the gods, unconcern or incompetence in high places.

Between four and five o'clock the Winer boy came by and Oliver was still out to watch him pass. In actual fact he had been awaiting him. Time sometimes weighed heavily on his hands and there were weeks that passed when the only words he spoke were to young Nathan Winer. He watched the boy approach with obvious affection. He had had a son once himself and though the boy, had he lived, would be in middle age, he always thought of him as being Winer's age.

When Winer was parallel with the house Oliver hailed him: "Boy, you better get in out of this mess."

Winer was sodden, his outsize shirt and pants flopping and his hair plastered thinly to his skull. He obediently turned from the road and crossed the yard to the porch's edge. In places the mud was shoemouth deep and sucked at his feet.

"Get in here out of that."

"It's too late now," Winer said. "I don't see how I can get any wetter." But he stepped onto the porch and leaned against a support. He pushed his hair back out of his face and wiped his eyes on a dripping sleeve. There was a curiously temporary look about him as if he must soon be off. "It's fell a flood, ain't it?"

"Like a cow on a flat rock," Oliver agreed. "You been workin out in this today?"

"No, we've been inside cleaning out the poultry house. Just shoveling it up and loading trailers."

"Looks like old man Weiss could've run you home."

"I guess he just didn't think of it."

"He'd've thought of it if he had to walk two miles through it," the old man said. "You want somethin dry to put on?"

"It'd just get wet again. Anyway, it don't bother me. I don't reckon I'll melt, I never have."

"Still, it wouldn't've hurt him. I had a car I'd take ye myself but I never owned one."

"I don't mind walking."

"Well, I don't reckon it hurts a man, I've done it all my life. Or so far anyway. You want me to heat up the coffee?"

"I got to get on. It's getting dark early tonight. Cooled off some too."

"Maybe a man can sleep then," Oliver said. "Here lately it's been so hot I ain't been able to get to sleep till two or three o'clock in the mornin."

The boy arose. "Go with me."

"I guess I better set around here." Oliver seemed to be scrutinizing the boy's feet. He got up stiffly from the swing. "I got somethin I been aimin to give you if it wouldn't make you mad. You reckon it would?"

"I doubt it." Winer grinned.

The old man went back into the house, Winer following. "I bought me a pair of shoes through the mail a year or two ago and then couldn't wear em. I expect my feet's about through growin too. I been kindly keepin a eye on them feet of yourn and I believe they've growed a size or two since spring."

They passed through the front room past the dead stove the old man kept up winter and summer and stepped down into the long, narrow lean-to that served as the old man's bedroom. The room was dark and lowceilinged and Winer stood uncertainly for a moment letting his eyes adjust to the cloistered gloom and watching shapes gain outline and solidity, ephemeral shapes halftransient lock themselves into recognizable form: an old chifforobe whose dusty mirror presented him with a warped sideshow representation of himself, an old rustcolored iron bed, boxes stacked on boxes nigh to the ceiling, old lavender and gray Sunday dresses fading and shapeless on their hangers, faint scent of lemon verbena out of some other time, or life. Oliver was fetching up from the bottom of the chifforobe a newlooking pair of black hightop shoes, freshly removed from their box and tissue paper like some memento covertly hidden from time.

"Here we go," the old man said. He handed the shoes to Winer. "Hold em up agin ye shoes there and measure em."

"I believe they'll fit. How much do you want for them?"

"Nothin."

"I'll pay you."

"Take em on. They ain't doin nobody no good settin here. I don't need em noway."

"I'd rather pay you."

"I may get you to sell my sang for me some Saturday. Either my legs ain't what they used to be or they keep scootin town a little farther west ever year."

After the fetid room the air outside seemed fresh and clean. With the shoebox turned upside down and tucked under his arm Winer stepped into the rain. He crossed under the pear tree through the spate of discarded scrapiron that lay like mutant fruit and onto the road. Oliver sat back in the swing. The chain creaked, tautened. He watched Winer out of sight beyond the hedgerow and then as he reappeared far down the road where the hedge broke in a curve of the road and the road ascended. The road crossed the creek there and he could hazily see the wooden bridge. Then dusk moved in unnoticed with the rain and a little wind blew chill out of the west and stung him with spray. Winer had disappeared in blue dusk. Dark gathered in the shadow of the pear tree and crept toward the porch and Oliver arose and went into the house to light his lamp.

These evenings Winer's mother would be in the front room awaiting him and she would be sitting motionless in the rocker before the dead fireplace. Tonight she had the lamp lit on the mantle and she was at the repair of some garment made soft and nigh shapeless by repeated washing and she did not even look up when he came in. A sallow young-old woman whose highcheeked face looked somehow androgynous, nunlike perhaps or resembling an ascetic priest at some vague rites. Coronaed by the yellow halo of light she looked unreal, a ghost at some vigil, faded sepia image on a funeral-home calendar.

His room was in the attic and he climbed a ladder to it, she did not even ask him about the box. He stowed the shoes in a wooden trunk then sat at the foot of his bed a moment looking at them. He figured Oliver could wear them. He sat staring at them in a curiously hopeless way and then closed the lid.

The loft room was unbearable during the summer and Winer had taken to sleeping wherever the heat would let him. Tonight the window was open and the attic cool. Winds had blown the curtains off and they lay on the floor, gauzy specters twice lifeless and crumpled. The floor was damp with blown rain. The roof formed an A above him, with the tin that comprised both roof and ceiling pockmarked by nails that had missed the rafter, and when he laid a hand against the tin it felt cold and damp. He changed hurriedly into dry clothes and went back down the ladder.

She seemed long taken by some vow of silence or a malfunction of whatever produced words or inspired them. He didn't speak either. He knew she would talk sooner or later, conquer momentarily whatever had closed her lips, anger or simply boredom with one day the same as any other.

She'd left his plate on the table with another upturned over it and he lit the kitchen lamp and sat down to eat. He ate hurriedly, seemingly without tasting the food, fried okra and greenbeans and new potatoes, fending away onehanded moths and bugs drawn by the light or driven in the open window by the windy rain. A candlefly guttered in the quaking heat above the globe, plummeted to the orange flame, convulsed, died in silent white agony behind the hot glass.

She was standing in the door watching him eat. "Did he pay you?"

"Well," he said, "it's Friday. He pays off every Friday." He pushed his plate back.

"I keep lookin for him to cheat you. You just a boy and him in a position to take advantage."

It was an old argument and he didn't care to reopen it. "If he does it's just me," he said. He arose, fumbling the money from his pocket, offered it to her. She took it wordlessly, he watched it disappear into her apron pocket.

When he had first gone to work for Weiss she had raged against it: a boy shouldn't have to do a man's work for a boy's pay. All she said now was that if he had a proper father to look after him things would never have come to this. To such a desperate pass. She looked at him now as if all this was some contrivance of his own.

"Just walk out and pull the door to," she said with an old bitterness. "Gone and never a word to nobody."

That was an old argument too and if he had any words of refutation now he kept them to himself. When he was younger and easier to hurt he had said, "He never run off."

She had gestured around the room with an expansive arm movement halftheatrical and halfdemented and shouted, "Well, do you see him anywhere? You reckon he's behind the door playin a prank on you?"

He had just watched her with eyes that were no longer child's eyes and he had had nothing to say.

When he went up the ladder at bedtime the rain still fell and it was still cool. Feeling carefully in the dark he found a box of matches and lit the lamp and then sorted through books in a cardboard box under his bed. The bedclothes were slightly damp but after the day's heat they felt comfortable. He lay down, positioned the lamp, and began to read, barely hearing the sibilant murmur on the tin. After a time he heard her come up the ladder and cross the floor with a kind of ratlike stealth.

"What are you doin in there?"

"Reading."

"It's gettin late," she said. "You blow out that lamp. Coaloil's high."

"All right," he said. He got up and took a quilt from the bed and laid it across the bottom of the door to block the light. He could hear her, satisfied, retreating back down the ladder. He read awhile longer and then blew out the lamp.

He lay for a time in a weary torpor, aware that he was in bed and yet still feeling the endless motions of the shovel, scoop and throw, scoop and throw. In another part of his mind he was still occupied with acquaintances real as the denizens who peopled his day, corporeal as Weiss or William Tell Oliver. He felt a vague anticipation of Saturday and town and at length he fell asleep.

The storm sometime in the night reversed its course or its brother passed for he woke in a lull of the rain, the air leaden and motionless and the night holding its breath. Then lightning came staccato and strobic, a sudden hush of dryflies and frogs, the walls of the attic imprinted with inkblack images of the trees beyond the window, an instantaneous and profound transition into wall-less night as if the lightning had incinerated the walls or had scorched the delicate tracery of leaf and vine onto the wallpaper. Then gone in abrupt negation to a world of total dark so that the room and its austere furnishings seemed sucked down into some maelstrom and consigned to utter nothingness, to the antithesis of being, then thunder came muttering balefully down the wall of ridges and a cool wind was at the trees, the calm eddying away like roiled water.

He could not sleep. He stood at the window for a time, watching across the bottom where the storm was forming, banked lightning pulsing and limning the landscape with a black-and-silver nightmare quality.

Downstairs the windows were raised to the cool night and the house was a house of the winds. It seemed enormous and barren in the dark, something abandoned to the windy reaches of space. He crossed the porch and went into the yard. The wind was stronger now and wove against the heavens a patternless and everchanging tapestry. Where three trees formed a triangle he had built a treehouse from old salvaged bridgetimbers and he climbed the ladder to it. The trees leaned their disparate ways, the treehouse creaking and popping, the branches above him a steady rushing sound.

It still was not raining. The storm passed to the south, the sky in a constant flux of electricity, sleek metallic clouds burnished orange and pink. Ovoid and tracking west they look composed of some gleaming alloy, a vast armada visiting upon the world a plague of fire then fleeing on to some conjunction of all the world's storms.

The treehouse rocked and yawed and here in the dark it seemed a craft adrift in roughening water, its decks tilting and sliding to the caprice of the seas, sails shredded and mast tilted and clocking like a gyroscope gone berserk: beyond it the night was unstarred, nothing for a mariner's glass to fix upon.

Rain came like an afterthought. A belated kindness rapping at the makeshift roof. Resting on the deck with his head against the listing bulkhead he watched through the cracks the lightning grow faint and fainter, the thunder dimming away, muted by the rain. Winer half dozed, listening to the rain intensifying, spreading surcease across the dark and sleeping land.

William Tell Oliver awoke sometime in the night. The storm had passed and smoothed out to a steady downpour with an air of permanence about it. He went back to sleep and when he arose at five it was still raining. Day came halfheartedly to a grim and sunless world. It kept raining all day.

Motormouth Hodges had in mind specifically a radio he had seen sitting on a bedside table. By standing on tiptoe and peering through a crack in the venetian blinds he could just make it out, it had a wooden case and an expensive look about it and it was a small radio that would be easy to carry through the woods.

He had found it by accident. He'd been squirrelhunting here back in the spring and come up for a drink of water and there had been no one about, the intense craving to possess the radio had not come until later. Watching the house from his makeshift shelter of windbrought tin he had no doubt there would be other knickknacks he could use as well and he had visions of himself sitting before a cozy fire next winter listening to the wonders the radio unfolded for him.

Knowing the habits of country folk he had waited until Saturday. Through the slanting rain he had watched the pickup leave. Taking into consideration the cornerstanding and talking and lunch, then buying groceries, he figured he had about all day. He hurried anyway. He came out of his shelter in the stand of pines and down a sawbriarchoked gully to the blacktop. He walked up the highway toward the house, elaborately casual, whistling to himself, hands in pockets, only removing the right hand when a car passed him, raising it then in a perfunctory greeting. They'd think he lived here, who knew.

There was a look of well-kept prosperity about the house. It was a white two-story with a steeply gabled roof and neat green trim. An enormous hiproofed barn painted red loomed behind it and it was surrounded with newlooking farm equipment, cultivators and combines, an outsize orange tractor. A small yellow Caterpillar bulldozer he'd have started up and driven had he the time and more clement weather. Beyond the barn a field of soybeans followed the curve of the road.

Prior reconnaissance had shown there were no dogs and no children so he scrambled down the embankment from the blacktop and across the drive. He followed a line of closecropped hedge to the front door, moving with some haste now, purposeful, fumbling the screwdriver out as he came.

The stormdoor was locked from the inside as he had known it would be. He had the hinges off and the door set aside before he noticed that the hinges of the front door were not accessible from the door jamb, apprentice burglar fallen afoul of the intricacies of doors and locks. He stood listening. All he could hear was the rain.

The back screendoor was not even latched. He came into a screened-in back porch used for the storage of a freezer and an aggregation of junk. Here he fared better. One side of the hinges was beneath the doortrim but the side screwed to the door was visible. He hurriedly backed out the woodscrews. He could feel a line of sweat moving down his ribcage. He set the door aside and glanced once toward the road, his vision of the outside world darkened by the filtering screen. A line of shadetrees all but blocked the house from whatever traffic might pass on the highway. Satisfied he pocketed the screwdriver and ventured inside.

He was in a hall. The floor was some richly gleaming wood not of his acquaintance and the house smelled like furniture polish. He concentrated on a mental floorplan, trying to remember where the radio had been. He turned into a bedroom and saw immediately that he had been right: there it sat as if it had been awaiting him all this time. He unplugged it, peering about the room as he wound the cord about the radio. A great profusion of red roses climbed the wallpaper. From an oval picture frame an old hawklike man watched him with fierce and impotent anger.

Small baubles on the dresser, old, heavy, awkwardlooking jewelry he judged worthless. Femininelooking gewgaws and jars of curious potions he stood smelling. A smell of lilacs. Tubes of bright lipstick like highpowered rifle cartridges. Some of these he pocketed, telling himself his wife might use them.

He was taken with a felt fedora he found dangling on a bedpost. He tried it on, turning it this way and that, flattening the brim. Eyeing himself in the mirror, he squared his shoulders, worked his face into a sneer, made his eyes cold and implacable. "Hell no I won't talk," he told the face in the glass. "You just wastin my time, cop."

Wearing the hat and carrying the radio tucked under his arm he went out of the room and up the hall and stepped into the kitchen just as a heavyset middleaged woman turned at his step from the sink. She had a plate in one hand and a soapy rag in the other. She cried out and dropped the plate.

Motormouth reeled back in shock, his eyes grown saucerlike and disbelieving in his freckled face. He made some terrorstricken sound deep in his throat and he was already whirling to run. Brandishing the dishrag like a weapon she started after him.

"They shitfire," he cried.

He went fulltilt down the hall in a rising crescendo of sound from his tennis shoes on the polished floor. He went out the hall door and through the screened-in porch without moderating his pace. He felt the radio slip from his hands and tumble, he grasped desperately for the cord, felt the radio wedge itself between door and jamb. "Broke my radio," the woman shrieked and he redoubled his efforts. He went through the hedge without slackening, bent over and his feet pumping madly. Ascending the bank he was running almost parallel with the ground. He crossed the blacktop swearing at a carload of startled faces that almost ran him over and went into the rainglutted bracken toward the hillside where the dark spruce beckoned.

He went far into the woods running in silence save the ragged tear of his breathing and the rain in the trees. When at length he ceased he fell to earth and lay gasping for breath. For some time he lay inert and then cautiously rose to a crouch and strained for any noises of pursuit. All there was was the sound of raincrows jeering at him from the sanctity of the treetops.

He looked ruefully at his fist, still clutching the plug and four or five feet of electric wire. He threw it disgustedly from him and sat for a time on a stump, still wearing the hat. A dark, inklike stain was seeping down his temples. He just sat listening to the wild hammering of his heart slowly begin to subside.

Monday Winer loaded the manure spreader and listened to the rain beat on the tarpaper roofing, for the rain to slacken so they could unload it, but it did not. In the middle of the morning Weiss came down to the chickenhouse. Herman Weiss was a short, thick little man with crinkly black hair shot through with gray. Winter and summer he wore a pith helmet and clean pressed khakis and walking boots as if perpetually ready to join a safari should the opportunity arise. Folks said he was impossible to get along with. Hardly anyone would work for him but Winer thought him not a bad employer. Weiss had a clipped, brusque way of talking that folks didn't take kindly to and no one knew where he had come from. They said he was a rich Jew, a hunky, an Italian. He was a white slaver, or a doperunner, or a retired motion-picture photographer, and his own tales were so convoluted and absurd that perhaps he no longer knew himself.

Winer didn't care what he was. To Winer he was just a poultry farmer. He had three enormous chickenhouses and each housed six thousand chickens. Winer fed them twice a day, watered them morning and night. When they were nine weeks old Weiss hired a few extra hands and the chickens were caught and crated on a trailer truck and hauled away. The houses were cleaned out, a new crop started.

All Winer knew was that he halfliked Weiss. Weiss had a wry, ironic amiability that amused Winer. He did not get excited. He was full of stories about far places and easy women and huge amounts of money and with the rain drumming on the roof, and Winer a willing audience, he told some of them again.

He had a thousand tales to tell and perhaps one or two of them were even true. He was a consort of presidents and kings. Generals sought his advice on military matters, he and Blackjack Pershing had been just like that. (Taking the chalk from Pershing's uncertain fingers, turning to the green chalkboard, signifying with dots and dashes the movement of troops across terrain contested by the maimed and the dying: No, the Germans'll expect you here. If you'll . . .) Had it not been for a crooked business associate he would have been a millionaire a hundred times over, for he had invented Coca-Cola. The formula had been stolen and sold out from under him.

"I bought one for a nickel in Topeka, Kansas," Weiss said. "In a drugstore. It was my drink, right down to the secret ingredient. I could have wept."

"I imagine so," Winer said. "Did you ever see your partner again?"

"As a matter of fact I did," Weiss said. "I saw him on State Street in Chicago in I believe it was 1922. He was driving a Rolls Royce Silver Ghost and he had a blondhaired woman with him who would have altered your heartbeat. Moseby just threw up a hand at me, casual, how do you do. And kept on going . . . but that woman. I'd have taken her on the White House lawn had the opportunity ever presented itself." He fell into a ruminative silence. "Or any other reasonable place of her choosing," he said after a time.

Weiss and his wife subscribed to several magazines and once a month or so they'd bundle them up and give them to Winer. Sometimes they'd give him books they'd accumulated, once Weiss's wife, Alma, gave him a new copy of Sandburg's *Complete Poems*. Winer's mother viewed this habit with suspicion, she kept thinking the gifts would be held out of the boy's pay or someday they would be tallied up and retroactively accounted for, annihilating an entire paycheck.

Another habit Weiss had that the boy liked was that about nine-thirty he looked at his watch and said, "Well, let's drink one," and they walked up to the porch of Weiss's house. Weiss opened the old icebox he kept stocked with Coca-Cola and homemade wine. He opened Winer a Coke and poured himself a glass of strawberry wine.

Winer studied his Coca-Cola, the slow rivulets of icewater sliding down the green bottle. "Did you bottle this one?" he asked innocently. "Or just buy it at the grocery store like everybody else?"

"What?"

"I thought maybe you just ran off a batch every two or three weeks."

Weiss studied him above the rim of the upraised wineglass. He drank, lowered the glass. "Respect for your elders is a trait not to be sneered at," he told Winer after a time.

"You might amount to something someday if you didn't work so damned hard," Weiss told him that morning. "A man works as hard as you do doesn't ever have the time to make something of himself."

"Do you not want your money's worth?"

"I'll get my money's worth. You go at every job as if it were the last one and you're trying to finish up. You've got to get out of that. There isn't any last job. You finish one and there's another one waiting for you. You've got to pace yourself."

Winer leaned on his spade, resting. Through the screened window the sky had darkened, clouds arisen in the west.

"Most of these folks around here are a little different," Weiss was saying. "You must be a throwback or something. A mutant. These woolhats or rednecks, whatever . . . I've lived here twenty-five years and I'm still a foreigner. I guess they're waiting to see if I stay or not."

"I guess some of them are peculiar all right."

"Peculiar? Trifling is the word I had in mind. I had that shack up by the mouth of the creek rented to a fellow named Warren one time. Boy, was he industrious. He liked to sit on his front porch and watch his garden grow. Only moved when the shade did or his wife yelled supper. Used to brag about that garden. 'Fine garden,' he'd say. 'Fine garden.' I was up there once when it all come in and I think he had maybe four head of cabbage. I could have carried off the stringbeans in this helmet and only made one trip. He only had about eight kids so I don't know what in hell he planned to do with the excess. Can it for winter, maybe. Truckcrop it out.

"And honest? While I built this house I lived over across the creek in a little place I threw up temporarily. When I moved I hired a couple of these fellows to help me. I lost a Browning automatic shotgun I wouldn't have let go for three hundred dollars. A pair of riding boots I bought in Spain and a silver-inlaid handgun my wife gave me. You understand we're talking about two or three hundred yards here. I hate to think what would have happened if I was moving to the west coast."

That night Weiss took him home. "There's nothing else to do inside," he said. "If this mess is still going on in the morning don't even bother to come out. I can feed myself. There's no point in soaking yourself getting here just to wait until feeding time."

The creek was already yellow and ominouslooking and had picked up speed and small sticks and debris that spun in gouts of foam. The branch behind Oliver's house came out of its banks and fanned into his piglot, festooning fenceposts and saplings with drifts of dead brush and cartires that looked like buoys left to navigate a world going to water, and from where he stood in the hall of the barn he could see it lapping upward out of the hollow.

A disgusted Dallas Hardin counted two days' receipts and grew tired of the company of Pearl and the girl Amber Rose and went out into the rain and stood on the lip of the pit and it seemed to him that he could hear turbulent waters deep in the earth. A change in the earth's pulse, a quickening, a curious occult change. He looked up at the leaden sky. He looked west and there was just more of the same as if the earth's weather had coalesced in this mode. "Then rain some more, by God," he told it.

It did. The third day the bridge between Mormon Springs and town wrenched free of its concrete pylons with a shrieking of timbers and lurched into the canefield at the creek's edge, spinning lazily in the calm eddies, drifting into the swift mainstream of the creek, where it picked up speed and went spinning crazily downstream like a calliope snapped free of its moorings. Half the road was underwater now and Oliver could sit on his front porch and look off into a vast wet world, a stretch of muddy water reaching all the way across the field to the creek unbroken save by the treetrunks and the tips of brush. He'd had to move the goats to higher ground and set pans and tincans under leaks he hadn't even known his house had. He sat on his porch like some grim and hopedrained survivor awaiting rescue or the ultimate cessation of the waters.

Winer had followed the ridge down through the woods. "Did you ever see it rain like this?" he asked the old man.

"I expect I have," Oliver said. "I don't know as I've ever seen it keep it up this long though."

Hardin watched the water in the branch rise. A thin line of foamy spray strung over the rim of the pit and increased even as he watched. When he came back out an hour later the hollow was filled with a rushing perpetual thunder and he could not even approach the abyss. A stream of muddy yellow water six or eight feet wide cascaded out of the hollow and he could hear it boiling and churning far down in the pit.

Late on the fourth day Hardin looked up toward the hillside where a quartet of dark and sodden figures hailed him. Four foolhardy souls driven by challenge or thirst to walk the six miles made twelve or more by the twisting and turning required to keep to the ridges and out of the waterglutted roads and hollows.

These hard travelers were the three DePreist brothers and a young whore named Bledsoe they had picked up somewhere. They wanted something to drink.

"Wolf ain't got a drop," they told him. "Sold out to the last dram and can't get no more."

They drank up what money they had and then a halfpint. Hardin set the DePreists to gathering firewood for when the day grew chill. While they cut lengths of rotten planking and last year's beanstalks and old sodden rails deposited by floodwaters the whore sat steaming by the fire and plaited her hair with a kind of demure and drunken dignity.

They kept saying they guessed they'd better get on but they never left. Like cats they slept on the floor before the fire and like cats fell to fighting over the whore sometime deep in the night. Great thumpings arose, overturnings of furniture, chairs thrown against the wall. Outraged squalling and swearing so that Hardin leapt naked from bed and drove them to the last brother into the rain at gunpoint, not even letting them shelter on the porch but backing them down the steps into the gray drizzle and going back inside and thumbbolting the door.

They made peace among themselves and conspired to burn Hardin out but possessed not a dry match amongst them. The youngest spent a drunken hour trying to strike sparks with a pocketknife and piece of flint. At last they gave up and retreated to the barn and left at first light, sullen and hungover, the whore abandoned.

The old man was asleep worrying some old dream when the rain ceased and when it did he awoke immediately. Water was dripping sporadically into a coffee can he'd set under a leak, then that ceased too. He could hear the creek. He arose from the swing he'd been catnapping in. In the west a band of clear sky lay above the treeline, a thin crescent of sun gleaming on the clouds above it. The clouds were the color of gold and they gleamed like something hammered from burnished metal.

Wearing an old black coat and a straw hat he'd resurrected from somewhere Oliver looked like a scarecrow made clumsily animate. Carrying an enamel waterbucket he crossed his juryrigged system of planks spanning the stream's meanderings, at last just giving up and wading in, the water swirling cold as ice about his thighs. "Waistdeep in water and havin to tote a bucket for more," he complained to himself. "If that ain't the beat."

Chestnut boards nailed in a V and shoved into an orifice in the limestone bluff fed the water into the springbox. The water was cold and virid. Mossgreen, it swirled against the lichened cedar planking of the springbox. Oliver stood immersed in the roar of water, the thousand seepings and drippings of a veritable mountain of water loosely contained by the fissured limestone, the continuous roar of the falls above him. It was deep shade here, cool and dark. The perpetually wet earth was a ferment of watercress and the air was drugged with peppermint. He set the bucket down by his feet and leaned forward, his hands cupping his knees. He peered into the springbox.

He'd caught a flash of white, not gleaming but dull like old discolored ivory. It was like peering into deep seas. From the shadows of the springbox slow strands of moss and fern waved like seaweed, echoed the slow circular movement of water. In these dark depths the object turned, winked a bright and momentary gleam of gold from beneath the near-opaque surface. He reached into the water.

He held in his hands a human skull. It was impacted with moss and mud, a salamander curled in an eyesocket, periwinkles clinging like leeches to the worn bone. Bright shards of moss clung to the cranium like perverse green hair. He turned it in his hands. A chunk of the occipital bone had been blown away seemingly by some internal force, the brain itself exploding and breaking the confines of the skull. He turned it again so that it seemed to mock him, its jaw locked in a mirthless grin, the two gold teeth fey and winsome among the slime and lichens.

It was concrete, irrevocable. Tangible vestige of old violence from chasms and channels so far beneath his feet light was not even rumored. To his hands. Mute sacrifice from the well of the world. He felt besieged by knowledge he had not sought and did not want. The past eddied and swirled about him as the waters had beleaguered the skull. For a bright moment he felt omnipotent, the years rolled by had opened a door and permitted him momentary passage through it, he knew he possessed knowledge denied all the world, save one other, but he had no idea what to do with it.

The wagon had stopped in the yard. Pearl turned, the gauzy window curtain strung from her hand. She was heavier these years and her placid face bore few traces of her former bovine prettiness.

"They comin in," she whispered.

"Then let em come," Hardin said. "I don't reckon the roof'll fall in on em."

She turned back to the window. Two women stood by the wagon in the earth yard, a third climbing down awkwardly from the wagonseat. Sunday finery, lavender and blue and green catching the summer light and flicking it away, a trio of radiant peacocks approaching halfquerulously this den of iniquity. Parasols slung along though the sky held no hint of rain. A knock.

"Reckon what they want?"

He made no reply save a gesture toward the bed where Hovington lay.

A knock, more assertive.

"Well, let em in."

"You."

He arose, standing his glass by the edge of his chair. He crossed the room and turned the wooden latch and opened the door six or eight inches, peered down into a smooth country face beneath a gathered bonnet. He didn't speak.

"We come to see about Brother Hovington," the woman said.

He opened the door wider and stood aside. Pearl turned toward them, awkward, gracelorn. "Come in," she said.

"How is he?"

Hardin took up his glass, drained it. "You can see for yourselves," he said. "Yonder he lays. Brother Hovington has fell on hard times."

Hovington lay under a comforter, an electric fan whirring the listless air toward him. In truth he seemed to know no times other than hard. He was skin and bones, his knees drawn against his chest. His skin was sallow, the bones delineating the yellow flesh. All that seemed alive in this face was the quick black eyes darting about. When he opened his mouth the teeth were long and wolfish and yellowed.

As the visitors entered the austere room Hardin went through the kitchen door with his glass. The women stood uncertainly looking about. All these decadent wonders. The silent jukebox. Stacks of cased brown bottles.

"Get yins a seat," Pearl told them. "Rose, you get some more chairs out of the kitchen."

The darkhaired girl arose silently and went through the doorway. She came back carrying three ladderback chairs and aligned them by the bed. Her longlashed eyes were downcast. Pearl fussed with the chairs, realigning them to her satisfaction. "Set down," she said. "Can I get yins bonnets?"

One of the women touched the girl's shoulder in a gesture of fleeting kindness. "Ain't she a little lady? And ain't she the prettiest thing you ever saw?"

The girl seemed not to notice. She seated herself in an armchair by the window and sat staring out at the yard, remote, as if in some manner she was able to will herself somewhere else.

The women subsided into chairs and took out cardboard fans and began to wave them about. Pearl stood behind them, harried, distraught, as if she were the uninvited guest here. "Can I get yins a cold drink? We never thought about no company."

The woman in the middle loosened her bonnet strings, let the bonnet fall onto her shoulders. Her gold hair lay in intricate rococo plaits. Sweat beaded on her upper lip, a glycerinous mustache. "Nothin for me, thank ye." The other two shook their heads. "We just come up here from church. Brother Hovington's name come up in the service as one afflicted and we prayed for him. We come by to see did he need anything."

From where Brother Hovington lay he seemed past the need of anything they might have about their persons. His eyes were closed, he might have slept. Or yet he might have been dead save the soft, liquid movement of the eyeballs beneath the near-translucent lids, the slow, hypnotic blue pulse of his throat. For Brother Hovington lay in agony, in an alteration of time juryrigged so by pain that its passage seemed scarcely discernible. In the molten fire where he lay he could watch the slow machinations of eternity, the cosmic miracle of each second being born, eggshaped, silverplated, phallic, time thrusting itself gleaming through the worn and worthless husk of the microsecond previous, halting, beginning to show the slow and infinitesimal accretions of decay in the clocking away of life in a mechanism encoded at the moment of conception, withering, shunted aside by time's next orgasmic thrust, and all to the beating of some galactic heart, to voices, a madman's mutterings from a snare in the web of the world.

"Pearl?" Hardin called from the other room and she arose, smoothing her skirt with her big hands, hesitated. "I'll be with yins in a minute. Let me see what he wants." (As if Hardin were the husband, the women would tell each other later. Not this frail vessel already faulted, life seeping from every fissure. Hovington might have been some stranger, or worse, an unwanted relative come to visit, remaining to die.)

Then voices, his mocking, conspiratorial, hers interrogative, faintly protesting, both made at once indecipherable and unmistakable through the thin walls, laughter vague and androgynous, and they all felt rather than heard the descension of flesh onto flesh, timeless, the protest of the bedsprings, an involuntary gasp, sounds they seemed to have possessed all their lives as inherent knowledge. Silence then save the whirr of the fan tracking in its mechanical orbit and then, unbelievably, the creak of the bedsprings commencing in earnest, intensifying, attaining the desired rhythm. The front door opened and closed and they saw that the girl Amber Rose had gone out.

The women sat in a hot, aghast silence. Color crept into their faces, they did not look at each other but all stared at the dying man who seemed charged with the performance of something that might break the furious agony of silence, propel them on to whatever their next action might be. When he made no move the woman in the middle arose, peered at the wasted face. "I believe Brother Hovington's gone to sleep." The other two arose with a thick rustling of silk, turned to the door. "Poor soul. I expect he needs his rest." The door pulled to when they crossed the porch and passed into the sun, parasols fluttering open, their foreshortened shadows darting attendance like dark fowl underfoot.

The horses turned to watch them come, moving a little already in anticipation, the wagon creaking, the traces rattling musically. The girl watched them clambering into the wagon, their faces flushed and flat with revulsion. "Come around here," one of them yelled peremptorily to the horses, snapping the lines. The wagon turned itself laboriously in the yard, dust billowing up from beneath the horses' feet, rising in a palpable cloud that had them at their fans again, turning the wagon then onto the road in a sigh of prolonged noise.

Amber Rose smoothed the dark wing of hair from her eyes. It seemed to her the world was full of things she had no control over, and she watched them go with no look at all on her face.

Weiss parked the car in front of the Utotem Market and cut the switch off. "Say he works in here?" he asked Winer.

"He did the last time I was in here. He was picking chickens and cutting em up."

"A man of experience then," Weiss said dryly. "Just what we need. I don't know whether I remember Hodges from the last time we caught. Was he the tall, redhaired one with the shifty eyes?"

"He's all right."

"Then get him. But if you can't, call me so we can get someone else."

"All right."

Winer got out of the car and crossed the sidewalk to the front of the grocery. It was hot on the street but inside the Utotem a fan whirred somewhere above him and he could feel cold air blowing from somewhere. It was almost closing time and there were few customers in the store. He walked past the checkout counter and down the aisle to where the drinkbox was. He had the lid back and was peering inside making his selection when a voice hailed him.

"Hey Winer."

He turned but he couldn't see anybody he knew. It had sounded like Motormouth but he was not about, only two women shopping, making their selections from shelves and putting them into shopping carts.

"Hey Chicken Man," the voice said. A chicken was ascending slowly past the chrome rim of the meatcase. Winer stood clutching a dripping Coke and staring at it. The chicken rose until its feet rested on the chrome rail. A human thumb and forefinger gripped each yellow foot. The chicken pranced across the length of the metal lip with delicate little mincing steps. It pranced back. It was halfplucked and its head lolled drunkenly on a broken neck. Its eyes seemed to be leering at Winer through their blue lids.

The two shoppers paused before the meatcase the better to consider this wonder. Perhaps warming to its audience the chicken began to dance, slowly at first, kicking out first one drumstick, then the other, a fey, loosejointed sort of shuffle to no audible music. Above the trays of hamburger meat and liver and the packages of its own dissected brothers it began a macabre country buck dance, its loose head whipping back and forth, its feet fairly flying on the chrome lip. A demented cackling sound issued from behind the meatcase. The two women stared at each other in awe or disgust when the chicken began a slow, lascivious bump and grind. They shook their heads and wheeled their buggies away.

Rapidly approaching footsteps across the waxed tile drew Winer's attention. He turned away from the chicken to see old man Christian coming down the aisle, taking off his apron as he came. His face was flushed and angry.

Winer judged the floorshow about over and he left. He paid his nickel at the counter and went out the door with its small chime and into the sun white and blinding off the tops of parked cars. Motormouth's Chrysler was parked down the block in its bristling array of antennas and lights and he got in and rolled all the windows down and sat in the heat and waited. He didn't figure he'd have long to wait and he didn't.

"He fired your childish ass, didn't he?"

Motormouth leapt and swore when his neck touched the hot plastic seatcover. "Old Christian was supposed to've been in Nashville till tomorrow. I been cuttin up like that all day. How's I supposed to know the son of a bitch was back?"

"I guess you weren't. Did he not think it was funny?"

"That whorehopper can't take a joke. He said it was disrespectful. I reckon he thinks the Utotem grocer store's a fuckin tabernacle or somethin."

"What's your old lady going to say?"

"No tellin," Motormouth said. "I guess she'll up and go home to Mama. She's been lookin for a excuse and this is made to order. She's always throwin up I can't hold a job. She thought I was clerkin anyway. She didn't know I was jerkin feathers off damn chickens and such as that."

He started the car and studied the sporadic traffic through the back glass. "I don't know. Seems like I squander myself huntin a job and then I ain't got the energy left to do it after I get it. I don't know what's wrong with me."

He began to back the car into the street. When he was turned to his satisfaction he barked the tires of the Chrysler and then squalled them again braking for the red light.

"Weiss catchin chickens tonight?"

"Yeah. He said if you want to catch be there before dark. I figured I'd ride up with you."

"I might as well I guess. Money's money even if you do have to breathe chickenshit to get at it. You want to ride out to my place awhile?"

Winer thought about Motormouth's wife. "Not really," he said.

"I'll show you all my carparts."

"I'm really not much on carparts. Besides, it's liable to get squally around your place when she hears you got fired."

"Yeah, I guess you're right. Listen, when you see Ruby don't say nothin about me makin that chicken dance. She's got even less of a sense of humor than old man Christian does."

"It's nothing to me."

"It's early yet. Want to shoot a game or two of pool?"

Late in the afternoon they drove up the road toward Weiss's place. Passing Oliver's gray clapboard Hodges said, "There's a feller lives there you don't want to fool much with."

"Tell Oliver? Why, that old man don't bother nobody."

"He may not now but he used to be rough. Back fore my time his old lady took up with some Ingram feller off at Jack's Branch. This was all a long time ago. Anyhow, she sent Ingram back with a wagon and team to pick up her stuff while Oliver was at work. He come in early and caught this Ingram feller draggin a chifforobe across the yard. They took to scufflin I guess over the chifforobe and he pulled a gun on Oliver. They was fightin over it and somehow Ingram got shot through the heart.

"They locked old man Oliver up and then let him out on bond. I guess he'd a got off, justifiable homicide or whatever, but the Saturday after he got out Ingram's brother jumped him in Long's store. Ingram come at him with a pocketknife and Tell Oliver jerked a axehandle out of a barrel and like to took his head off. They give him some time over that. I reckon two in one week was a little hard to take. Or else they figured they better get him out of the way while there was still Ingram breedin stock left."

"That old man's had a lot of bad luck."

Hodges glanced at him curiously. "I don't reckon you could say them Ingrams exactly come up smellin like roses."

A tractor-trailer rig sat parked before the long chickenhouses. A muscular black man dozed behind the wheel, a checked golf cap pulled over his eyes. Seven men or boys were grouped before the truck telling jokes and lies and waiting for dark to make the chickens drowsy enough to facilitate catching. A floodlight set in the eave of the chickenhouse washed them with hot bright light.

Hodges walked from the group toward the corner of the chickenhouse and unzipped his pants. He stepped around the dark corner. Out of sight of the men he leaned to avoid the lowering branches of sumac and went at a dead run toward the far corner of the building where it intersected the woods.

He worked rapidly, chuckling to himself. Beneath a window he constructed a makeshift cage of old chickencoops. Two high and six square. Standing atop them he took from his pocket a pair of cutters and scissored a triangular cut in the wire mesh covering the window and then leapt back down. He pocketed the cutters and went back up the ammonia-smelling alley into the light.

He came back into view blinking his eyes and zipping his pants ostentatiously under the acerbic eye of Weiss and his frail wife. Weiss fixed him with a hawklike look of suspicion but Hodges paid it no mind. It was a known fact that Weiss was suspicious of everybody and besides Hodges was busy computing his money and planning the trip to Lawrenceburg tomorrow to sell his chickens. He fell to thinking of a pair of cowboy boots he had seen in a shop window, a pair of low beam foglights from the pages of a parts catalog.

With good dark Weiss awoke the packer and gave the men the word to proceed. "Be easy with my babies," he told the catchers. Though they were already doomed to the meatpacker's knife he could not bear to see them handled roughly or maltreated. The packer took his place halfreluctantly on the truck and opened the first row of coops and prepared for the onslaught of chickens.

Four chickens in the left hand, three in the right. Groping in the musty dark where the chickens huddled, rising, out then into the white glare of the floodlights where the packer waited and Weiss watched the proceedings with a critical eye. Weary arms loaded with somnolent chickens upraised for the packer to take. Fourteen chickens to the crate, an inordinate amount of empty crates to be filled. Six thousand divided by fourteen, Hodges thought wearily. The precise figure eluded him but he knew it was a lot.

The packer would fill the crate and slam the lid closed and whirl with it to stack it on the rear of the truckbed. Empty crates at the front of the truck, full ones behind. Coming out with their armfuls of chickens the catchers would glance surreptitiously at the number of full crates, the number of empties left to fill.

In the hot, fetid dark the air was full of down and small feathers drifting in the windless air and they stuck to the sweaty skin of the catchers and in their hair and eyelashes and in the white fluorescence the catchers took on a look curiously alien, like vaguely sinister folk lightly furred.

Winer's arms grew weary. He was used to working and he knew to pace himself but even so six thousand chickens is a lot of chickens and the pace they had to keep was numbing.

Motormouth fared far worse. He grew hot and sweaty, his face so infused with blood he looked flayed. When he stood with his chickens aloft waiting for the packer to accept them his thin arms trembled spasmodically and he had a panicky look in his eyes as if he worked always a few degrees past the limits of his endurance.

"What the hell's Hodges doin with those chickens?" Buttcut Chessor asked Winer. Buttcut was a friend from school who had been an athletic hero on a scale almost mythic and he had never quite gotten over it.

"Beats the hell out of me," Winer said. "With Motormouth you never know. He may have another truck parked around there."

Every few loads Motormouth would make a sidetrip to the window he'd rigged and dump his armload of chickens unceremoniously into the night. They lit in his homemade cage with soft, quarrelsome mutters, their chicken dignity affronted, their tickets punched for someplace they'd never been.

The only thing that kept him going was the boots. He'd about decided on the boots. They had cunning silverlooking chains draped about the ankles that had a Mexican look and when he'd hoist up the chickens he'd think of the musical clinking the chains would make as he strode into the poolroom.

At last they were through. The driver was booming down the coops while Weiss passed among the stunnedlooking catchers with his thin sheaf of dollar bills.

Motormouth shoved his carelessly into a shirt pocket and went to watch the truckdriver, giving him unwanted advice and meaningless handsignals. "Pull up, back a little now. Cut ye wheels hard to the right." At last the driver rolled down the glass and called, "Fella, would you kinda get the fuck out of the way so I can turn this damn thing? I ain't got all night."

"Turn the motherfucker over then for all of me," Hodges said, but the driver wasn't paying any mind. "Uppity upnorth nigger," Hodges told the rolled glass, the racing motor, the big wheels crushing the sumac.

He went and hunted Winer. "You want to go over to Hardin's and get a sixpack?"

"Not me. I got to get up again tomorrow morning. Tomorrow's old workday."

"Well, it ain't for me. I aim to get me a sixpack and ride around awhile."

"If you're set on riding around you can drive me home. I've got to take a bath and get to bed."

"We'll do her."

"Before you get the sixpack."

Motormouth drove back up to the Mormon Springs road and turned left toward Weiss's place and parked in a sideroad below the house. He opened a bottle of beer and listened to the wall of night sounds start up again around the silent car. Through the trees he could see no light from Weiss's windows. He turned the radio on and listened by its warm yellow glow to the halffamiliar jocularity of disc jockeys and to plaintive music and then after awhile to a seemingly demented preacher ranting and raving and pleading for money. "Send me that foldin money," he cried. "The Lord's work don't get done with them old clankin nickels and dimes. The Lord likes that quiet money." Listening, Motormouth pondered what sort of radioland congregation of mad insomniacs this postmidnight preacher might have and as he ranted the preacher began to make spitting noises into the microphone, so choked with emotion was he. Motormouth began to wonder could this spit possibly short out his radio when this preacher calmed himself and began to tell Motormouth of a wonderful cloth he could have for a ten-dollar donation. It was a prayer cloth and spread over any afflicted area it did wondrous things. It had cured cancer, made whole an exploded appendix, repaired ruptures. Crutches and trusses thrown away hundredfold by folk cured by this miracle fabric.

"Reckon it would make my dick grow an inch or two?" Motormouth asked the preacher.

He drank beer and waited. He knew he should be at home and he guessed his wife wondered where he was but he wasn't even sure of that so he sat cradling the bottle and listening to the incessant crying of whippoorwills. He knew that it was not just the chickens that kept him here and he knew subconsciously that some vague hunger for doom drove him, kept him tightrope-walking the edge, he knew he was consumed by some fatal curiosity as to what nature of beast lurked beyond the abyss. Some affinity for ill luck that fed the grocery money nickel by nickel down the mechanical throats of pinball machines and drew and bet to inside straights.

Faint thunder came from somewhere behind him and turning he saw lightning bloom above the western horizon and flicker there bright and soundless and after a moment thunder came again. He got out and unlocked the trunk and took out the burlap bags he'd been hauling around for this occasion and climbed down the embankment and went up a concrete tiling higher than he was tall, his feet echoing strangely on the subterranean floor. He came out through a clump of blackberry briars ascending toward the head of the hollow. It was very dark save when the lightning came. He increased his pace, an anticipatory exhilaration seized him. He could smell the leather of the new boots, feel the crinkly tissue they came in.

He'd decided to bag all the chickens and move them into the woods to safety and then carry them down to the car two bags at a time. He only had two bags filled with the querulous chickens when the light hit him. He leapt up glaring wildly toward the source of the light but all he could see was the white glare and he stood for a moment frozen as if the light had seared him to his tracks. In that moment various excuses crossed his mind but none seemed adequate. Found them where they lost them off the truck. That nigger stole them and I took them away from him and brought them back.

"I'm armed," Weiss called. "Don't you make a move."

But by the time the voice came he had made a series of them. He threw one bag across his shoulder and sprang into the sumac dragging the other. The chickens began to squawk angrily and brush and brambles tried to wrest the bags from him. A report came and a bright blossom of fire and shot rattled off in the trees like hail falling. Bits of chopped leaves drifted unseen. He released the bag he was dragging and increased his pace, running blindly into the dark while intermittent lightning showed him stumps to dodge and deadfalls to leap. The sack bounced madly on his back and he ran constantly through an outraged din of protestation. Lightning bloomed and died and in the inkblack pause for thunder he ran fulltilt into the bole of a tree and went tumbling into the hollow in a riot of squawks and curses.

He sat stunned for a moment clutching his spinning head. The sack had opened and chickens were running into the night. He held his breath and listened for Weiss. All he could hear was an angry muttering from the pullets. He arose and took up the empty sack and began to stalk the chickens, trying to lure them back into the sack. They wouldn't come. Then he began to run after them one at a time but they fluttered away, cackling and flapping their wings, and finally he threw the sack away and began to curse them. He went shambling on down toward the mouth of the hollow and all about him the chickens were taking to the trees like pale spirits rising.

Over the years Hardin had taken on the lineaments of evil. You would sometimes see him on a Saturday streetcorner, the center of a group of men itemizing the faults of the world. When he spoke men listened. He seldom laughed but when he did the rest of the men laughed too in sporadic bursts of mirthless noise. No one wanted to be in his disfavor, it had come to seem that being in his disfavor was tantamount to being homeless.

There were folks in the bootlegging trade who had decided they might be in the wrong line of work. The Moon family had been at it for three generations and within a fortnight of Hardin's decision to shut them down two of them were in Detroit bolting doors on carbodies and the third was logging for Sam Long. That was Bud. Bud was the first one to the still after the explosion rocked the hills and when he got to the head of the hollow the still was just not there. It was scattered over a larger area than Bud would have thought possible and there was no piece of it that would not have fitted comfortably into a shoebox. A week or so later they attempted to sell off what stock they had on hand and Bud's house mysteriously burned.

Hardin's vulpine face was leaner and more cunning than ever, the cold yellow eyes more reptilian. Or sharklike, perhaps, lifeless and blank save a perpetual look of avarice. And he went through life the way a shark feeds, taking into its belly anything that attracts its attention, sucking it into the hot maw of darkness and drawing nourishment from that which contained it, expelling what did not.

There was a gemlike core of malevolence beneath the sly grin, beneath the fabric of myth the years had clothed him in. In these myths he supplanted the devil, the tooth-and-claw monsters of childhood darkness. "You behave yourself or I'll give you to old man Hardin," women told their children. "You better get to sleep," they cautioned them at night. "If you don't mind, he'll slip in that winder and carry you off so quiet we won't even hear him." His spirit moved in the night, rustled the branches outside their windows, his familiars crouched in the brush where the porchlight faded away.

"He shot and killed old Lester Sealy just as sure as I'm settin here," a man might say in the poolhall.

"Why, shore he did. Everbody knows he was goin with Lester's old woman. But how you goin to prove he killed him? Bellwether tried that hisself."

"Well, them kids of Lester's could I reckon. At the first. You know they first told Hardin done it but I reckon they might've been persuaded Lester done it hisself. Old Mrs. Winsor told that that oldest girl of Lester's said that Hardin was there with her mama when Lester come in and caught em. He cut for the bathroom and was halfway out the winder when Lester busted in on him. Said Hardin shot him through the heart and climbed back in and Lester's wife fixed it so it looked like he shot hisself."

"Course, Hardin birdhuntin with Judge Humphries ever few days didn't hurt nothin."

"I spect not. Nor all that money passin under this table and that."

He prospered during these years. The war brought him a seemingly endless supply of thirsty soldiers and their women. The lights stayed on all night at Mormon Springs these years, the jukebox he brought from Memphis sang sad songs to closedancing couples, bereft or lonesome women, men touched by the shadow of war, the shadow of something dread that was creeping up on them.

Shifting hues of red, white, and blue neon dissipated these shadows, bathed the dancers in the romantic hues of the unreal. The songs and the lights and the quickened pulse of their lives made them larger than life so that they saw themselves as figures of myth and tragedy. Overalled farmers side by side with furloughed or shellshocked stateside soldiers, momentary virgins from godforsaken hollows where the owls roosted in the shade trees, old painted women washed up like refugees from the poolhalls, the all-night cabstands, the shotgun coaloil shacks. Old stringy women with ribald mouths and furious, outraged eyes as if life had done them some grievous wrong.

Among these demifamiliars Hardin moving like some perverse host, eyes watchful for the salesman on his way to Memphis, the cattleman back from the auction, the fat leather wallets on plaited fobs hanging like fruit for the harvest. For those with high tolerances for alcohol he had envelopes of white powders folks did not resist so well and he had knuckles fashioned from the handles of a galvanized washtub and what he called his Sunday knucks made from brass. An amorous drunk might step into the bushes, Pearl's arm about his waist, or he might just ease out into the bracken to relieve himself. Where Hardin would relieve him as well, rising from the brush like some grim specter, the handkerchief-wrapped knucks finding just the right spot, quick hands to the pockets and fading back into the dark.

Morning. A hot August sun was smoking up over a wavering treeline. Such drunks as were still about struggled up beneath the malign heat slowly and painfully as if they moved in altered time or through an atmosphere thickening to amber. The glade was absolutely breezeless and the threat of the sun imminent and horrific. The sweep of the sun lengthened. Windowpanes were lacquered with refracted fire. Sumac fronds hung wilted and benumbed as the whores and smellsmocks rose bedewed from the foxglove and nightshade. Strange creatures averse or unused to so maledictive a sun, they were heir to a curious fragility as if, left to the depredations of the sun, their very flesh would sear and blacken, their limbs cringe and draw like those of scorched spiders.

The cool breath of the abyss drew them through the undergrowth like a magnet aligning iron filings on a glass slide. Hardin went down with his morning coffee. Silent, unjocular. In fact, the glade seemed permeated with silence, an appalled hush in response to the night's bedlam, as if ultimately all things must balance. The air rising from the pit seemed to emanate from some reversal of the seasons at the earth's core. The far-off voices were murmurous, vaguely placating. The undergrowth was more luxuriant here, darkening perceptibly toward the pit, the earth mounding in a fashion curiously vulval, the cleft in the rock mysterious, enigmatic.

And how would you lock him out? Short of killing him, how would you ensure the sanctity of your home, your family? Doors will burn, windows melt and slide viscous and flaming down the sills, locks blacken and lie unrecognizable among the ashes. If you expect him you can prepare, but he is cunning. When will he come, what will be the hour? He has all the time in the world, he can pick and choose, all the time you have is the moment of his arrival. He is a bearer of grudges, trifles drive him to limits an ordinary man only reads about.

"Wood will burn," the note he sent the widow Bledsoe said. It was unsigned, ambiguous yet final. She carried the note into town and laid it on the high sheriff's desk.

The high sheriff that year was a young man named Bellwether. Bellwether had been wounded at Pearl Harbor, badly enough to be discharged but not badly enough to prevent him from performing the duties of a sheriff. He was discharged just in time to be elected in an early wave of patriotism. Bellwether was a hero. He had a Purple Heart and a Distinguished Service Cross to prove it. He had a series of scars climbing the length of his right leg and a starshaped explosion of scartissue on his back where shrapnel had struck him. He was a local boy. The best thing you could say about him was that he was honest, the worst that he was a sorry politician. He washed his hands all by himself. He did not work well with the local judges, both of whom Hardin carried folded like banknotes in his pocket. He had been born poor and doubtless would so remain.

Bellwether had light, wavy hair going prematurely gray. His mild eyes were gray as well and his smooth face calm and reassuring. He had the note unfolded on his desk. The three words were blockprinted on a leaf of foolscap from a nickel tablet. They looked like the work of a child. Bellwether shaking his head.

"What do you want me to do?"

"I want him put away."

"There's no way I can even arrest him on the strength of this. His name's not on it. It's not even a direct threat. Even if I sent it to Nashville no expert could tell me anything about that printing. It may just be a prank. What did you get into it with him about?"

"My daughter went out there with them DePreists and took to hangin around down there at Mormon Springs. Runnin wild, layin drunk down there. I went after her a time or two and the last time Hardin cussed me and run me off. I told him what I thought of him. I told him I was goin outside the county if yins wouldn't do nothin."

"And then you got this."

"In the mailbox but it wasn't postmarked or nothin. He just slipped it in the box. It's scary, somebody sneakin around like that, peepin in your windows, spyin on you."

"What happened to your daughter?"

"Last I heard she was still down there livin with Hardin. Her and that Hovington trash too. God knows what kind of devil's nest of meanness they've got down there. But I've give up on her. All I want is not to be burned out."

"I'll talk to him."

"What good'll that do?"

"Maybe none. But it'll let him know you know who wrote the note and that if anything does happen we'll know where to come lookin. It might scare him."

She arose, an angry, heavyset middleaged woman clutching a shiny black pocketbook. "If you plan on scarin Hardin you just might as well set here in the courthouse," she told him. "I knowed all the time it wouldn't do no good but I come anyway. All right. You go talk to him. And I'll tell you what I aim to do. I'll lay for him with a shotgun. And the next time I need you it'll be to gather him up out of my back yard."

"I'll talk to him anyway," Bellwether said.

Bellwether talked but as he did he got the distinct impression that Hardin was not even listening. His eyes looked abstracted and far away as if he were already experiencing what he knew he was going to do and perhaps could not have been deterred from doing even had he been willing. They sat in the shade on Hardin's porch and as Bellwether talked a slight, pretty girl with violet eyes that in the shade looked black as sloe came out and stood leaning against the screen door. No sound came from the house save the constant whirr of an electric fan. A drunk man naked to the waist and wearing army O.D. pants and dogtags reeled around the corner of the house. His mouth was already open to speak but when he saw Bellwether in his neat pressed khakis and badge he veered suddenly back out of sight. The girl smiled a small, secret smile and said nothing.

When Bellwether appeared finished, Hardin said, "You care for a little drink?"

"I reckon not. I ain't ever been much of a drinkin man."

"I didn't mean nothin illegal, Bellwether. I got two–three cases of Co-Colas icin down in there."

"I reckon not."

They fell silent. Hardin's hands were composed. He kept studying his shiny wingtip shoes. "Damned if I know what to tell ye," he finally said. "That old woman's crazy. And that girl ain't even here no more. She took off with some soldier from Fort Campbell. But that old mother hen . . . you know how some women gets in the change of life. Some goes one way, some another, and I reckon she went crazy." He paused, seemed to be in a deep study. "I hate to say this about southern womanhood," he said. "But she got to horsin. You know how some of these women gets to where they got to have it. Well, she got to horsin and kept comin around here tryin to put it on me. Hintin around. Finally she spelled it out to me and I turned her down flat. Hell, I can pick and choose."

Bellwether did not believe one word of this story but at the same time he divined that Hardin didn't care if he believed it or not. He was spinning out the tale for his own amusement, just something to pass the time. Just keeping his hand in.

"Everbody knows she's about half a bubble off of plumb," Hardin said. "Didn't she hang a Co-Cola bottle up in her that time and have to go to Ratcliff and have the bottom busted out of it fore they could even get it out? They tell it on the streetcorners. Ain't you heard that?"

Bellwether stood up. He felt an intense need to be elsewhere, he'd stayed not only past his welcome but past the limits of his endurance. "It don't matter if I've heard it or not," he said. "As far as I know there's no law against it. There is a law against threatenin people, and torchin off their property, and my job is to enforce it."

"Shore," Hardin said thoughtfully. "Folks always got to do their jobs. You got yours to do, I got mine."

"It might be easier on both of us if they never overlapped," Bellwether said.

"I was thinkin that very thing," Hardin told him.

From the edge of the wood Hardin watched her get out of the truck, heard the door slam. The widow Bledsoe crossed in front of the old pickup, a square, unlovely woman with a masculine walk. She opened the door on the passenger side and a few moments later reappeared burdened with two grocery sacks, going up the walk to the front door. He unpocketed and glanced at his watch. "Go on in," he told her softly. "It's time for ye stories. Time to see what's happenin on the radio."

He sat in silence for a time seeing in his mind her movements about the house, a vivid image of her before a cabinet, arm raised with a can of something. Folding the empty bags, laying them by for another time.

When he judged her finished and listening to the radio he arose, followed the hillside fence as it skirted the base of a bluff. It was very quiet. Once a thrush called, in the vague distance he could hear the sorrowing of doves. The timber here was cedar and the air was full of it, a smell that was almost nostalgic yet unspecific, recalling to him some misty past, incidents he could not or would not call to mind.

He had waited until she had her hay cut and stored and the loft was stacked with it nigh to the ceiling. A good crop, it looked to him, for a year so dry. The barn was made of logs and situated in the declivity between two hills and it sat brooding and breathless under the weight of the sun. The hills were tall and thickly timbered and the glade was motionless. Not a weed stirred, a leaf, heat held even the calling of birds in abeyance.

Latticed shade, the hot smell of baking tin and curing wood and dry hay. Eyes to a crack in the log, he watched the house. It lay silent as the barn. Some old house abandoned by its tenants, reliving old memories. Drowsing in the sun. "I guess you thought it was all blowed over," he told the house. Eyes still to the unchinked crack he urinated on the earth floor, spattered his boots with foam-flecked bits of straw and humus. He straightened and adjusted his trousers. A core of excitement lay in him like a hot stone. He ascended through dust-moted light a ladder to the loft. Under the hot tin dirtdaubers droned in measured incessance, constructed their mud homes along the lathing. Hardin was already wet with sweat. He turned toward the house, he could see the sun wink off the metal roof, instill in the wall of greenery a jerky miragelike motion as if nothing were quite real. Near the end of the roof the wind had taken a section of tin and the bare lathing showed, he could smell the hot incendiary odor of the pine. Harsh light trapped in a near-translucent knothole glowed orange and malefic as if already an embryonic fire smoldered there.

He underestimated the dryness of the chaff and last year's hay: when he threw the match it very nearly exploded. An enormous wall of heat assailed him, knocking him backward. He scrambled down the ladder swearing and feeling to see was his hair afire. There was a fierce muttering above him and he could smell the clean scent of the hay burning. He wasted no time. He went past the tractor parked in the hall of the barn and through an eight-foot wall of pokeweed and through the fence and began to climb the hill, his breath coming harder, the white shirt plastered to his sides and stomach.

He paused halfway up the hill and watched through a gap in the cedars. The glade below danced with heat, a fierce quarter acre of hell consigned here shimmering and vibratory with menace, smoking bits of lathing falling into the dry sedge and small, bright flames darting playfully into the lot, a growing tide of fire that rode the crest of sedge toward the house like a wave on water. A landscape from a palette of fire. The tin curled and was blown off smoking into the wilting pokeweed and he could hear the enormous *whoof whoof* of the fire sucking, drawing off air from the hollow like a flue.

When she finally did come out he knew it not by seeing her but by the screech of her voice and even that seemed strange in the glassy air, something grating and mechanical, a shrieking of metal on metal. The voice through the fire came distorted and fragmented, foreshortened then elongated. When he heard the grinding of the truck motor even that sounded like nothing he'd heard before. Filtered so by the fire it intercut with her voice, became surreal, a garbled electronic shrieking there was no one about to hear.

A warrant was sworn out and Bellwether arrested him. Pearl followed the squad car back into Ackerman's Field and he was on the street within the hour. In a week he appeared before Judge Humphries and the case was bound over to the grand jury. When the jurors met they threw it out. They decided there was insufficient evidence for prosecution and that they all owned barns.

Weiss's wife was named Alma. She didn't have much to say and when she did speak her voice was a wheeze like air leaking from a broken accordion in one endlessly sustained note. She had asthma attacks. Each breath she took was audible from several feet away. Winer caught himself waiting for her to breathe, holding his own breath. Then it would come, the tone of the wheeze breaking off in an agonized pause when her lungs were filled, changing then, the pitch lowering as if some tension had been relieved, then the battle for oxygen would begin again.

She had a small dog she perpetually clutched in her arms and she swore it had saved her life during three separate asthma attacks. It was a breed Winer was unfamiliar with and it was the ugliest dog he had ever seen, possibly the ugliest anything he had ever seen. He judged it some model of lapdog. It had a mouthful of tiny needle-sharp teeth like some malign form of life dredged up by appalled fishermen from the keep of the sea. It did not like Winer any more than he liked it and it would bare its teeth and snap at him from the safety of the woman's cradling arms in a gesture curiously catlike. It had black, shiny, bulbous eyes devoid of any emotion remotely doglike and with its bulging eyes and spiderlike limbs it looked like some grotesque insect the old woman had taken to her bosom. Their fates were intertwined, for when she died in September that year the dog was put to sleep as well and placed in her coffin, a talisman whose own luck had run out.

"They say he went crazy and pulled a gun on Ratcliff," Sam Long told Winer in town the Saturday after she died. Long was arranging the boy's purchases in a cardboard box, totting them up in a ticketbook. "Ratcliff doin all he could to save her and Weiss throw down on him with a pistol thataway. Ratcliff said he was just a rippin and a rarin. Said he said, 'You let her die and by God you'll die with her.' Old Ratcliff told him, 'Son, can't nobody but God Almighty blow breath back into a dead woman and he ain't no more impressed with pistols than I am.'"

"Are they burying her around here?"

"Lord, no, boy. You think the ground around here is sacred enough for old man Weiss? I reckon not. He hired a ambulance all the way to Nashville. Puttin her in one of these aboveground tombs, what I hear."

Winer remembered the Sandburg book she had given him. In the dust, he thought. In the cool tombs.

He took up the cardboard carton and balanced it on his left shoulder, steadied it with a hand. He moved toward the door and opened it onto the hot sidewalk.

"I'll see you."

"You come back," Long said automatically.

The door closed behind Winer with a soft ching from the bell and burdened with the box he went on down the street toward the cabstand.

Motormouth came out of the pasture past the looming bulk of the barn and halted where the moon threw cedared shadows, paused a moment to gain his bearings. A thin figure propelled by sheer anger dark to dark and shadow to shadow past the barn and on to the house. The world lay in a grail of silence, the only color a square of yellow light a window threw misshapen into the yard. One shadow among others less mobile, he moved past the truck in a soundless lope through unprotected light, the gun clasped across his chest, gaining invisibility momentarily in the accumulation of shadows against the wall.

He lay in the grass. It had just been mown, he could smell it, could feel it, wet with dew, adhering to his bare arms. Slowly he began to rise, straightened to a crouch, scarcely daring to breathe. The screen was cool against his cheek.

The room was yellow. He could see three-quarters of the bed and a man's freckled arm, a yellow wall bare save a door and a calendar with a scene of a lovable waif wending his way down a country road, fishing pole on his shoulder. Unloved and perhaps unlovable, Motormouth straightened further when the door opened and a young woman came through it. She was young, pretty, Motormouth's wife. She wore a peachcolored slip and now she drew it over her head in one smooth motion, tossed her hair, breasts bobbing, turning toward the lightswitch. He stared at the darker thatch of her pubic hair as the room went down to darkness. He fumbled open his clothing, spent himself in an act of bitter solitude, affected more by the sight of her naked now than in all the nights she'd willingly shared his bed. He moved limberkneed back to the truck, more confident now that the lights were out.

He brought out a packet from his hip pocket, unwrapped it. A soft avalanche of sugar down the throat of the gastank. "One lump or two?" he asked it. He moved on toward the barn, a figure curiously simian in the cold night. Somehow the sugar did not seem enough. He could smell the sour ammoniac odor of the horsestalls. He brought out his wirecutters and knelt in the grass. He could hear the soft snuffling of the horses. The woven wire clicked when he cut it, when he was through he went on to the barbed wire. The barbed wire was taut and it clanged when he cut it and sprang away into the darkness. The moon slipped behind a cloud and the horses were lost to his sight. He could hear them moving about the pen fretfully, almost furtively.

He pocketed the cutters and took up the rifle and turned hurriedly back toward the woods. The cloud passed the moon then and its huge shadow paced him, dreamlike, through the surreal field of silver weeds.

In Hovington's last days they moved his bed out of the long front room and into a side room as if the sight of his dying might offend the sensibilities of such drunkards and whores as the nights seemed to draw ever more of. The long room held more cardtables now and the jukebox and sometimes late at night couples danced in the end where his bed had been. He'd lie in the darkness and listen to their laughter through the slatted walls, to the thump and slide of their feet on the rough floorboards. Perhaps in these last hours he was grateful for the jukebox. This world is not my home, the Carter family sang. Oh Lord, what will I do? Or perhaps he lay in the darkness and thought no thoughts at all, not even dwelling on the thousand deeds and nondeeds that had brought him to such a pass.

The room had one fourpaned window and he used to lie curled facing it and peer across the weeds to the branch and past that to where the hills gave way to autumn sky.

Visitors didn't come much anymore and with the cessation of a need for appearances Pearl had stopped shaving him and his thin cheeks were covered with a soft black beard flecked with gray. He might have been a fanatic consumed from within by the fires of some fierce and obscure religion.

The girl used to come sit by his bed in the ladderback chair and watch him without speaking. In these days she could study his face at leisure. His eyes would be closed, the eyes unmoving beneath the yellow lids, and she guessed he didn't dream much anymore.

She remembered his laughter from a childhood so long ago it might have been a tale she'd read in a dusty schoolbook. Then a little at a time silence had taken him over and there had been a time when she had wanted to scream at him, "What's the matter with you? Why do you let him run over us like you do?"

When his back began to bend like something folding what was left of his life inside it, and the perimeters of where he could go and not go were marked by the dimensions of the bed, he had grown more silent yet. Sometimes he'd come awake from dozing and she'd be a slim, dark presence by the window, watching him, her face as unreadable as his own. And he had no words to say, no deeds to do. Everything seemed said, nothing left but waiting.

He lay steeped in pain and oblivious of his surroundings like a dying rat preoccupied with the pellet of poison slowly dissolving in his belly. Death by misadventure, a garbage can explored better left alone.

"He's coughin up blood again," she told her mother. Pearl laid aside the dishtowel and went into the near-dark room.

Hardin shuffled a poker deck and dealt himself a full house, the cards rippling smooth as water. He reshuffled and dealt a jackhigh straight flush, conscious of the sounds from the sickroom, of the door opening. The shiftless shuffle of her houseshoes ceasing. He could feel her behind him, silent and somehow accusatory.

Then she said, "He's dyin."

Bored with straight flushes, Hardin laid the cards aside. "Well," he said, "there's no news in that. He's been dyin ever since I knowed him."

"He's bad off."

Hardin went to see. Hovington's flesh was gray and clammy. Hardin's hand came away moist with cold sweat when he touched the sick man. He wiped his hand on a trouserleg. It seemed to him he could already feel a rigidity seeping into Hovington's flesh, stealthy, covert, he could already smell the sweet, carrion presence of death.

"You reckon he needs a doctor?"

"Undertaker is more like it." Hardin passed through the door and paused and lit a cigarette. He went on through the house and onto the porch, then sat on the edge of the porch in the sun. Pearl followed him out, the door closing nigh soundless behind her. "Stay with him," he said. "It's him in there dyin, not me out here."

Pearl was silent awhile. "He's wantin somethin," she finally said.

"I don't doubt it for a minute," Hardin said. "In his place I might could think of a thing or two I'd want myself."

"He wants that Winer woman brought up here. He wants to talk to her."

"Say he does?"

"That's what he asked for."

"He's out of his head."

"Maybe, but he ain't never asked for nothin else."

"That's crazy and a waste of time besides."

"All these years and he's never asked for nothin," she persisted. "Nothin only what a preacher could give him and he never even got that. Just laid there all this time and took what come."

"That's all any of us can do, take what comes."

She looked stricken, the flesh of her cheeks folded on itself, her lips trembling. A damp and fearful blue eye. He thought she might cry.

"Just shut it up," he told her. "Don't you think it's a bit late in the day for this? He made his bed and by God you made yourn and all you can do now is lay there with the cover pulled up around your chin and rest as best you can."

Yet there was a stolid immutability to her he hadn't known was there, an immovable weight of stubbornness that held her rooted before him as if he were wedded to her, condemned alike to her tardy sense of guilt. He thought suddenly that to move her aside he'd have to shove her, cut a path through her with a hawkbill knife. He dropped his cigarette and ground it out with the toe of his boot.

"Then by God get her. But get her on your own book. I've got more to do than run up and down the road." He stepped off the porch and strode toward the barn. She went back in.

The girl came out and hurried across the yard, a momentary hand raised to shield the sun. It was early yet, the morning sun resting above the green treeline. A day brimming with incandescent light and filling up with birdsong and she thought she'd never seen a brighter day. So bright a day to lie dying on. She was touched with horror, with a desperate need to hurry.

Her shoes made flat little plops in the roadbed and little clouds of dust arose like phantoms pursuing her. She increased her pace and the harsh green world became a world in motion, a bobbing wall of greenery like murky water, and even the cries of birds were muted and distorted like sound filtered through fire.

Amber Rose did not believe in miracles. He is dying, she thought. She thought of a casket lid being closed. No one will open it, ever, she thought in wonder. The concept of forever struck her with the force of a blow. It yawned before her, all-engrossing, awesome. She stopped in the curve of the road and looked back.

The house sat full in the sun, its roof growing dull green, its walls myriad shades of weathered gray. Brooding so in the morning light it seemed pulled magnetically by the anomalous shadows from the hollow. She whirled and hurried on.

Through the moving windshield of the Packard he watched with wry amusement their progress up the dusty roadbed, two figures imbued with haste, hurrying jerkily toward him like puppets dragged along by strings.

He slowed the Packard as he neared them, braked to a stop when they were almost parallel with the car. He cut the switch and sat watching them, an arm on the sill of the window.

"Looks like you had a long, hot trip for nothin, Miz Winer,"

Hardin said. "Brother Hovington passed away a minute ago. I thought I'd save you the rest of the trip."

"It wadn't no trouble," the woman said. Her voice sounded stilted and formal from beneath the rim of the bonnet. "I hate to hear about Mr. Hovington."

"Well, I guess he can rest easy now. Get in and I'll run you back home."

"I'll just go on I reckon and see if I can be of any help to Mrs. Hovington."

"We can manage. I'm just sorry we drug you into our troubles."

"Folks got to help one another."

"I reckon. We'll manage though."

The girl came around the side of the car, opened the door, and got in without speaking. The woman stood awkwardly in the roadbed as if awaiting enlightenment. "What was it he wanted me for anyway?"

"He never said," Hardin told her.

The girl sat staring across the fence where Oliver's goats grazed the bright tangle of bitterweed, though she did not see them. She thought, They will have to break his back to ever get him in a casket. A sense of horror suffused her, she fell to thinking on how this could come to be. Surely there were tools for this, no ordinary hammer would suffice. Beyond the grazing goats her mind dreamed implements of brass and gleaming bronze, folds of purple velvet to mute the blows.

Hardin had said something.

"No, I'll just walk," Mrs. Winer said.

"Suit yourself then," Hardin said. He started the car and began to turn it in the road.

She sat watching her hands fold pleats in her blue skirt. She thought she ought to cry but she didn't.

William Tell Oliver straightened from the milling goats amidst the halfmusical clangor of the bells to watch the stately passage of the hearse, the corn spilling forgotten from his hands, the polished black of the hearse winking back the midday sun, its sides already dulling with a film of dust.

Hovington, he thought, fascinated by the windows curtained by red velvet, the hearse's low, sinister configuration somehow profound and appalling against the border of sumac and blackberry briars, diminishing then, content this time with another.

Winer went three times to the Red Diamond Poultry Farm. The first two times there was no one about at all and no sign of Weiss's car. The chickens were halfstarved. He fed and watered them. The third time was on a Wednesday and Weiss's car was parked in the drive and the front door was ajar though no one answered his call. He stood uncertainly in the clutter of the porch and after awhile he sat in a lawn chair and waited. He felt restless, bemused, time was a commodity in short supply and he must ration his.

Everything seemed to be in disorder. The porch held stacked boxes of white cylinders that turned out to be photographs rolled tightly as window shades. A box was upended and the pictures scattered about the floor. He unrolled one. Another. They all seemed to be photographs of military units, hundreds of soldiers posed before barracks that looked makeshift and temporary, perhaps as temporary and fragile as the men they housed. Only the faces were different, a multitude of them, stern faces with overseas caps cocked jauntily, and then after awhile even the faces seemed to merge and lose identity, become multiple exposures of some soldier posed in limbo, awaiting a ship that would bear him to a war fought long ago.

A noise drew him up and through the halfopen door. This room as well was in disorder, suitcases open, clothing strewn about the floor as if kicked there. Weiss lay on the couch. His mouth was open and the room was full of his noisy breathing. A stain fanned out from an overturned wine decanter, a red seeping as if the room had been the scene of gruesome carnage. Weiss slept in his clothes and his boots. The pith helmet lay tilted on the carpet.

When Winer shook him Weiss's eyes opened and he started, rose on his right elbow, peering wildly about the room.

"What? What is it? What's the matter?"

Winer suddenly found himself bereft of anything to say. Weiss's startled face struggling up from sleep wore an expression somehow akin to madness as if whatever had happened in the last week had marked him, left him deranged. Weiss had always worn the helmet and looking down at him Winer saw that he was almost bald, the scalp pink and vulnerable through the kinked black hair.

"It's morning," Winer said. "The sun's way up."

"Fuck the sun," Weiss said.

He struggled toward a semblance of erectness, abandoned the effort, settled back against the couch cushions. His eyes were open but unfocused, his fingers going awkwardly through all his pockets. At last he came up with the remnants of a pack of Camels, took one out and stuck it in his mouth, and sat without lighting it. His big head was propped on the heel of his hand, his elbow kept sliding off his knee.

"Jesus," he said. "Oh, Jesus Christ."

Winer stood in silence peering out the window. The sun fell through the window, a rectangle of merciless light. Where the yard fell away he could see the fence bordering it and through broken greenery the red road itself. He wished he were already on it. When he turned back toward the man on the couch Weiss's eyes were closed to slits and were watching him speculatively as if surprised to find him still there.

"What do you want anyway?"

"Well. I came to work. To feed and all."

"There's not any work," Weiss said. He had taken up a table lighter and was turning it in his hands this way and that, dropping his eyes to stare at it bemusedly as if uninitiated in its complexities.

"Not any work?"

"That's what I said. I'm gathering up some stuff and getting out of here. I'm getting the fuck out and I don't know if I'm ever coming back or not."

"What about the chickens?"

"What about them? You can have them. Give them to these rednecks around here and let them have a barbecue to remember me by. Give them to your friend Hodges, he wanted them badly enough to try to steal them."

Winer stood awkwardly without speaking, unable to articulate his thoughts. Finally he said, "Then you don't need me?"

"Hell no, I don't need you. What would I need you for? I told you, there's nothing. I'm getting the fuck gone and you may as well do the same."

"I guess that's plain enough. I'll see you."

"I doubt it." When Winer was halfway to the door Weiss said, "Look. Goddamn it. For what it's worth I'm sorry, Winer." He raised his hands, dropped them. "There's just nothing. How much do I owe you?"

"Eight dollars."

"All right." He withdrew his wallet, sat for a time staring into it so that Winer thought he had forgotten his purpose in extracting it. Then he tossed it to the boy. "Here. You get it. My vision seems somewhat impaired this morning."

Winer counted out a five and three ones and folded them down into his shirt pocket. He handed Weiss the wallet.

"No hard feelings, Winer. You did me a fine job."

"No hard feelings. I was sorry to hear about your wife." Winer turned to the door. When Weiss didn't reply he went into the hot sunshine.

Dreading what she might have to say he didn't tell her until the next morning.

"Ain't I told you?" she wanted to know. "That's just like him, I always knowed he was no account. Come in here throwin his money around and buildin his big chickenhouses and now where is he? I reckon now you'll take up for him and argue your own mama down. Read a book one time and think you know it all."

He let the screendoor fall to behind him and sat for a time on the doorstep. This day was a world of distances, of silence. This was the first day there'd been a hint of coolness in the air. He was surprised to see a few leaves already turning. There was a winey smell to the air, an immeasurable blueness to the sky. He was still sitting there when she came out. There did not seem much else to do.

"Well?" she asked him. "What do you aim to do now?"

He didn't say anything.

William Tell Oliver had known Winer's father for a long time. He remembered seeing him going to work in the mornings, Oliver as well was an early riser and back before the boy was born and Winer had no horse much less an automobile to ride to work Oliver used to hear him pass about four o'clock in the morning. That was before Winer started carpentering and in those days he used to walk all the way to Big Sinking to offbear at Hickerson's sawmill all day and even in the summer it would be dusk when he got home, in winter dark would have long fallen. Old even then, Oliver if he happened to be on the porch would hear out of the cold dark Winer's measured footfalls, see him pass wraithlike, the stride determined, constant. He might raise an unseen hand in the spectral dark. Winer needed no light to find his way, needed only the constant repetitions of his journey to guide him.

He did not know the woman that well. She had been a Hines and like the particular branch of the family she sprang from Oliver thought her dour and overly practical. She had no interest in anything that happened in a book, on the radio, in France or Washington, D.C. Nothing that was not readily applicable to her life. If you can't eat it, fuck it, or bust it up for stovewood, she's got no use for it, Oliver thought one time with sour amusement. So when he saw the boy coming up the road in midday he thought, So Weiss has lit a shuck and he's out of a job. And they have been into it about it.

"I guess I'm fresh out of a job," Winer told him without being asked.

"That's about the way I figured it. He's gone, is he?"

"Yeah."

"You want some coffee?"

"I might drink a cup."

Winer followed him into the kitchen. Oliver poured coffee from a blue enamel pot. The food on the table was covered with a clean white cloth to keep the flies off.

"Help yeself to anything ye see."

"I don't want anything," Winer said. He raised a corner of the cloth, peered. "What kind of cake is that?"

"Storebought. Coconut. You can eat it, I didn't cook it."

Winer sliced a wedge of cake and stood eating it.

"Come on out to the edge of the porch where's it's cool."

When they were on the porch and Oliver back in the porch swing he said, "Old man Weiss was a funny sort of feller."

"He acted all torn up about her death."

"Hell, I guess he is all tore up. Look at it this way. He's been here twenty year and don't have friend one. Which I guess was more than not his own fault. Nobody to talk to, drink with, nothin. Everbody has to have somebody like that and he had her. Now he ain't."

"I guess so. They thought the world of each other. They got along better than any folks I ever knew."

"Hell, he may be in South America by now."

"South America?"

The old man grinned. "Weiss said some funny things sometimes. Told me one time, said, 'I got open channels to heads of state and access to banana boats to South America.' Said it like he was braggin. Ain't that a hell of a thing? Course, I didn't mind. I never envied anybody their access to banana boats."

"He told me one time he invented Coca-Cola. But whether he did or not, I've still got to find a job."

"Boy, why don't you just ease up and be your age for awhile? School'll be startin pretty soon anyway, won't it? Don't you finish this year?"

"I may not go. I may take a year off and work and then go back next fall. I don't know what difference a year makes anyway."

"I guess at your age you feel like you got more years than anything else."

"I don't guess it matters."

"How much was you makin if you don't mind me askin?"

"Two dollars a day."

"Great God, boy. I wouldn't grieve long over a job like that. You ort to be jumpin up and down turnin summersets. You can make more money than that trompin the woods for ginseng and blackroot."

"I might could if I knew what it looked like."

"I'll show ye. It's got me through some mighty tight places back when times was really hard. But we got to hurry. We need to get started right now. You can't find it after frost."

"Well. We'll go then. I've got to do something while I'm waiting on a job to turn up."

Oliver dreamed his wife was shaking him awake. "Tell, Tell," she kept saying. He dreamed he was awake and she was leaning before him in her nightgown with her hair all undone and the room was lit with the cool, otherworldly glow of moonlight through the glass. The weight of her hand still lay on his shoulder. "Get up, Tell," she said. "He ain't come in. Willie ain't. I heard him at the door awhile ago but he ain't come in."

He got up and pulled on his overalls and shoes without putting on his socks. The dream was so vivid he didn't know it was a dream. It was wintertime and he could feel the cold, stiff leather against his bare feet and the icy metal of his galluses against his naked shoulders. He did not know the hour but in a detached part of his mind he knew he was in a strange, clockless world set apart from time.

He went out the door and into the moonlit yard. The Mormon Springs road lay white and cold and dusted with moonlight. He went past the pear tree and onto the hardpan and stood for a moment undecided, he didn't know which way to go. He turned back toward the house and she stood in the doorway watching him. The shadow of the porch fell across her, beheading her with darkness, but he could see her eyes glowing out of the dark like cat's eyes. He turned and went on toward the apple orchard.

Nothing looked right, by subtle increments everything was changing. He was venturing into a world going surreal before his eyes, reality was being stepped up, warped by heat. The bare branches of the apple trees writhed like trees from a province in dementia. A coarse whispering came from the orchard, furtive, conspiratorial, almost but not quite intelligible. Then he saw that the branches of the trees were alive with birds, curious dark birds he could not recognize, birds a fevered brain might hallucinate. Unfeathered salamandrine birds with strange lizardlike heads and skin textured like wet leather. He could see their yellow eyes about the trees like paired-off fireflies. The whispering increased in pitch, became intelligible. He stood transfixed by the hypnotic buzz of sound from the apple orchard. Willie, Willie, the birds were crying, over and over. Willie, Willie.

He was touched by a cold engendered by more than weather. He turned in the road, north, south, searching the silver fields for sight of the boy. Random stones gleamed like details in a mosaic. Weeds sheathed in ice were glass reeds in the moonlight. He began to walk aimlessly down the white road. He could hear a fluttering from the trees behind him as the birds took wing. Looking up, he could see dark shapes shifting patternlessly above him. A few alighted in the road and paced him with a ducklike gait he found repulsive and whirling he kicked viciously at one and it hissed like a snake and spread its unfeathered wings and stood its ground.

"Get," he told it. "Get, Goddamn you."

Willie, Willie, they were calling above him.

The bird had stopped at the edge of the road. Turning, he went on a few feet then looked back and the bird was following him taking delicate, mincing steps as if it were tiptoeing. He went on through country he had known all his days that was slowly altering before his eyes and at length the road he had known faded out and the metamorphosis was complete: he was somewhere he had never been. A barren twilit world of winds and sounds.

The road began to descend toward some great declivity, an enormous pit like an amphitheater excavated out of the ground. When he reached the edge he paused and peered down. He stood in frozen awe. The bottom seemed hundreds of feet away. All he could see of the earth looked red and raw, freshly dug, as if all there was of the world anymore was this ravaged, bleeding ruin. He knew intuitively that he had been following this moonlit road all his life and that this was where it led. The pit was profound, imbued with meaning, and he felt he must absorb every detail: he was being shown something of the workings of life. He must remember this place and whatever tale it had to tell. The birds began to alight in the dead vestiges of trees on the precipice of the pit. The trees leaned as if they bore the weight of some perpetual wind. The chanting from the birds ceased and turning at the sudden silence he saw multitudes of them descending, their leathery wings beating the air.

He began to descend the sloping shoulder of the pit over icy whorls of frozen earth and bulldozer tracks seized in ice like something vague and prehistoric preserved for all time. In the bottom of the pit water had seeped and pooled and it had frozen white as milk. He went on. He could hear the thin crystalline breaking of ice beneath his feet and he was held by a sense of impending doom, an apprehension of things beyond his command, forced onward yet possessed of a foreknowledge of what was to be.

A rusting yellow bulldozer sat cocked long silent on a mound of earth. Veering toward it, he thought he might ask the nature of all this destruction but beneath the dozer's cowl the operator was an eyeless skeleton in leached khaki rags, a faded blue hardhat tilted rakishly on yellowed bone. A rusted black dinner bucket lashed to the cowl. Oliver turned without surprise and went toward the bottom.

The floor leveled out and he seemed in some lifeless manmade valley that went on forever. He moved moonlit though shadowless to the edge of the ice then a foot onto it and stopped where the white face of his son lay pressed against the underside of the ice, eyes open, dark hair fanned and listless in the still water.

He cried out in a strangled voice and fell to his knees. He could feel hot tears flood his eyes and course down his cheeks unchecked and bitter grief lay in him like a stone. He clawed at the whorled ice until his fingers were torn and bleeding and he ceased and looking skyward exhorted the fates who'd glanced aside for a moment and let this thing happen. All he saw was the seamless heavens and the slow drift of a dead and foreign moon.

The birds began to call again and their voices had the mournful cadence of doves. Willie, Willie, they called. When he looked again through the ice the face was gone and all there was beneath the translucent ice was motionless water and black frozen leaves.

He awoke breathless in the hot dark with his chest constricted and an ache in his throat and it was a few seconds before he knew where he was or that he had been dreaming. He lay with his mind sorting through the fragmented images separating real from imagined and he thought of her saying, Where's Willie? What have you done with him? and did not know whether it had ever happened or if it was some curious halfwaking progression of his dream.

Willie will kill Dallas Hardin, he thought. Then, confusedly, No, no, not Willie, Willie's dead himself these fifty years. Young Winer will kill him.

He got up. He lit the lamp on the dresser and crossed the room to the chifforobe and opened it. He took down a shoebox and unwrapped the skull from its bed of tissue and looked at it. Course I got to do somethin, he thought. He had thought at first to bury it and be done with it but somehow that had not seemed fitting. It was unfinished, there were too many loose ends. Wrongs needed someone to right them and words ought to be said but he did not feel worthy of saying them.

In the yellow halflight from the coaloil lamp he and the skull formed a curious tableau. Kneeling so before the chifforobe he might have been an acolyte before an oracle, a disciple seeking wisdom from this hard traveler newly raised up from the bowels of the earth. Could it speak what tales would it tell him? Had it seen its doom? Had its eyes unbelievingly traced the trajectory of the bullet that splintered it?

If he ever finds it out nothin won't stop him from killin Hardin and he'll live out his life in the pen, Oliver thought. If I wasn't soft in the head I'd a killed him myself a long time ago.

There were three of them. They were there at first light, coming up the road or simply coalescing out of the mist, the sound that portended their coming clean and clear and halfmusical and lending an anticipatory air to their arrival, though there was only Amber Rose Hovington there to hear them or to see them, sleek and arrogant and graceful, quartering at the road and singlefile following the branch, halting to feed on the dewy clover that grew rankly on the stream's bank and nuzzling the clear limestone water, raising their heads from their roiled reflections to stare contemptuously at the house, their eyes not yet admitting its existence.

Their steel shoes rang hollowly on the slate, moving on toward the abyss, which had already claimed two heifers that summer. Turning aside only when they came upon what Hardin liked to call his garden, four rows of defeated corn yellowed and bent askew by stormwinds, pale beans wrinkled and dried on their tripod arrangement of sticks. Nothing thriving here save ragweed and Spanish nettles.

"There's horses in the garden," she called into the house.

The dry snap of breaking beansticks drew Hardin onto the porch with his coffeecup still in hand. The horses had trampled most of the ruined corn as if scorning whatever poor nourishment it might contain and were at the pole beans, raising their heads and staring toward the sound of the girl's voice, the stallion disregarding them and turning toward the rich green at the hollow's mouth.

"Horses I reckon," Hardin said. "Them's Morgans. Look at that big beautiful son of a bitch. Ain't he somethin?" He drained the cup and set it by a porch support and eased into the yard. "Be a shame to see horseflesh like that go end over end down a hole in the ground. Go in there and roust Wymer out. He's on that old carseat."

Hardin sat on the doorstep and watched the horses. "Easy now," he said. He tipped a cigarette from a pack and lit it with a thin gold lighter, sat smoking and turning the lighter in his hands. The lighter was initialed, though the initials were not his own. He had on a pair of tailored slacks and he was barefoot.

The stallion stood facing him across the branch-run, peering up at him cautiously from its lowered head. Hardin watched the smooth, oiled play of its muscles beneath the roancolored hide. "Look at me then," he told it soothingly. "Get your eyes full, you sweet bastard. Fore this is over you aim to see a lot of me."

From past the weatherboarded walls he could hear the voice of the girl and another voice raised in querulous anger. Sounds of protest, disbelief, anguish. The girl could go get fucked, Hardin learned. Hardin himself could go get fucked. A suggestion Wymer continued to issue indiscriminately and to the world at large. The door opened, the keeperspring creaked it to.

"He won't come. He just cussed me."

"The hell he won't," Hardin said. He tossed the cigarette into the yard and arose. "You go down there and get me a bucketful of that sweetfeed and bring it here. Go around the far side of the house so you don't spook them horses."

He went in. After a few moments of silence sounds of commotion arose. The splash of water, cries, curses. The door burst open and a little man ran drunkenly out onto the porch and with Hardin's now-shod foot to propel him continued down the steps and into the yard. His thin hair was plastered away from a pink baldspot and rheumy gray water dripped off his nose and chin. Half an eggshell was tangled in his hair like some fey adornment. The white shirt he wore was spotted with esoteric bits of food. His hands shaded his eyes as if to shield them from deadly rays. He stood swaying limply for a moment then dropped his hands and stared at the red orb of sun burning away at the mist, peering at it as if he had never seen it at just this angle before.

"Get on up there by that hole and stand," Hardin told him. "When that girl brings that feed, if she ever does, me and her'll try to toll em down to the lot. If we can't we'll have to drive em. And if you let that big red son of a bitch stumble off in that pit just make damn sure you beat him to the bottom."

Wymer had his shirttail out wiping his eyes. He raked the dripping wing of hair back out of his face. "Why, shore," he said. "All you had to do was ast."

Hardin had the bucket of sweetfeed now and his fist knotted in the stallion's long auburn mane and he was whispering into its ear. The horse tossed its head in tentative defiance but Hardin's calm assurance aborted it, its eyes rolled heavenward and his fist knotted tighter, pulling the neck down. He went on whispering, a ripple of motion ran across the horse's smooth hide. The girl stood by the doorstep watching. Pearl had come out and stood leaning in the doorway. Wymer was waistdeep in the bracken, bent hands to knees peering apprehensively into the weeds for snakes. The voice went on, conspiratorial, equal to equal, halfsoothing, halfobscene banter, dark secrets he shared with the stallion. He took a step, halfturned, his voice coaxing, slackening his grip in the mane, raising the feedbucket to the horse's muzzle. He took another step toward the stream and this time the stallion's feet echoed it. They came down the embankment with his arm still about the horse's neck and into the stream where the horse paused for a moment, head bent to the cold water rippling across the slick black slate. He stroked its shoulder.

"Get that lot gate open," he told the girl. "Now." The two mares had ceased worrying the bean vines and stood watching the stallion. After a moment one of them lifted her head and took a tentative step to follow him.

Such a fence as it was, they were in it. Hardin and the girl fed them cracked corn and more sweetfeed and then stood by the fence watching them eat. The fence seemed held together more by honeysuckle vines and cowitch than by wire and half the posts were rotting and canted and held up by the towering pyramids of poisonoak that clotted them.

Wymer hunkered in the shadow of the barn wiping his face with his handkerchief. Hardin reached him a cigarette and Wymer took it and stuck it in his mouth. When he made no move to light it Hardin proffered the gold lighter.

"Who do you reckon they belong to, Wymer?"

"Nobody around here got any Morgans but them Blalock boys over on Harrikan. They got to belong to them."

"Man owns horseflesh like that ought to tend his fences."

Wymer gestured with his cigarette. "You won't never keep em in there."

"I will when you get through patchin it and proppin them posts and loopin me three strands of bobwire around it," Hardin said.

"Lord God," Wymer said. He peered toward the sky as if beseeching the intervention of some more authoritative word. The sun was in ascension now and the sky was a hot, quaking blue, it seemed to pulse like molten metal. Against the deep void a hawk wheeled arrogantly, jays came to tease it and it rose effortlessly on the updrafts from the hollow like an intricately crafted kite, climbed until it was only a speck moving against the infinite blue.

Hardin put an arm about Wymer's shoulders. "Now, it won't be so bad," he told him consolingly. "It won't take long and while you're doin it you know what I'm goin to do? I'm goin to take a case of beer and put it in the freezer, and it'll be there icin down just waitin on you."

Wymer didn't say anything. He just stood there staring at the leaning fenceposts.

"You tell Pearl I said give you some money and take that truck and go get me two rolls of bobwire."

"Why, I ain't even got no license," Wymer protested.

"I never knowed one was required to buy bobwire," Hardin said.

"It likes to grow on the north slope of a hill," Oliver told him. "Shadier there I reckon. It's funny stuff, some places it'll grow and some places it won't. And it don't come up ever year. You won't find none in no pineywoods or in a honeysuckle thicket. Lots of times you'll find sang up on a hillside from where a branch runs. But then lots of times you won't."

Winer followed the old man down a steep hillside, Oliver negotiating his way tree to tree, pausing to point with his stick toward an arrowheadshaped fern.

"See that? Now, that's pointer. Where you find that you'll generally find some sang though it ain't no ironclad guarantee, it just grows in the same kind of ground sang does."

They had been out since daylight and Winer's legs ached from clambering up and down the hillsides and he did not see how the old man held up. He was agile as one of his own goats and he seemed possessed by a curious sense of excitement.

"It's like gamblin or drinkin or runnin women or whatever you get habited to," he had told Winer. "You get started huntin sang and it just gets in your blood."

Oliver paused, peering groundward. "Come here a minute, boy."

Winer came up beside him. Oliver was pointing out with his snake stick a plant growing in the shade of a chestnut oak. He dropped the point of his stick back against the earth and rested his weight on it.

"What would you say that was there?"

Winer laid his sack aside and knelt to the earth, raking back the leaves and dark loam from around the delicate stem of the plant. He studied the wilted top he carried for reference.

"It's ginseng," he said.

"Are you right sure now?"

"Well, it looks like it." He studied his top some more. "Sure I'm sure."

Oliver grinned. "That's just old jellico," he said. "See how the limbs grow out of the stems on it? One here and one there? Now look at ye ginseng. See how them limbs grows out right even with one another? That's how ye tell it."

"Well, it looks like it to me."

"It ain't though. Folks dig some peculiar things thinking it's ginseng. Back in the depression it couldn't a stalk peep out of the ground without there was somebody there waitin on it. I never like to dig it myself fore it sheds its berries. That way you always got young comin along."

"It must be hard to learn to recognize it."

"No. And once you do learn nothin else looks exactly like it. You can spot it as far as you can see it. Though I do remember old man Hovington when he was a boy dug half a tow sack of poisonoak fore he learned the difference. He found out in two–three days. He might never've learnt sang but I bet he knowed poisonoak from then on."

They went on under the lowering branches of a chestnut oak, gentle wind out of the south stirring the leaves. The woods smelled yellow and brittle. The hollow was deep and below them Winer could hear the rush of water over stone. Occasionally the old man would stop and punch a hole in the loam with his stick and drop in one of the reddish-brown berries he carried.

"Nature's a funny thing," he said thoughtfully. "Now, you take that jellico. It's like sang but it ain't. It grows in the same kind of ground and it looks about like it. Everthing in nature's got a twin and jellico's sang's twin. I don't know for what reason. Protection maybe. Whoever laid things out made it look that way so some folks'd go ahead and dig it up and let the sang be, where it wouldn't die out. Sort of like iron pyrites, you know, fool's gold. You could learn a lesson in all this was you lookin for one."

Winer didn't say anything.

"Now, I know you at a age where you don't want folks teachin you lessons. But you'll learn em sometime and this here's the easy way. Sometime up ahead you'll think you found what you been lookin for. Lord God, you'll think. What a mess of ginseng. You'll fly in and dig it up thinkin you really got somethin. But you won't. All you'll have is a sack of this old jellico."

"The whitecaps came down this ridge right about here," Oliver said, pointing toward the stony sedgefield. Below him Winer could see Hovington's house and outbuildings, the corncrib almost swallowed in a riot of pokeroot. "Them Mormons had their church built down some from where the spring is and I reckon two or three brush arbors and lean-tos or some such. The old foundation pillars is I guess still there."

"Why did they do it anyway?"

"Lord, boy, I don't know. I long give up on wonderin why folks do all the things they do." He hunkered in the windy sedge, began absentmindedly to massage his stiff knee. "Though I guess like everthing else it was a number of things. I guess they was drinkin a little and just wanted to raise hell. Them Mormons was a different breed of cat too and I reckon bein different's always had its occupational hazards around here. And you get a bunch of them old hardankles like used to be around here together, specially with pillowcases to hide who they are, and you need to make sure wherever you are's got a back door to it."

"I thought the story was they were worried about their womenfolks. That's what I always heard."

"Well, that was the tale but it was just so much horseshit. But then folks in these parts always had some curious ideas about women. Had to be protected and all that. Sheltered. I never knowed one couldn't take care of herself and I never knowed one to park her shoes under any bed she hadn't crawled into by herself."

"Did they have any women from around here at their camp?"

"They had two or three I think but they was here on their own hook. Nobody tolled em off or drug em screamin by the hair of the head."

Below them came the faint slap of a screendoor and a man entered the back yard. He took up from against the weatherboarding a shovel and advanced onto a cleared area where a large rectangle was marked off by stakes and batterboards. He pulled off his shirt and began to shovel earth from beneath the line. His back was very white. He worked fiercely for a few seconds then stopped and stood leaning with his foot cocked on the shovel studying the distance left to cover.

"Who all was it?"

"I doubt you'd remember any of em," the old man said dryly. "There was a good bunch of em. Tom Hovington's pa, he was one. Not no ringleader or nothin, just one of the bunch. A follower, he was good at that sort of thing. Never had an idea of his own but was the first to jump when somebody else did. Kind of a suckass. They talked it up for a week or two before they done it. They come around the house and Pa, he run em off. Pa never was much of a joiner. Old man Hodges was I guess the worst. He had a daughter down there. She would've been, let's see, Motormouth Hodges's aunt. She'd done run off with everbody else and maybe she figured she'd see if the Mormons had come up with some new way of doin it. That mob come up here long about daybreak and set in to whip em but them Mormons must've had mixed feelins about bein whipped. They started shootin back and forth and the whitecaps ended up killin ever one of em cept four or five women. They tied em up and whipped em, among other things."

"How old was you?"

"Fifteen or sixteen. Old enough to know not to be here but not bright enough to come up and warn em. That's always bothered me some."

"Why didn't anybody else let em know?"

"I guess everbody figured it was all blow. If Hodges'd killed all the folks he threatened this county'd be mighty thin settled. Anyway, folks thought they was just takin a hickory to em, that's what the whitecaps was famous for. I doubt they knowed theirselves they was goin to be slaughterin people right and left. It just got out of hand."

The boy did not reply, seemed lost in the subtle gradations of umber and burnt sienna, the dull green of rampant summer's growth turning sullen and sulfurous with its coating of dust, the old house bleached field gray, somehow oblique and alien in the harsh light, the bracken darkening and becoming more luxuriant near the spring and the hidden dark orifice of the abyss.

He wondered what the truth was, secretly doubted there was any truth left beneath the shifting weight of myth and folklore. Truth had changed the way the landscape had changed to accommodate progress, altered by each generation to its purpose. He had learned from the talk of old men that there was no such thing as truth, truth was always shaded by perception and expectation. And the old man's truth might not be Winer's. Hodges had said that the old man himself had killed two men, but Oliver had never spoken of it. Now that too was layered with time, had held truth only in the bright millisecond of all time it occupied, now there was the old man's truth, the dead men's survivors' truth, the court's truth, all of them separate truths men had sworn to. Winer disregarded them all.

"One thing about gettin old," Oliver was saying. "You can watch another feller work and not feel guilty about it. Though whether or not what that feller's doin qualifies as work depends on whether you're payin or gettin paid."

The man had forsaken the shovel for a mattock and was flailing at the earth. A darkhaired girl came out and took up the shovel with what from a distance seemed reluctance. The pale man ceased and stood gazing thoughtfully off into space then recommenced with renewed enthusiasm when a tall man came into the yard and stood watching them.

"I guess they'll get it now," the old man said. "There's Old Nick in the flesh."

"Hardin?"

"Whatever he's goin by now."

Winer turned as if to share Oliver's jest but the leathery face showed no sign that the old man had not been serious.

"What do you suppose he's buildin down there?"

"More room for his meanness, I guess." Oliver braced himself on the handcarved stick and arose, gaunt and ungainly against the blue void, a figure himself of myth perhaps, an Old Testament patriarch marvelously transported to 1943 and finding the world not entirely to his liking. "The harder times get for everbody else the better they get for folks like Hardin," Oliver said.

Motormouth's wife, Ruby, had left him for what she described as good and all in August. Ruby was a bitch but there was no news in that. She had always been a bitch. He had divined that even when she had been a little girl in white crinoline and white shoes holding her father's hand on the way to church she was already a bitch, though a more diminutive and less strident one. She had been a bitch in her cradle, a tiny, toothless bitch at her mother's breast. Motormouth had known all this and had married her anyway, planning to reform her.

The ink had scarcely dried on their marriage license when she had cuckolded him. He had caught them at a deserted racetrack, naked in the backseat of an old Ford. She had been with a high school junior who was not even seventeen years old. He had been scared so badly he could not even get his pants on, had both feet stuffed into the same trouserleg and was just madly jumping up and down as if he were trying to drive himself into them and escape from sight. Motormouth had been appalled. "Why, he's not even on the Goddamned football team," he had told her.

He used to get up in the mornings after she had left him and make himself a pot of coffee and just head out. He didn't have a job

the long home

anymore and he subsisted on whatever he could eke out. As time
drew on his wants became simpler. He used to work some for
Abner Lyle at the service station. He would patrol the main highway west of town. He had the old rustcolored Chrysler tricked out
with a removable redlight and a siren and he used to cruise the
highways like a predator, a hawk on the wing, riding the updrafts
and scanning the earth for a victim. Motormouth's victims were
little-old-lady schoolteachers on vacation, elderly couples who appeared prosperous and looked as if they did not know much about
automobiles.

"Looks like you about to run a wheel off," he would tell them
once he got them stopped. They always looked apprehensive even
before he told them, for there was nothing reassuring in his ap-
pearance, Motormouth with his old junker like something from a
junkdealer's dreams, encrusted with blinking lights and reflector
mudflaps and various animal tails depending from high, looping
police antennas. Him with his cap in hand, puckish face hangdog,
the bearer of bad tidings, wheelbearings shot, rearends about to fall
out. His fey leprechaun's eyes were halfmad and the lies strung
from his mouth like spittle, a demented spider who would draw
them into his web. "Just drive right slow down to Abner Lyle's fillin
station," he would tell them. "I'll foller ye case ye have trouble."

"Thank you," they would tell him uncertainly.

"Lots of folks would just drive on and go about their business,"
he would tell them. "But I believe in helpin my feller man."

As the autumn drew on he lived an increasingly precarious existence, sleeping wherever dark or exhaustion overtook him, a curious nomad, homeless as a gypsy, the old Chrysler parked in brush
by the river's edge, out of sight at some roadside table. He took to
carrying soap and a razor and a change of clothing and he would
just stay out for days at a time.

Listening to the radio in the falling night by the river the disc
jockey's voice overlay an incessant crying of frogs and the voices became his consorts, all there was of friendship left in the world.
Silences elongated, for there were fewer and fewer people who

would listen to Motormouth's troubles. His face in these solitary hours between waking and the drugged unconsciousness he accepted as sleep took on a peculiarly serious look, a kind of slack-jawed thoughtfulness as if all his resources were locked in concentration, devising a way out of the quandary he found himself in. Sometimes while the voices and guitars underlined his plight he feared madness, thought, I've got to get a hold on myself, but he could not find the handle. By day he'd spend the kickbacks Lyle paid him at Hardin's or wherever temptation and opportunity coincided, sure of an audience as long as he parceled out his worn greenbacks.

His theory was that all would have gone well had it not been for the Blalock brothers. "If I could just keep the son of a bitches away from her," he told Hardin one day. "If me and her was off to ourselves and let alone I know she'd be all right. But they're like a pack of Goddamn dogs around her. I had it all to do over I'd marry somebody so ugly nobody would even fuck her."

"There is nobody that ugly," Hardin told him from the height of his experience. Hardin was whittling with a big bonehandled Case pocketknife, carving something unrecognizable from soft red cedar. He favored Motormouth with a look of sour condescension. "People will fuck anything," he said. "Chickens, cows, sheep, each other. They'll fuck watermelons and cucumbers. Anything with a hole in it or that's soft enough to cut one, somebody somewhere will fuck it."

This romantic's view of the world of Eros did not sit well with Motormouth. "Ruby ain't like that," he said sullenly.

Hardin would listen to Motormouth's incessant monotone as long as there was money left to spend but when Motormouth began stretching out his last beer and letting it warm in his hands Hardin would know he was broke and he would grow restless, wanting him gone, his sad stories falling on other ears. "I'll tell you how it is, Hodges," he said. "It's a fact of life and you might as well face it. When you lay down with the hogs you ain't got but two choices. You can waller with em in the mud or you can get clean away from em. You can't have it both ways."

Motormouth lurched drunkenly to his feet, the Coke crate falling behind him against the house. "I didn't come here to be made sport of," he said, running a big freckled hand through his hair, his face seized with besotted dignity. "And furthermore Ruby ain't no hog."

He looked for a moment as if he might reseat himself, then thought better of it and shambled around the corner of the house. After awhile they heard the Chrysler cough and start.

"Hodges had to draw light in ever pot he was ever in," Wymer told Hardin. "But he really outdone hisself on that Blalock deal. Cecil Blalock took to wantin to screw that gal Motormouth was married to so he got his brother Clyde to go over and get Motormouth to go coonhuntin. They was coonhuntin heavy there for awhile. Motormouth was always braggin about it, he thought they wasn't nobody like Clyde Blalock. Me and Clyde this, me and Clyde that. What fine coondogs Clyde had. And all the time Cecil screwin her right in Motormouth's bed and then him and Clyde sniggerin about it."

"It does sound like he's missin a face card or two," Hardin said.

"Hell, he used to ride em around in that old car. Him and Clyde in the front and her and Cecil settin in the back."

"He talks like he thinks a right smart of her."

"Yeah, I guess so. But he done it to himself. He's just too dumb to live."

Hardin sat for a time in silence, just listening to Wymer talk. Hardin lived in a world he manipulated day to day, you never knew when a piece of information might have a use. Life was a jigsaw puzzle someone had kicked apart on the day Hardin was born and he was still putting it back together a piece at a time, turning each section this way and that to see where it fitted. He sat listening and whittling while Wymer talked on and the evening shadows lengthened.

She had been gone for over forty years and Oliver would have thought her forgotten long ago. Wherever she was she was old or maybe even dead but that was not the way he remembered her, for in some curious way she had transcended the ravages of the years. From where she waited in time she still looked the way she had that morning long ago when she had walked through the door with no backward look, not even pulling the door to, just across the porch with her shoulders stiffened and into the road.

He seldom thought of her except in fall, and he could not have said why that was. Something in the way the skies looked or the woods smelled sent him reeling down the years. The leafy hill he and Winer were climbing became transient in time, could have been the same hill forty years before.

Course, I wouldn't change things now if I could, he thought hastily. Except about Willie and maybe if that changed the rest would too, for that was the root it growed from. But I wouldn't beg her to stay even now. I never begged man or woman for any blessed thing. But if it would do any good I would about the boy—

"Let's blow awhile," he said aloud. "I can't tramp these hills like I used to."

Winer paused and seated himself on a stump on the hillside.

"We ain't goin to find no sang in this holler anyway," William Tell Oliver said. "Damn cordwood trucks and saws has ruint it. I reckon they'll keep on cuttin till all the timber biggern a broomhandle is hauled off to them chemical plants."

"I guess the country around here's a lot different than it was when you were a boy."

"Oh Lord, yes. But you know, you always hearin about how things is growin but I don't know. The way I see it it's gone down. They was thirty-five hundred people livin at Riverside then and now they ain't nothin but a grocery store. That and them old wrecked furnaces. The railroad tracks run all the way to Centerville then and the trains run ever day haulin out pigiron. Boy, that was a rough place. Saturday nights Riverside was lit up like a Christmas tree.

"And Napier was boomin then too, they was minin iron ore over there. I worked over there for a while. Me and this other feller swung fifty-pound sledgehammers. All this raw ore come down a big chute with water runnin through it to wash the dirt out. They had it rigged where it come out of the river, didn't have no pump or nothin like that. These big chunks of ore come tumblin off the chute and we had to bust em up. He'd swing and I'd swing. All day long. They Godamighty. Fifty-pound hammers. Now I doubt I could pick one up."

"I bet it was rough around here back then."

"Well. It was tolerable rough. That bunch around Riverside was more roughhouse than mean, though they was a few cuttins and the like when they got to drinkin. But I'll tell you what, I'd take a week of it over thirty minutes down at Hardin's on a Saturday night. We used to have a lot of dances down there back then. Wasn't much else to do. Course, they wasn't enough women to go around but everbody would get drunk and listen to the music."

The night he met her the fiddle played: You ought to see my Cindy, she lives away down south. . . .

They came out of the dance arm in arm to balmy Saturday night and the local boys had run off his mule. She'd been tied to a tree in the school-house yard but she was long gone now. He'd walked Cindy home and kissed her. As he'd been walking (twelve miles, and to this day he could not remember passing through Rockhouse, or crossing the river, though that was the only way. As if he'd floated through or been in a trance) home out of Riverside someone had thrown a railroad spike at him and it had sung past his head, turning end over end. He could still hear the vicious flut-tering sound it made in the air. He'd whirled but there'd been no one there.

"They say folks was mean at Napier back then."

"What? Oh well, I reckon they was. Riverside couldn't hold Napier a light for rough. They had a bunch of them whitecaps over there tried to run everbody's business. Take folks out and whup em, that sort of stuff. But the truth is people don't change much. Individuals change, me and you change, but people in general just keep on bein people. All you can do is just try to pull yourself up as high as you can. Your own self, that's all you can be helt accountable for. Sometimes you'll think folks is gettin a higher foot on the ladder, and then here comes a son of a bitch like Hardin and it all goes out the winder with the dishwater. But you can't worry about that. Leave that to the preachers, they get paid for it."

Winer was silent a time. Past the timbered horizon the west was awash with purple. Whippoorwills began to call one to the other tree to tree. With falling night the woods took on a quality of ambiguity, as if nothing were quite what it seemed.

"Don't it bother you living by yourself all the time?" he finally asked the old man.

"Well, I don't reckon. It did awhile, some time ago. Course, a man don't always get his druthers, he has to make do sometimes. Why?"

"I don't know. I was just thinking about Motormouth Hodges. Him and his wife split up and his wife took up with somebody else. He acts like he's about halfcrazy. Tryin to get her back all the time."

"He ort to let it lay, but it ain't for me to advise nobody. And Lord knows a man can't always do what he ort to. Me, I got used to livin by myself. When you come right down to it, a man's always by hisself anyhow. When push comes to shove all you got's yourself."

'Leavin? Leavin where?' He'd come in off the third shift and she had her suitcase already packed. He'd come home an hour early, had the furnace not broken down she'd have been down the road and gone. 'It come up mighty sudden,' he said. 'And mighty hard too for you to set out walkin four miles to town.'

'It's nothin to me. I'm goin and you can't stop me.'

'The hell I can't.' She'd been standing by the bed and he'd pushed her back, gently laid his weight against her, his hands cupping her face. He'd kissed her, but the face was dead, she lay quite still without looking at him, staring at the ceiling, he did not exist anymore. He laid a wrist across her throat: he'd been feeding the boilers at Napier then, loading them three times an hour with iron ore, and his arms were thick and corded with muscle. He had never hit her but he was dizzy for a moment with an awareness of his own strength. He could have broken her neck, crushed her

*throat in his hands, but he could not get what he wanted or make her do
anything but what she had already made up her mind to do.*

'It's that son of a bitch on Jack's Branch, ain't it.'

'Jack's Branch or China, it's all the same to you. I'm leavin.'

It was a week before Rayner came by.

*'Rasbury talked to Clyde and knows you ain't sick. He said tell you
he'd hold your job twenty-four hours and then that's it. He's hirin somebody else.'*

'You tell Rasbury I said hold it or drop it, or just whatever suits him.'

*'Oliver, what the fuck's the matter with you? You look like death
warmed over and this place is a Goddamned pigsty. What're you doin?'*

'What does it look like I'm doin?'

*'It looks like you're tryin to crawl down the neck of a whiskey bottle.
And to my way of thinkin makin pretty fair progress.'*

"I lived by myself a lot of years," Oliver said. "Used to work
twelve hours and walk home and feed the stock by lanternlight.
Cook and eat and hit the bed and up in the mornin tryin to farm.
Back that night at the furnaces. A man that busy don't have much
time for feelin sorry for hisself." He looked westward, arose stiffly.
The last of the light had drained off, the night crept up like rising
waters. "We stayed longern I meant to. We don't get out of this
mess of tops fore good dark we'll be here in the mornin."

Nights Motormouth spent time like linty change fished up
from the pockets of his jeans. Drinking in the Snowwhite Cafe,
Hardin's. In the Snowwhite a slanteyed whore with a mop of curly
black hair gave him a halfsmile he carried with him into the cool-
ing night, where his only other comfort was the slow drift of the
Chrysler's wheels in the gravel, his only absolute the moonlit road
coming at him like gleaming cable unreeling dizzily from a spool.

Out of town then, where the last streetlights were sentries
marking civilization's end, all that dark beyond them a world in
flux, unclaimed, provinces without dominion. A world up for grabs,
where a man with an eye for the angles might make a stand. Here

where the light pooled and gave the slick pavement the gleam of dark glass he went, reflected headlights tracking below like something sinister pacing him just beneath the surface of the earth, car and anticar snaking past the city limits and gone, looking perhaps for the deceptively simple curve where matter and antimatter collided in a brief and fatal explosion, the slow rain of falling glass, the tilting headlights limning panoramic birches white as bone, the grinding wrench of crumpling metal, sweet peace.

For there were nights when Hodges sought death like a brother, courted it like a longlost lover, a bitter and unnamed grief lodged in his breast like a stone. If I can make it at seventy-five, can I make it at eighty? he'd wonder, the mysteries of physics spread before him, a clinical coolness settling over him. Hands steady on the wheel, the fruitjar cocked between his thighs, the spiel of disc jockeys a dislocated and demented commentary on the onslaught of night coming at him faster and faster, a dark frieze of trees and mailboxes and nameless tenant houses. Then at the moment he was sure of control a feeling of elation almost orgasmic would seize him, he'd slow and raise the fruitjar and drink to the fates pacing him who'd seen fit to spare him once again, some joy perverse and sweetly erotic.

And down the line. Past sleeping houses behind whose walls sleepers spun dreams he'd never know, let alone share. A thousand lives woven like threads in a patternless tapestry and if he died here on the highway it would alter the design not one iota. The world was locked doors, keep-out signs, guard dogs. He figured to just ease through unnoticed and be gone.

Maybe down to Hardin's, he might think, fingering the scant sheaf of bills, the ball of greasy change. Who knew who'd be there? A blond whore from Memphis watching him from beneath mascaraed lashes. "You wasted in this onehorse town, Daddy," she'd tell him. "Let me take you away."

Rounding a curve on the Mormon Springs road he came upon them framed in his headlights temporary as startled deer, the old man and Winer stepping from the hedgerow of sumac onto the roadbed and turning frozen in momentary hesitation as if unde-cided whether to flee or wait and take their chances, will he stop or not? A madman coming at them in a two-thousand-pound carton. Motormouth locked the wheels and slid sideways toward them.

"Lord God," the old man said. He leapt backward as the car ca-reened past, flailing at it with his stick as if he might head it off like an animal, the stick striking the front fender and rebounding into the night, Oliver scrambling up swearing from out of the sawbriars and gravel, fiercely red and diabolic in the brakelights. The backup lights of the Chrysler came on then and the car fishtailed drunkenly back toward them.

"He's seen he missed us," the old man said. "I reckon he means to try his luck again."

"It's just Motormouth Hodges."

"I know who it is," the old man said irritably. "Why do you think I was scoutin the bushes?"

Motormouth had rolled down a window and was peering my-opically into the night. The Chrysler idled throatily. Past the dark horizon the first stars were out, a pale band of them strung east-ward. "Yins want a ride?"

Oliver was silent a long minute. "Not hardly," he finally said.

"What are yins doin out here anyway?"

"Hunting ginseng," Winer said.

"You must have needed some real bad," Motormouth snig-gered. He lit a cigarette, the flaring match giving his face a yellow, wolfish cast. "I never knowed you had to slip up on it in the dark," he said.

"We got turned around back on Buttermilk Ridge. Cordwood cutters got the woods so changed it's easy to get on the wrong road."

"I been on that wrong road myself," Motormouth said. "Get in. I ain't got all night."

"Well, I have," Oliver said. "And hopefully two or three more. I wouldn't slide my bony ass across them seatcovers for a hundred-dollar bill with the ink still wet on it."

"Get your gimlet ass in here, Winer. I got a thing or three to show ye."

"Not tonight, Motormouth. We've been out since good light hunting sang. We're trying to get what we can before frost."

"That's what I'm doin myself. Tryin to get what I can fore frost. Get in and I'll run ye home anyway. Don't you think I'd let ye out, or what?"

Winer grinned. "I'm not even sure we'd get there." His fingers traced the long scrapes on the Chrysler's rocker panels, straight furrows like clawmarks as if the car had barely escaped some dread beast. Lines like hesitation marks on the wrists of an aspiring suicide. "Looks like you been cleanin out a ditch-run or two."

Motormouth put the car in gear, the pitch of the engine rising. "Well, they never did build the roads to suit where I wanted to drive," he said. "If you old folks don't want to ride, you can walk then. I got things to do. I'll see you." He released the brake, left in the small storm of dust and rocks the wheels flung.

The old man watched as the taillights winked from sight. "You take a little bitty crazyhouse and put a wheel on each corner and give it a kick down the road and you'd have somethin about like that," he said.

Several years back William Tell Oliver had gone out to his hoglot one morning and found a curious phenomenon. He had kept a few sows and a boar then and what he saw so surprised him that he set the bucket of feed he was carrying aside and stood leaning against the fence, ignoring the riotous squealing of the pigs, just staring out at the lot.

There were two holes there, craters almost, ovals roughly five or six feet in diameter and almost two feet deep. After a time the old man climbed the fence and passed among the milling hogs and inspected the holes closely, expecting who knew what. They were a wonder to him. He squatted in the offal of the lot examining them. The manure and rich black earth mounded their rims and the bottoms were smooth. He peered closely at the bottoms, perhaps looking for the remnants of some molten star, thin, bright layers of celestial slag. Hurled here at random or by discernment.

There was nothing. Only the dark earth beneath the layered manure and what he took to be spade marks. "Be damned," he said to himself. With his walking stick to part the thick weeds about the fence he searched for signs. He had no idea what he expected to find. Old bones replevied from the curious graves, new bodies so destined. All he found was the hot ferment of the weeds and a copperhead moving sleek and burnished in search of deeper shade. He let his mind wander. What would there be to steal? He counted the hogs three times and all three times they were all accounted for. "What else in a piglot," he asked himself, "save pigs and pigshit? A manure thief?" He looked for tiretracks without expecting to find them, for there was no road through the weeds and his mind could conceive of no one so desperate for pigshit they must steal it under cover of darkness and cart it away on their backs.

It was a mystery and he didn't care for mysteries: an old man who suspected chaos and disorder beyond the curtain of swirling dark, he hungered for order and symmetry in what remained of his life, a balancing of the scales.

He fed and watered the hogs and returned to the house. When his chores were completed he sat for a time in the shade of a pear tree, his eyes closed, feet up on a Coke crate, listening to the drone of bees glutting themselves on the ripe and windfallen fruit. Before the day was over he had returned to the lot to puzzle anew over the holes. He learned no more than the nothing he already knew.

In the morning there were three new holes, somewhat shallower but spaced over a wider area, as if someone had been digging for something at random. "Be damned," he said again. He stared at the harried earth, suspecting perhaps some magnetic anomaly that sucked meteors and asteroids from the dusty band of space he hurtled through. He stared upward, seeking some cosmic mirror whose reflections marvelously cast chaos into order, righted the perverse and disordered, but he peered only into blue emptiness, past shapeless wisps of clouds that fled westward ahead of the sun. He stood listening to the morning sounds that mocked him with their familiarity. He could hear the crinkling of hot tin, the pop of barn rafters warping in the heat. The furtive scuttling of a lizard. A thin film of perspiration crept across his shoulders, dampening his chambray shirt.

He counted the pigs again without expecting to find one gone. They were all there and he was halfdisappointed, surprised to find himself willing to sacrifice a pig for an explanation. A pig thief he could have understood, there was reason in it, sense. There was no sense in these holes pitting his hoglot. After awhile he got a manure fork and began halfheartedly to shovel the earth back into the holes.

He took a long nap that afternoon and about dark he made himself a quart jar of coffee and carried it with him down to the barn. He had an old Browning over-and-under and he carried that too. In the hayloft he arranged bales of hay into a comfortable chair and settled himself out of sight to see what transpired.

For a long time nothing did. Dark deepened and shadows took the world. He sat immersed in the cries of insects, in the timeless tolling of whippoorwills. There was something of eternity in these sounds, at once bitter and reassuring. He'd heard them as a boy, as a young man, they sounded the same then as now. In this curiously altered stillness he felt he might even hear his wife open the kitchen door and call his name, his son might be on the spring path following him, a small form forever stalemated by time. He drank from the jar of bitter coffee and wiped his mouth on a sleeve, forced his attention to the barnyard below him. It lay in darkness but after an hour or so the moon cradled up out of the eastern trees and the pale illumination crept across the face of the land, tree and fence and stone imbued with significance like images in a dream.

The moon was high over the treeline and he judged it ten o'clock or better before he saw anything stir. When the boy came he came up from the branch-run with silent stealth, easing through the border of gum and persimmon, peering all about, cautious as a grazing deer. Apparently satisfied, he came out of the brush and approached the fence, carrying a burlap bag and a shovel whose handle was longer than he was tall. It was the Hodges boy. Why, he ain't no morn nine or ten year old, he thought. The boy threw the sack over and leaned the shovel against the fence and clambered over. He took up the shovel and immediately fell to work, selecting a fresh corner of the lot to dig in. Just clock in and go to work, the old man thought in puzzlement. The boy dug for some time and then unpocketed a flashlight, knelt on the scattered manure he'd dug from the hole, raking carefully through it with his hands. Kneeling so in the earth he raised his face to a moon clocking on westward and then arose and commenced shoveling again.

The old man was at a loss. For a moment he thought of Hodges's grandfather digging for money on the Mormon place, perhaps some genetic quirk had encoded it in the third generation, a trait so degenerated by now that nothing remained save the compulsion to dig at random just on the offchance someone might have buried something worth replevying.

Oliver rose as stealthily as he could, even so his knees popped and he stood still and silent until he saw the boy hadn't heard. Then he moved cautiously toward the ladder and climbed down it. When he eased into the moonlit piglot Hodges was still digging. Oliver approached within a foot or so of his back. "Hidy," he said. The boy dropped the shovel as if electricity had coursed through it and leapt five or six inches into the air. When his feet touched earth they were already pedaling as if he rode an invisible bicycle and he was almost immediately at the fence. Oliver caught him as he was scrambling over the topmost slab and lifted him, kicking and squirming and cursing, and set him back to earth.

"Let me alone," the boy was yelling.

"Whoa, young feller. Hold on a minute here. Nobody aims to hurt you. I just want to know what you're up to."

Hodges was trying to jerk his arm free. "None of your Goddamn business. Now, let me alone."

"You're young Hodges, ain't ye?"

"What's it to ye?"

"Well, they don't call ye Hodges, do they? What's ye first name?"

"Yeah, I guess you'd like that, wouldn't ye? Me tell ye my name so's you could run straight to the law with it."

"Hell, son, I don't need no name. I got you in the flesh, right by the seat of the britches. I'se just askin to be polite."

"My name's Clifford."

"All right. That's some better. And just so you'll know, I ain't never been one to run overquick to the law. Now, you reckon if I turn you aloose you can control the impulse to jump that fence?"

"I ain't done nothin."

"You move right pert for a feller just takin the night air. Ain't none too qualmy about these copperheads neither." Oliver released his grip on the boy. "Now, what's my hoglot got you can't dig up nowheres else?"

"Wouldn't you like to know?"

Oliver had been wanting to smoke but had been afraid of setting the hay in the barnloft afire. Now he packed the bowl of his pipe and struck a kitchen match on his thumbnail and lit the tobacco. When he spoke his voice was furred by the smoke. "What was you diggin for?"

"It ain't none of your business."

"Well. I reckon it's your shovel. But it's my lot and my hogs been standin around losin sleep and watchin you diggin like a fool. Now, what is it? Do you just like diggin or is there somethin particular about my hoglot that appeals to you?"

The boy seemed to be considering, there was a shrewdness to his features, a transparent cunning. Oliver watched the play of thoughts on the small freckled face. Half is better than nothing, the face was thinking. Oliver grinned. The face was already trying to devise a plan for cheating him out of his half of whatever it was he didn't even know about yet.

"Well. I guess we could split."

"I don't see why not."

The boy squatted on the earth before him. In the moonlight they were dwarfed by the dark shapes of trees above them. A warm wind smelling of summer going overripe came looping up the hollow and across them. Faint surcease scented with rich opulence, the ripe pears and musk of honeysuckle. An owl called lonesome from a hollow negated by dark.

"Well. It's pigs."

"Pigs?" the old man asked in disbelief.

"Hell, yeah. I'd a thought a man as old as you are would have figured it out hisself by now."

"Boy, you've lost me. Figured out what?"

"Diggin up them pigs."

Oliver felt like a participant in some surreal conversation in which the answers bore no relation to the questions, lines had been fragmented and shuffled indiscriminately. "They Godamighty. Is that what you been doin out here of a night? And them sacks . . ."

Hodges was nodding. "To tote em home in," he said.

"Lord God, boy. You don't dig pigs up out of the ground like taters or somethin."

"You want em all for yeself," the boy said craftily.

"Whoever told you pigs was dug?"

"My mama did and I don't know what cause she'd have to lie."

"I see," Oliver said.

"I ast her where they come from and she said the old sow rooted em up in the hogpen."

"And you not havin a hogpen . . ."

He sat in a ruminative silence, just smoking the pipe and listening to the crying of the nightbirds, somewhere far and lost and streaking down the night the whistle of a train. "And what'd you figure, just kindly eliminate the sow? Bypass her sort of? Just dig the pigs up ahead of her and sell em?"

"Yeah. A person's smartern a hog ain't he?"

"We won't argue about it," Oliver said. "I suspect folks listening to us might work up evidence for either side."

He sat watching the boy. This diminutive hog rustler, self-confessed and unrepentant thief of unborn swine. He with his fallow burlap bags and eye cocked to livestock futures. Oliver saw little that was lovable. He had a moment of clairvoyance, an insight of weary foreknowledge stabbed with regret. He knew that Clifford Hodges would always be slipping in at night and digging up somebody else's pigs. He would always be playing the longshot or taking a shortcut, figuring the angles in somebody else's game. And he would never have a game of his own. If he lived until he was grown he would be shot then or shoot someone else in a failed inept holdup. He and a cohort halfmad as they looked aghast at each other across the body of a fallen grocer or gaspump operator. If he won the game he'd be in Brushy Mountain penitentiary, if he lost the graveyard. Oliver felt a pity for him, a commiseration for the things that had been and the things that were yet to be. He wished for words to encourage him, to enlighten him, but none came. And his own life did not lend itself to examples.

"Well, what about it?"

"What about what?"

"About them pigs. Are we goin to split like we said or are you goin to dig em up after I leave and keep em for yeself?"

"Boy, they ain't no pigs there to dig."

"You done got em."

"Goddamn it. Son, that ain't where pigs comes from. I done told you that."

"So you say."

"Well, there's a considerable body of evidence to back it up."

"Then where does the old sow get em?"

Oliver took a deep breath. "All right," he said. "They grow there in the sow. Then when they're big enough, when they're made, they come out."

"Come out," the boy echoed. He was shaking his head, staring at Oliver in wonderment. "Everbody says you're crazy and by God you are," he said. "You're crazy as hell. I never heard such a crock of bullshit in my life."

"Well," the old man said, "don't blame me for it. It's not like I laid it out or anything. It's always been like that."

"I'm goin to tell Mama," Hodges said. He arose and took up the burlap bag and the shovel and hurled them over the fence and clambered after them. "Keep ye damn pigs," he said. "I don't mind ye bein greedy but I hate to be took for a fool."

Oliver grinned to himself. "You watch for snakes," he called. After awhile he could hear Hodges scurrying down the embankment, a small bright angry thread in the pastoral tapestry of night sounds. He hunkered still in the barnlot awhile listening and then he arose and went on back toward the house.

The horses had been gone for three weeks before Cecil Blalock even learned where they were. He had covered almost all the county asking and had come to think they must have started back toward west Tennessee, where he had bought them, for everyone in the county knew him and he could not imagine anyone just putting up his Morgans and not telling him. Blalock was the only man in the county who raised Morgans.

"You hear about them fine Morgans Hardin's got?" a man in the poolroom asked him.

"No. What sort of Morgans are they?"

"Big stallion and two mares. Finelookin horseflesh."

"Where'd he get em?" Blalock asked, though by now he knew.

"He told me he found em."

"The hell he did," Blalock said.

This was late on a Saturday evening and by good light on Sunday morning he was up and breakfasted and had the sideboards on the truck. A redhaired woman clad in a slip stood in the door and watched him make ready to leave. "You be careful," she called but he didn't say if he would or he wouldn't.

He had turned in at the yard and was backing toward the outbuildings when Hardin stopped him.

"You tearin my yard all to hell, Blalock. Ain't you had no raisin? I never heard you say could you cross it or kiss my ass or nothin."

Blalock looked down from the driver's seat of the truck, his face tight and angry. He had been about halfmad all night anyway and he wanted his horses but an innate sense of caution had made him hope Hardin would still be asleep. By all odds he should have been after Saturday night but here was Hardin all wide awake and cleareyed at six o'clock of a Sunday morning, playing the country squire, smiling upon him despite the harshness of his words, a benign smile so transparently crafty it would not have deceived a child.

"I come after my horses."

"Can you prove they're yourn?"

"You know damn well I can."

"I sort of thought you could. Get out awhile and we'll talk about it." He crossed over to the porch and stepped onto it. He hitched up his dress slacks and squatted not on the porch but on the heels of his shiny shoes.

"There ain't nothin to talk about. I come after em. Figure up what I owe for their keep and send me a bill."

"Whatever you say, you're the doctor. I guess we could dicker about it. I figure you owe me somethin in the neighborhood of eight hundred dollars."

Suspecting some defect in his hearing, Blalock sought clarification. "Eight hundred dollars? For what?"

Hardin arose and crossed the branch. Curiously birdlike, a graceless bird all joints and angles. Imprints of his shoulderblades through the thin yellow dress shirt he wore, morning sun off a gold cufflink when he pointed across the stream.

"I had me a damn fine corncrop there and they done wiped me out before I knew they was on the place. They came in the night."

Apoplectic with rage Blalock swung open the door and leapt out. He slammed the door so hard the truck rocked on its springs and he strode past Hardin and across the stream and up the stony bank. Past the tilting dead cornstalks all he could see was Spanish nettles and sawbriars and great slabs of white limestone. He turned. Hardin was watching him amiably, a grin on his crooked face, hands pocketed and thumbs tucked in the loops of his trousers.

"And where is this fine corncrop?" Blalock asked.

Hardin had a sharpened kitchen match in his mouth for a toothpick. He withdrew it and threw it away. "I thought I said," he told Blalock. "It's gone. They eat it. They wiped me out."

"Why, there ain't a Goddamned thing out here but rocks and sawbriars. You couldn't hire a fuckin stalk of corn to grow here."

Hardin was deferential. "I admit it don't look like much now," he said. "But you ought to seen it before your horses got in it."

"They shitfire."

"I had some beans too but I'll just throw them in."

Blalock climbed back down the abutment and this time waded right through the branch. He was watching Hardin's pocket trying to see did he have a gun there but he couldn't tell. If he did it was a small one.

"If you think I'm givin you eight hundred dollars for a few bales of hay you're crazy as hell. I'll give you what I think's fair and you can like it or not. Just whatever suits you. And I'll tell you another thing. Anybody else would've let me know where them horses was. It takes a damn sorry feller to put up another man's stock and not say a word about it. Especially a stallion worth as much as that one."

"How'd I know whose they was? They ain't got no license plates on em like say a automobile nor collars like a coonhound, and this old free-range shit has about played out. Most everbody keeps their stock up nowadays."

"I do keep em up, Goddamn it. Somebody cut my fences."

"Well." Hardin shrugged. "It wasn't me." He walked back toward the truck and Blalock stood awkwardly for a moment and then followed.

"Why don't you buy your own damn horses and leave mine alone?"

"Well, I'll make you another deal. I'll count you out five one hundred dollar bills for that horse right here and now. Then we'll go have a little drink and forget we ever had words."

"That horse ain't for sale and you know it. And even if it was that wouldn't make a down payment."

"Whatever you think. Whether you go loaded or unloaded is all the same to me."

"I'll go loaded or by God know the reason why."

Hardin turned. "All right," he said. "This is the reason. If you so much as trespass a foot further onto my property, so much as open a gate or cut my fences, they will carry your dead ass out of here on a stretcher. They will load you up and haul you away. Do you understand me?"

"You're crazy, you're the one that's goin to be hauled away."

"Not so crazy I don't know whose property we're standin on."

"Nor me either," Blalock said. "Thomas Hovington's."

Watching the yellow eyes fade to slits Blalock thought for a second that he was a dead man. Had Hardin been carrying a pistol perhaps he would have been. There was a moment when things could have gone either way, and then the eyes widened a little and Hardin said, "Like I said it's on you. You can bet or fold."

"I'm suin you," Blalock said. "I'm gettin me a lawyer right now."

"That's fine. I'll get me one too and while our lawyers is dickerin back and forth and runnin up the tab, the price on the horse is goin down and the corn's goin up."

"I can't talk to you," Blalock said. He opened the door on the truck and climbed in. "I'll be back," he said. "I'll get them papers and I'll be back."

"That don't surprise me," Hardin said.

There was a faint wash of light on the window curtains, a cessation then of the sound of an engine somewhere down the road.

Hardin rose on his elbows and peered at the phosphorescent hands of the clock. It was after one o'clock. He lay back stiff and silent, listening, thinking, Well, why not? If they're goin to try it they'll try it now. Hovington's dead and buried. He had always known without articulating it that Hovington was a kind of insurance policy as long as he lay dying. He knew the curious decorum of country folk, their superstitious fear of death and dying, and he had slept a little better at night, had not been afraid of the windowlights being shot out, the house being torched. That policy had lapsed now, and he thought of another, the Winchester leaning in the corner, a 30-06 in a land of .22-caliber squirrel rifles.

There was a long elastic interval between the faint hushing of the motor and any other sound so that he lay completely wide awake now, straining for any aberration in the night, his ears amplifying the whir of dryflies, and he thought, Well, is there anything or not? A carload of drunks? He immediately discarded that, he had never known drunks to remain so quiet. A courting couple, someone getting them a little? He had halfrelaxed when the first sound came, though less a sound than some suggestion of difference, of disquiet, some delicate change in the balance of the night, so that he was off the bed and halfway to the gun when the first firm step came on the porch. By the time the shoulder or whatever heavy it was slammed against the front door he was on the floor with the rifle in his arms and scrambling toward the back door aware of Pearl awakening in the bed behind him, her saying, "Dallas?" Then, "What is it, Dallas?" And of the girl crying out in the front room, the noise the latch made flying off and skittering across the linoleum. He was swearing running into and around dark objects that seemed conspired to snare him, as if the house and ultimately the night itself were aligned against him.

There were already two of them at the back door, garbed in white, faces obscured by masks, featureless save dark eyeholes. He felt hands clutch at him, jerk him forward, he could hear their grunts of triumph and something, a club or cudgel, caught him alongside the shoulder so that for an instant his left arm went dead and he was conscious of a great rush of relief, thinking, Sticks. The son of a bitches have just got sticks.

The moon was shining and the dusty yard gleamed like mica. He was down in it for an instant, twisting a cheek against the ground, the cold rifle still beneath him, his elbows holding it against his naked stomach. "Help me hold him, Ray. The son of a bitch is gettin up." He staggered up with one of them astride his back, an arm about his throat, and struck blindly with the barrel of the rifle, felt metal strike bone again and again till one of them said, "Can you get aholt of his fuckin gun?" The other man kept swinging the stick. The voice behind him said, "Goddamn, Ray, you hittin me, not him. Try to hit him just ever now and then." A glancing blow to Hardin's head knocked him halfsenseless and he felt his legs buckle.

He whirled and the man on his back slipped free. Hardin's momentum spun him halfway around and he fell, sitting with one leg twisted beneath him, the rifle in his lap, momentarily disoriented, seeing rising above him the gray bulk of the house and the play of flashlights at the windows, above the inkblack pyramid of the roofline the luminous fabric of the sky, all of it swimming sideways in a sick illusion of motion as if he alone were stationary, all the universe spinning dizzily past him.

He could hear Pearl and the girl screaming, he was dimly aware that they had been herded into the yard. He heard blows without knowing where they were coming from, who they were directed against. One of the men dove behind the hood of the truck just as Hardin fired and simultaneously there was the whang of the bullet and then the more solid thunk against the engine block. He could hear running footsteps, they seemed to come from everywhere. A man was sprinting desperately for the road, bobbing in the moonlight. Hardin aimed, took a breath and held it, squeezed the trigger almost gently. The man did an eerily comic dance in the roadbed, his right leg flung out rubbery and unhinged, the knee shot away.

Then he fell forward, balled up in the driveway. Hardin could hear him moaning. The man halfrose and began to vomit.

Hardin wiped the blood out of his eyes. The hair at his temples was wet with it. He could hear the brush popping in a diminishing flurry and in a multitude of directions. In a little while the car cranked somewhere down the road and he could hear the tires in the gravel. Hardin grinned. He thought, The first son of a bitch there took off with the car and left the rest of them to walk it. There'll be some sore feet and mad whitecaps in Ackerman's Field in the mornin.

"Shut it up," he told the girl. She was sitting on the doorstep crying. She did not cease. Her face was hidden by her hands and twin wings of long black hair.

"Did they hurt you?"

"No."

"Then shut it up."

Pearl was leaning her head against a porch support. Her eyes were closed.

"Are you hurt?"

"They hit my legs with a big old stick or somethin. They never done me and Tom thisaway. This never happened before."

"Nor is it likely to happen again. Can you walk?"

"I reckon. Let me see about your head."

"Let it go. Just help me load him in the car. Get a bedspread or quilt or somethin out of the house and put in the back. Bastard's bleedin like a hog with its throat cut."

She arose, stood massaging the flesh of her thigh. She seemed dazed or drunken. "You ain't aimin to kill him, are you? I can't stand no more trouble."

"Just get it like I told you."

Hardin backed the Packard up to where the man lay and opened the right rear door. He knelt beside the man. Apparently he had passed out. He lay unmoving but Hardin could hear the steady rasp of his breathing. He took out the bonehandled Case pocketknife and tested the blade with a thumb, slit the pillowcase and folded it aside like a caul.

Pearl stood looking down, a quilt draped across her arm.

"Who is he, Blackwell, Blackburn, Blacksomethin. I've seen him."

"Why, that's Mr. Blackstock," Pearl said. "He runs the drygood store in town."

"He'll run the son of a bitch out of a wheelchair now if he runs it at all. No, I ain't goin to kill him. If I killed him I'd have to hide him, and I don't want him hid. I want him where folks can see him, ever day of his life, right there in that drygood store. Get that quilt laid out in there."

The man was heavy and slack, a seemingly boneless weight they could hardly handle. When he was almost in Hardin fell to swearing at him and shoved him the rest of the way in with the door, leaning his weight against it until he heard the latch catch.

"Where do you live, Slick?" Hardin asked, neither expecting nor receiving an answer, glancing upward at the rearview mirror and not seeing the man either, just the top of the upholstery and the back glass where fled a landscape in motion, a retreating moonlit world with a blacktop highway snaking away down the middle of it. He looked forward again and the night was coming in wisps and tatters of fog like clouds blown past the speeding car. The countryside was remote, locked in sleep. Off the blacktop then and back to chert and past old man Oliver's unlit house and the orchard of dead apple trees, tree on tree looming at him from the silver roadside, unpruned branches gnarled and twisted and dead, charred bone juxtaposed against the seamless heavens like some childhood witchwood of myth or nightmare. Taking the curve the headlights yawed across the unkept yard and touched the windowpanes with illusory life, leapt past the hedge of alders gleaming white as bone, the road straightened here and he accelerated onto the long stretch to town.

The old man roused from whatever state of halfsleep he habited and watched the wash of light across the faded wallpaper, arose and rested on his elbows till the light faded, the wall momentarily disappearing and then regaining visibility in the moonlight. For a moment he had thought the car was coming here, for a moment past and present had merged and he was unable to tell one from the other, dream from reality. Old days of crisis in the night, the knock at the door, the light at the window. Then he recognized the deepthroated roar of the Packard's muffler and lay back listening to it fade away.

The town was in restless slumber as well but there was an all-night cabstand out of which a man named Wolf de Vries ran a bootlegging establishment and an almost perpetual poker game. Hardin parked in front of the cabstand and cut the lights and switch. He went in the front and passed by a desk where a woman slept with her mouth open and her head pillowed against a telephone and down a narrow hall to a locked green door. He knocked.

"Who is it?"

"Dallas Hardin."

After a moment the door opened a crack and a face studied him. The door opened wider. Stale blue smoke boiled out and Hardin coughed. He fanned the air wildly. "Jesus Christ," he said. "They goin to find ever one of you sots in here smothered to death some mornin. Does this place not have a winder?"

"Deal Hardin in," de Vries called. De Vries was a quick little man with a slick, evasive face like a failed politician's. "His money's as good as anybody else's."

Hardin studied the men circling the green baize table. "Looks like you got a full set of fools without me."

De Vries had noticed the blood drying at Hardin's temple. "What the hell happened to you? You been sortin cats?"

"No." Hardin didn't smile. "You know where a feller name of Blackstock lives? Runs a drygood store."

"Charles Blackstock? Sure. West Fourth Street, right behind the school. Why?"

"I got him out in the car. Him and some whitecaps or Kluxers or some damn thing come down to the house to teach me a lesson."

"Is he dead?"

"No, but he may have wished he was a time or two."

The men at the table arose and followed Hardin back through the cabstand. The woman had awakened and her face wore a stunned, vapid look as if she did not know where she was, or care.

Blackstock was conscious as well. He stirred on the back floor-board, said something unintelligible. His eyes stared at the faces ringing the windows of the Packard but did not remark them. He flung an arm across his face as if the light bothered him. His trouserleg from the knee down was saturated with coagulating blood.

"Shitfire," de Vries said. "You better get him to a hospital fore you're lookin a murder charge in the face."

Hardin got behind the wheel, cranked the engine. "By the way," he said, "you didn't by any chance know anything about this, did you? Or know anybody else who might be in it?"

"Hell no, Hardin. They may hit me next."

"No. It was me they wanted."

The man remained conscious all the way to his house, mumbling something incoherent, prayer, blasphemy, benediction. When Hardin opened the door and laid a hand on either side of his shirtfront the eyes opened and then when Hardin jerked as hard as he could the face blanched lifeless and the eyes rolled back and he went to sleep again. Hardin laid him in the dewy grass and sat down breathing hard. As he arose a black dog loped around the corner of the house, paused, its hackles rising. It growled deep in its throat.

Hardin had the pocketknife out. "Try it if you feel lucky," he told the dog. The dog hushed and then dropped to its belly and began to inch along the ground toward the wounded man.

Hardin got back in the car and blew the horn. The dog turned and lay watching him across the fallen man. Hardin lit a cigarette with the gold lighter, turned to study the house. It was silent and dark. He blew the horn again, longer, puffed the cigarette, his image reflected back by the windshield fiercely orange, a curious fiery face with black recesses for eyes.

The porchlight came on. The door opened and a woman stood under the lightbulb tying the belt of a yellow robe. She raised a hand to her face and stood staring at the crumpled man on the lawn. She opened her mouth to speak but the Packard abruptly cut off whatever she said. Hardin glanced back once and she was running down the walk.

Sometime after four o'clock in the morning William Tell Oliver was awakened again, this time by a heavy and determined pounding at the door. He lay for a sleepy minute listening to it, perhaps thinking that if he ignored it it would go away. It did not. It intensified and after a time a voice began to call, "Hey. Hey."

What on earth, the old man wondered. He got up slowly, began to pull on his pants. The voice kept calling. "All right, all right," Oliver said. "I'm comin." He took down the Browning over-and-under from the rack above the bed. He lit a lamp and with it in one hand and the gun in the other crossed to the door. He leaned the gun against the wall and opened the door slightly.

The moon had set by now and the porch was in darkness, fainter darkness framing the bulk of the man standing before the door. The door opened wider, allowing the seepage of yellow light to spread, illuminating a tiredlooking man leaning against the doorjamb. He swayed slightly as if drunk or exhausted.

"What is it?" Oliver asked.

"Well. I'm in kind of a bind and I need some help. I need to get you to run me into town."

"Have you got a stick?"

The man looked startled. "A stick? What kind of a stick?"

"Well, you wanted run to town. I shore ain't got no automobile."

"Shitfire." When Oliver didn't comment the man said, "I'm Cecil Blalock."

"I know who you are. But I still ain't got no way to town. What's the trouble, ye car play out?"

"Yeah, and it's a hell of a piece to town. Seems like I been wanderin around in the woods half the night."

"Where'd ye have trouble?"

"Down by Hardin's."

"Why, Lord, that ain't over a mile. It ortnt took but a few minutes to walk that."

"Yeah. Well I might've got turned around or somethin. How about lettin me use your phone to call a cab?"

Oliver was silent a time. "I'm sorry," he said at length. "I just ain't bein no help at all. I ain't got no telephone neither."

"Hellfire." Blalock stood as if undecided what his next move should be. A cool wind blew across the porch, rustled through the leaves. The light wavered in the quaking globe, guttered, flared up. "Thanks anyway," Blalock said. He descended the steps and crossed the yard toward the road. He was out of sight but Oliver could hear the walking. "Hey," Oliver called. The steps ceased. "Ain't no use wakin up them Winer folks. They ain't got no car neither." There was no reply save the steps commencing again and after a moment he went back inside and closed the door.

Like aging birds aligned on a winter wire the row of old men sat before Sam Long's cold stove and endlessly refought Hardin's set-to with the whitecaps. On creaking Coke crates and upended cuts of wood they refurbished or delineated the story to its marrow according to their whims.

"I hear they takin his leg off," Horace Hensley said. "What of it Hardin didn't take off with that highpowered rifle."

"Some say Hardin didn't do it," a man named Pulley said. "Blackstock hisself says he had a fight with a feller he caught ransackin his house."

"Yeah. A burglar."

"A man tells a baldfaced lie like that I wouldn't believe him if he was standin in Buffalo River and he told me his feet was wet."

Sam Long dumped William Tell Oliver's poke of ginseng onto the scale, watched intently the fluctuation of the needle. "I make it just under thirty-nine ounces, Mr. Oliver. You want it in cash or credit?"

"Well, I took me on a partner. You might ort to just let me have it in cash."

"That must've been a purty good to-do, though," Long said. He punched No Sale on the cash register and began to count bills onto Oliver's palm. "Shoot Blackstock's leg off and kill a Diamond-T truck. All in the same night. Well, I guess Blackstock was astin for it since he didn't have no business down there. But that truck was just a innocent bystander."

Horace Hensley had been listening in silence. "I'll tell you what Hardin told me one time," he finally said. "And it was the damnedest thing I ever heard tell of, I still don't know if it was so or not. You never could tell when Hardin was tellin the truth and when he was talkin just to hear hisself.

"It was right after he come to this part of the country. Back before Hovington died and right after Hardin moved in with Pearl. Times was tight then and by God I mean tight. They wadnt no soldiers blowin money nor judges birdhuntin with him nor none of these sharptittied Memphis whores down there. He wadnt drivin no Packard back then neither, all he had was an old Diamond-T truck and he won that off old man Pennington in a poker game."

Pope raised the lid of the dead stove and spat into the ashes. "Which he probably rigged," he said.

"Which he probably did," Hensley agreed. "Anyway, somebody had busted his still up, just teetotally demolished it and busted all his whiskey, and he worked up some kind of deal with Homer McCandless over in Hickman County and bought a bunch of whiskey off of him. I don't know how, he probably beat him, you know how slick he could talk. The hell of it was Hardin couldn't drive a car. Here he was a grown man and he couldn't even drive. Oh, he could I guess hold one in the road but nobody had never showed him the gears nor how to start and stop one. Course he can now, he drives that Packard, but he couldn't then. So he come to me.

"I didn't want no part of him. He just didn't look right to me. He looked like a feller who'd do anything and already had a start on all of it but drivin a car, but I had three kids contrary enough to want to eat ever day or two. And he laid a twenty-dollar bill on the table, I never will forget it. It looked as big as a bedsheet, and I believe I could have warmed my hands off of it. I got to thinkin about grocers.

"Hovington had about five or six hundred pounds of cotton down there in a crib and we loaded it on that truck. He had some old sideboards he'd cobbled up. We headed out to Hickman County and got that whiskey, and I was on pins and needles all the way. I never fooled none with whiskey, didn't even drink. I think that's why he wanted me. He had the whiskey hid under that cotton and a tarpaulin stretched over it and lit out like we was headed to Lawrenceburg to the gin. Made it all the way back and turned down the Mormon Springs road and a rod in that old truck started knockin. I was wringin wet with sweat, and it October, I knowed we wadnt goin to make it. I knowed I'd be settin there in the middle of the road with fifty gallon of whiskey and a blowed-up truck and I'd done made up my mind to take to the bushes.

"Then to top it off the law stopped us. Amacher was hid out in a sideroad and he stopped us. I don't know if he'd been watchin

Hardin or not, I do know he didn't have em bought off like he does now. Amacher come up and checked my license. Wanted to know where we was goin. 'Just takin off cotton,' I told him. 'Takin it where?' he ast. We was headed the wrong way and I hadn't even thought of it. Then Hardin spoke up calm as you please. He told Amacher we was headed to Lawrenceburg and the truck started tearin up and we come back.

"Amacher made me crank it up. It sounded like a cement mixer with a armful of brick throwed in it. Amacher just nodded and waved us on.

"Anyway, we got there and got the whiskey unloaded. Hardin took him a little drink and got to braggin. Spread hisself a little bit. That's when he said what I started out to tell you that was the damnedest thing I ever heard of. He said he was a walkin miracle, that nothin bad couldn't ever happen to him cause the worst already had. He said he was a walkin dead man.

"He told me he was born in a casket. Said his mama was killed when a horse run off with a buggy and throwed her out and broke her neck. They had her laid out and everthing and was preachin her funeral, and in a way I guess his too, when they heard a baby squallin. Folks didn't know what on earth to do. Some just jumped up and took off runnin out of the church. Some of the women finally got up and looked. Godamighty. He was a down in her clothes. He'd crawled out or got jarred out by them handlin the casket or somethin. Anyway, there he was."

"Not that I believe any of this horseshit for a minute," Sam Long said. "But that's the strongest argument for embalmin I ever heard. She'd a been embalmed he never would've been."

"It just sounds like a damn lie to me," a man named Pope said.

"I don't know. I've thought about it a lot and I don't know why a man would make up a tale like that to tell on hisself. But I don't know why he'd tell it if it was the truth either."

"Hardin never done nothin without a reason."

"Yeah. It makes you think though. This ain't nothin against religion but looky here. It looks like somebody slipped up and let him get started in the first place and then seen what they done. They tried to wipe out that mistake with anothern and let the cagey son of a bitch slip through anyway. I guess when they seen how set on gettin into this world he was they just throwed up their hands and said let him go."

The car blew one peremptory blast of its horn but by the time it did Winer had already opened the door and stepped onto the porch. He stood peering into the yard. Dusk was deepening, the western sky beyond the darkling stubbled fields mottled with bloody red where the day's light was draining off the rim of the world.

"What say, Winer?" The Packard sat gleaming dully in the yard.

"Hidy."

"You got a minute? I got a little business I need to talk with you."

"I reckon so."

Winer approached the car. Hardin cut the switch and the lights and swung the door open a little way though he made no move to get out. He sat facing Winer with his arms on the door panel, chin resting on his forearm. "Come on up, boy. I reckon everbody's peaceable."

Winer thought the face curiously asymmetrical: the nose had been broken and healed crooked, tipped slightly toward the left side of the face. The right side of the face was lanternjawed, the cheek perpetually swollen. There was an imbalance to the jaws as if God Almighty had laid a hand on either side of the face, slipped one side a notch up and the other a notch down. The eyes were pale yellow, some peculiarity about the pupils. The eyes were goatlike. The left lid drooped sleepily as if his guard never dropped, as if one eye must watch while the other rested.

"I hear you run out of a job."

"Yeah. I was working for Weiss."

"Me and you might be able to help one another. You need work and I need it done."

Winer hunkered in the yard, absentmindedly took up a stick, began to scratch meaningless hieroglyphics in the earth. A whippoorwill abruptly called from the woods, as if at some occult signal others took up the chorus. As dusk drew on the face faded out, there was only the voice and the pale gleam of the Packard, which seemed to emit some cool black light.

"What was it you wanted done?" Winer asked.

Something in his voice, caution perhaps, made Hardin grin. "I ain't tryin to hire you to kill somebody," he said. "I don't sub that work out." He shook a cigarette from a pack, offered the pack to Winer, returned it to his pocket when it was refused. A match rasped on metal, flared. "You know that buildin I'm puttin up up there? I need some help on it. Reckon you can drive a nail? You ever done any carpenter work?"

"What I don't know I can learn."

"I hear your daddy was a carpenter."

"That's right."

"I heard he was a damn good worker. I heard a lot of folks say you're a pretty damn good worker yourself."

"I don't know about that."

"I want that place finished before cold weather. I want it dried in before the rains start and I ain't gettin it. I got Gobel Lipscomb down there piddlinass around and he's cryin he ain't got no help. I done hired him two helpers and they quit him. Hell, he ain't no carpenter nohow. I can pick up plenty of these old boys but as soon as they get enough worked out to buy a halfpint of whiskey you don't see em no more till next Thursday. That ain't what I want. What I want is somebody'll be there to work ever day the weather's fit and give me a day's work for a day's pay. From what I hear that's you, Winer."

"What are you paying?"

"Well, I'm payin fair wages. What are you worth?"

"I don't know."

"I might tell you a dollar an hour and be underpayin you. I might say two dollars a day and be payin you too much. What say you come down Monday mornin and we'll try each other out."

"Well, that sounds fair enough to me."

"I guarantee you a fair wage. I ain't astin you to work for nothin, and man nor boy don't enter into it. I pay what a man's worth. Me and you just might hit it off. I been lookin for a likely feller I could trust. A young man wants to make his mark."

Winer arose. "I'll see you Monday then."

"You got any tools?"

"I got my pa's. I reckon he had about everthing I'll need."

"You get in there and rest up then. Me and you's got a honky-tonk to build, Winer. A hell of a honkytonk. I'm gonna have a nig-ger cook fryin hamburgers for them that's hungry. I'm gonna run poker games for them with money burnin their pockets and whores for them inclined in that direction. I'm gonna feed em, bleed em, and breed em, all under one roof. And you're gonna build me that roof."

Winer dragged the box of tools from the back room out to where the light was. Hands gentle and respectful to the tools. He wiped the framing square with an oiled rag, tilted it toward the white globe of light to read the spill of numbers. Something awe-some, almost occult, ageless, in this sheer condensation of knowl-edge.

"What are you doin?"

"Getting ready to go to work."

"For him?"

"Yes."

"Buildin that Godless mess down there at Hovington's."

He laid the square aside. "Well. I haven't noticed any preachers coming around to hire me to build a church."

"You think God Almighty'll ever allow a roof over such a snake's den as that? No, he won't. He'll burn it down with a bolt of lightnin before the first bottle's sold or the first blasphemy's said. Then where will you be? If it was me I'd want to be as far away from a sight like that as I could."

"Well. God Almighty let him sell it off Hovington's front porch and I never even heard any thunder."

"Yeah. Yeah. And him gettin bolder ever minute and darin folks to stop him. Shootin em and goin scot-free, burnin houses over folks' heads. And you defendin him to your own mama and gettin a mouth on you needs a bar of soap took to it."

Winer didn't reply. He tried a tape measure, dripped oil into the case, tried it again.

"And you gettin more like him ever day. Usin his tools. It's a wonder he didn't take em with him when he went, I reckon he figured there wadnt a dollar in them." Old bitter anger long unhealed imbued her with vehemence. "Storm in here mad at nothin and gone with never a word of why to anybody."

He still didn't reply. He seldom did anymore.

Oliver had always expected his fences to outlast him but in the last year or so it seemed to him that he spent most of his time repairing them where the goats had pushed through.

"I aim to kill em," he said. "Ever last emptyheaded one of em. I'm goin back to the house soon as I fix this fence and get my gun and lay out ever last goat I own."

"If I was going to kill them I'd just let the fences go," Winer said. He was grinning, he'd heard death sentences passed on the goats before but the old man's herd always seemed to increase rather than diminish. Even as Oliver spoke a baby goat was rubbing its head against the old man's arm.

He was weaving a temporary deterrent of seagrass string among the rusted strands of wire. "I sort of like to hear the bells but by God I can string the bells on wire and let the wind ring em." He knotted the string. Already goats were pushing against the wire. "And say we're out of the sang business?"

"I reckon. I told him I'd be there Monday."

"Just as well, I reckon, it'll be gone fore long. I look for a early frost and a long winter. Long and cold. Signs is there if you know where to look."

"You reckon I ought to go work for him or not? I'm a little undecided."

"Boy, you got to do what you want to do. You suit yourself. As long as you keep your head straight and stay out of his business you'll be all right. Just drive nails and draw your pay on Friday and go on home. Besides, I know you. You're goin to do what you want to anyway."

"But you don't like him."

Oliver straightened when he finished the fence, stood halfbent a moment then with hands on knees, his fingers kneading recalcitrant flesh and bone. "No," he said. "But there ain't no law says you got to like a man to do his work and draw his money. All you have to do is get along with him. I just worked for bosses I liked, I guess I'd a spent a good portion of my life settin on the front porch."

"Would you work for Hardin?"

"Lord, no. I'd scratch shit with the chickens before I'd take a nickel that passed through his hands."

"Why? Because he's a bootlegger?"

"No. I got nothin against bootleggin. I lived around it all my life. Thomas Hovington was a bootlegger and I never had nothin against him cept he let folks run over him. Never would stand up for hisself. Let Hardin do him out of his business, his place, even his woman. A man like Hardin, now, he can spot that in a feller and use it, he knows who he can shove around and who he can't. Just see he don't get started off that way with you. The way I see it there's a way of doin things, a way they ort to be done. Hardin strikes me as a feller that won't cull much if it'll get him what he wants."

"Well. It's your business anyhow," Winer said. "I just wanted you to know why I won't be over Monday."

"You a good worker. Don't sell yourself short and don't let him run nothin over on you."

Watching the boy go back up the roadbed Oliver knelt back in the sun and rested a moment. Well, go then, he thought. I can't stop you. The sun was a warm weight on the paper lids of his eyes but it already had a quality of distance to it, a subtle eclipse of the seasons he had an affinity with, a clocking of the earth's time he felt in sync with, he and the earth growing old together but never able to give up.

That spotted horse, he thought, remembering *the hoofbeats and almost concurrent with them the horse and rider appearing apparitionlike and immediate out of the brush and morning fog, the bunched muscles of the horse's hindquarters when Hardin sawed the reins and the horse rearing, its eyes wild and muddy but no more wild than Hardin's own, the look of surprise lasting no more than a second then going blank and serene, all surface you could not penetrate. There was a Winchester cradled in the crook of Hardin's arm and as the horse calmed he laid it across the pommel of the saddle. Just resting it there.*

'What the fuck are you doin out here?'

It was fall of the year and the woods were the color of bright copper and the wind was blowing, shifting the depth of the driven leaves like water. The forest became surreal, a place he'd never seen or dreamed or heard rumored, a dark corner of childhood night, and he thought, This son of a bitch is crazy. This madman is goin to shoot me where I stand and leave me where I fall. He would rot in these woods, black millipedes sleep in his chambered skull, the teeth of predators score his bones. 'Just mindin my own business,' he said. 'A pastime I ain't noticed much of around here.' There was a sharp, metallic taste to his saliva, like cankered brass.

'Your business, hell. I reckon you think anything moves in these woods is your business. Don't think I ain't seen you prowlin. Stickin your long nose in my business.'

There was a hot seeping of anger in Oliver's chest. 'You don't own this property,' he said. 'You better check your lines.'

'My lines is where I make em,' Hardin said. 'And I make a new set ever day.' He spurred the horse and almost as an afterthought quartered the horse toward Oliver, the horse's shoulder catching him in the chest and spilling him backward into the brush, the spotted horse passing almost

over him, he could hear the creak of leather and smell the horse, then the hot, acrid leaves he lay in, breathless. His lungs were emptied as if he'd fallen from some great height. His mind was a torrent of rage and disbelief. He lay stunned for a moment. He heard the blood singing in his veins, the fallen cries from blackbirds winging above him. Falling his mind had seen what his eyes had not remarked, the shovel across the saddle, not a proper shovel but a military entrenching tool, the blade wet with fresh clay. The shapes in a gunnysack tied to the saddlehorn.

Them was fruitjars, he thought. *I just like to caught him buryin his money.*

He thought of the jars packed with greasy coins and wadded bills, overflow from the money machine Hardin was hooked to, tucked into graves like the hasty and unforeseen dead.

The sight of the rifle had raked his forehead and a fine, bright line of blood crept down his face unnoticed. *I will lay for him and shoot him,* he thought, but he knew already he wouldn't. *I am old,* he admitted for the first time, *old, tired of it all. All I want is to be let alone, all I want is for things to run along smooth. All I want is peace, and an old man ought to have that, if nothin else.*

BOOK TWO

The girl had black hair as coarse and glossy as a well-kept horse's mane and it was cropped straight across below her shoulders as if it had been sheared. The first few days after school started Winer would see her come out and await the schoolbus, her books clutched against her breasts, her face self-absorbed and touched with a kind of sullen insolence, staring down the road the way the bus would come. Then after a few days she didn't come out of the house when the bus blew its horn. The bus turned and paused momentarily a few mornings and then it didn't come anymore.

These warm days of Indian summer she used to bring out an old metal lounge chair and sit on the sunny side of the house and watch them work. Winer, looking up from the pile of corners and tees he was nailing together or the blocking he was cutting with a handsaw, would see her sitting with calm indifference, her fingers laced across her stomach, watching the progress of the work not as if it interested her very much but as if it were just something to watch, just motion, like a cat watching anything that moves.

She would sit with a kind of studied unawareness of her spread legs, the glimpses they stole of her white thighs. Her eyes were halfshut beneath the weight of her long lashes and she might have been asleep but she was not.

"She's got a case on one of us," Gobel Lipscomb told him. "And somehow I just don't believe it's you." Lipscomb was the carpenter. He took to working shirtless so she could watch the play of muscles in his sunbrowned back, to ordering Winer around more. He used to drop his tape or hammer and stoop floorward for it and pause staring upward at the juncture of her thighs and he'd straighten with a look on his face near pain. "Black drawers," he would say. "Godamighty damn. Black drawers."

Hardin's business seemed to keep him pretty well occupied but sometimes on slow days he would come out and sit beside the girl and watch. Once he laid his hand on her knee and said something to her and glanced toward Lipscomb and laughed and she smiled a small smile and said nothing. When Hardin was about, Lipscomb found a higher gear in his nailing arm and seemed unaware of anything that transpired beyond the maze of partition walls he was erecting.

Carrying a beachtowel the girl came out of the trees above the abyss. Her bathing suit was wet and her black hair plastered seal-like and glossy to her head. She passed the building where they worked without glancing toward them and walked on toward the house, her hips rolling like something meshing on ball bearings.

Lipscomb was suddenly frozen, the hammer frozen in midstroke as if it had come up against some invisible barrier. Even the jaws that were perpetually kneading tobacco were still. He stood for a moment and then with great deliberation he laid his hammer aside.

"If that ain't a invite then I don't know one," he said. "Here goes nothin."

He stood before the bedroom window with his hands shading the sundrenched glass.

"Hey," Winer called.

Lipscomb might not have heard. He didn't turn. Stood leaning back to the sun staring into the room. Whatever he saw there seemed to have rendered him immobile as stone.

"Hey, Lipscomb," Winer called again.

When Lipscomb turned he threw a hand to his eyes as if struck blind or perhaps paradoxically illuminated by divine revelation and he staggered across the yard. "Oh Lord," he said. "Oh Lord." He wiped his brow and flung off imaginary beads of perspiration. He crossed the yard in great rolling seafarer's strides. "Please, Jesus, hold me back," he cried. He halted suddenly and thrust his pelvis forward spasmodically, his hands and hips miming masturbation of an enormous phallus. His tongue lolled, his eyes rolled in his head.

"How high a fever you run with them fits?" Hardin asked him. Hardin was leaning against the corner of the house smoking a cigarette. "You reckon I ought to send that boy after Ratcliff?"

Lipscomb ran a hand through his sandy hair. He seemed tonguetied. His face was so engorged with blood it looked swollen. "There ain't nothin wrong with me," he finally said.

"The hell there's not," Hardin told him.

Winer fell very busy. He knew intuitively that he had never seen a man so close to dying. His hand was counting the nails in his nail apron. One, two, three, his busy fingers counted.

Hardin didn't say anything to Lipscomb all day. He just got in the black Packard and left. At lunch they ate leaning against the wall they'd erected. "You see that bastard, how he looked at me?" Lipscomb asked. "If looks killed I'd be lookin at the underside of a casketlid right this minute. I've about decided he's got the hots for that little gal hisself."

Winer didn't reply. He drank cold coffee from a pint fruitjar and ate his sandwich and thought about the way Hardin had looked at Lipscomb. Winer did not anticipate ever being looked at by anyone in just that way.

"Hell, he looks like one of these killdees," Lipscomb said. "And they ain't nothin to him but legs and pocketbook." He studied his own thickly muscled forearms, his big hands. He seemed to draw comfort from them. "He fucks with me I'll fold him up like a rule and stick him in my pocket," he said. "Or else come upside his head with a clawhammer."

Winer judged he'd about decided Hardin wasn't going to say anything.

A few minutes before four they heard the Packard drive up and the door slam to, then Hardin came around the corner of the house. He stood there for a time watching them.

"Lipscomb, you want to step around here a minute? I need a word with you."

"Here it comes," Lipscomb said in a low voice. He slid his hammer into the strap on the leg of his overalls.

Winer went on nailing a wall together. He kept waiting for threats, blows, the sound of violence. All he could hear when he paused in his nailing was the murmur of the brook, doves mourning softly from the hollow.

Lipscomb was gone only a few minutes. When he came back his face was red all the way down into the collar of his blue chambray shirt and he was not pleased. He had an old plywood toolbox with a length of rope knotted through each end for a handle. He began gathering his tools up and slinging them into the box.

"Get your shit gathered up," he told Winer. "We're draggin up."

"What?"

"We're quittin, by God. We're goin to the house."

"We, hell," Winer said. "I didn't know we came in a set like salt and pepper shakers."

Lipscomb straightened with a square in his hand. He looked as if he'd just as soon take it out on Winer as not.

"What are you, some kind of Goddamned scab?"

"I'll make up my own mind when to go to the house. You never hired me."

"Why, you snotty little bastard. I ought to just slap the hell out of you."

"Why don't you just fold me up like you did Hardin?"

"By God, I believe I will." He took a step toward Winer but Winer still held the hammer and he did not retreat under Lipscomb's tentative advance, just stood waiting with an almost sleepy look in his eyes. Lipscomb dropped his hands and stood staring at him, his eyes fierce and malignant. "You little backstabbin shitass. You set this whole mess up, didn't you? Now you think you got the job and the girl too. All you had to do was holler, but hell no."

"Why, hellfire," Winer said. "I called you twice but you was so busy making a damn fool out of yourself you couldn't be bothered."

"Ahh, the hell with you and him both," Lipscomb said, turning away. He laid the square in the box and took up the box by its rope handles. He started toward the door.

"I'd like to stay and see the mess you'll make out of things. You couldn't build a fuckin chicken coop if you had a book to go by."

After awhile Hardin came out and climbed onto the subfloor. He sat on a box of nails watching Winer work. He had a slim cigar clamped in his jaw. He wore expensivelooking gabardine slacks and a yellow shirt. He began paring his nails with a bonehandled knife.

"Well, I had to let ye runnin mate go," he said. "I couldn't afford union scale for winderpeepin."

Winer went on working.

"Hold up a minute. You ain't gettin paid by the nail nohow."

Winer ceased and stood waiting.

"Ain't you worked past quittin time anyhow?"

"I don't know. I don't have a watch, we used his. Besides, I wasn't sure what you wanted."

"I told you what I wanted when I hired you. I want a honkytonk built. Can you do it?"

"Well, I can do most of it. There's some things it's hard for one man to do, like puttin up the joists and rafters. And I can't raise the walls and plumb them by myself."

"That's all I wanted to hear you say. You measure em and nail em together and I'll grab a handful of these highbinders I'm always waistdeep in and we'll raise em for you. You run into anything requires more than two hands, just holler. All right?"

"I'll give it a try."

"Shore you will. You can do it. Ain't you goin to ast me about the money?"

"What about it?"

"About how much I was payin him. I'm payin it to you now, you're the architect and the carpenter and the hired help too. You fuck up we'll know who to blame it on."

Winer grinned.

"Come on and I'll run you home. Can't have my builder walkin to work totin his tools. Folks'll be talkin about me."

Winer was still wonderstruck. I am rich, he thought. I am a wealthy man.

Lately Winer's mother had taken to cleaning herself up more and doing her hair. She seemed always to have on a clean dress and there was something foreign about her. Winer realized for the first time how much she had let herself go down through the years. She was not pretty but had she been less dour and practical she would have qualified as plain.

He noticed the tiretracks even before she got the pans.

"Had company today?"

"No. A salesman stopped by."

"A salesman? Selling what?"

"Sellin pots and pans," she said irritably as if there were no other kind of salesman, as if he were interrogating her.

A week later she had the pans. He saw them when he came in from Hardin's, a great motley collection of them, coppercolored, gleaming, skillets and cookers and spatulas and doubleboilers and seemingly a pan for every purpose the mind of man could devise.

"Great God," he said.

"What?"

"Where'd you get all that stuff?"

"I bought em."

"Bought em? Why?"

"Because I wanted em is why. I always wanted me a set of cookers like that."

He was a little awed by them. "Well." He paused. "What'd they cost?"

"Never you mind what they cost. It won't be a nickel out of your pocket."

He took his razor and mirror and a bar of soap down to the branch. Beyond the barn it curved and there was a hole of water deep enough to swim in. He washed and shaved and came back out of the woods and onto the stoop and she was awaiting him. Apparently their conversation was not yet over.

She laid a hand on his arm. "I got a friend," she said. "Sells them pots and pans."

He thought, a friend, not understanding at first. Then he saw in her sallow face some commingling of shame and pride, the eyes imbued simultaneously with humility and stubbornness, and he thought, She means a man. He didn't know what to say though her face expected something, she looked as if she were ashamed of whatever it was she was doing but had no plans to stop.

"I think you'd like him, Nathan. He wants to see you."

"Well. Sure." He was looking all about. "Where is he?"

"He's supposed to be here next Friday," she said. Not "He'll be here Friday," Winer noticed, not yet with sureness or even confidence, she was uncertain of her hold on him, or did not believe it yet.

Monday he was there long before worktime planning his day. There was more to know than he had realized and now there was no one to ask. Old questions on the pitch of roofs, the cuts on rafters, troubled him. Yet as the week wore on he discovered an affinity for planes and angles, for the simple rightness of things. His corners formed perfect squares and they stood as plumb as a level could plumb them. There were things he did not know how to do but he found there were several ways to do everything and that even if he took the long way it did not matter if the end result was the same.

He seemed always to work with an audience. With the weather holding fair Hardin's coterie of convivial drunks used to follow the sun and in the afternoon they'd align themselves on Coke crates or folding chairs or old ladderbacks as spindly and loosejointed as themselves and against the whitewashed concrete blocks of Hardin's addition they took on the character of a sepia daguerreotype, old felthatted and overalled rogues watching time pass with attentive eyes out of dead faces. Watching anything that life chose to parade before them. There was a great calm about these old men, they seemed to have arrived at some compromise with life long ago and nothing much surprised them anymore.

The young men were mostly furloughed or shellshocked soldiers or over-the-hill sailors far from any seas and they would be inside drinking and trying to get the girl to ride down the road with them. Finally drunk they settled for whatever whore chanced to be in attendance or even Pearl herself should the need be acute.

Winer was comfortable with the old men but he could never become comfortable with the soldiers, there was an air of desperation about them. They acted as if time were the commodity they were shortest on, as if they did not have the leisure to take life as it came but were eternally seeking shortcuts, must twist each moment until it suited their purpose, bend every event to their own amusement. Something had to be happening for them every minute. They were wound too tight, Winer thought. He knew why and he didn't guess he blamed them but he thought they were wound too tight anyway. They reminded him of a war being fought that had heretofore been just a disembodied voice in a radio and he knew that unless things changed it would not be long before he was fighting it too.

All the soldiers looked alike to Winer and he thought if he ever saw one sober he might think about them differently but around

Hardin's he wasn't likely to. All the ones he saw were a little drunk and a lot belligerent. They always wanted to fight the sailors but if there were no sailors they'd fight each other.

One afternoon he paused in nailing weatherboarding on the walls when a fight erupted inside and boiled out the back door, the old men picking up their jars or jellyglasses or whatever and retreating to more neutral territory. Two soldiers were rolling in the yard and when a stringyheaded blond broke a beerbottle over the topmost one's head a girl with red hair knocked her down with a two-by-four and fell upon her. Winer, watching their exposed white thighs and rent clothing, ultimately counted eighteen participants and he wondered how they kept up with who was fighting whom and which side they were on.

They fought all over the backyard pulling hair and cursing and falling over one another. Winer swung himself onto the top plate the better not to be mistaken for a participant. Hardin tried to yell them down, then he and Wymer moved among them like dogs snapping at the heels of milling cattle, first with blackjacks then Hardin slipping on his Sunday knucks and wading in.

When they subsided no one seemed to know what the fight had been about and they all went back inside to discuss it save one soldier sitting crying in the grass with his jaw hanging crazily. He sat there awhile by himself and then he got up and hobbled around the corner like a very old man. Winer went on back to work and after awhile the old men came up from the branch laughing and seated themselves again.

Leo Huggins sold throughout a three-county area what he described as waterless cookware. He canvassed the backroads in his old green Studebaker, sitting with housewives on their porches, beseeching, wheedling, his eyes black and glossy with whatever obsession bulged behind them, the present one being that this waterless cookware was the only thing of moment in all the world.

He'd demonstrate it in the comfort of your own home. He'd
have you invite the neighbors over and he would go into the
kitchen and prepare and serve a meal in these marvelous pans.
Many a husband came in hot and sweaty from the sawmill to find
his yard clotted with cars and the house full of folks he hadn't expected. Huggins's Studebaker likely blocking the driveway.
Huggins himself humming busily in the kitchen, his sleeves rolled
up, supper on the stove. The wife sitting waiting with mounting apprehension, wondering how she had let herself be talked into this.

So there were times when Huggins had to depart in haste, the
meal left halfprepared, the pots and pans abandoned until another
day when the husband was once again at work.

"Your mama tells me you a wood butcher."

"I reckon."

."I reckon it's all right if you can make any money at it,"
Huggins said, then turned the conversation neatly to himself. "I
never could make a livin at public work. Had to do what I could
with my brains."

And your mouth, Winer thought, then immediately decided he
wasn't being fair, that he did not know Huggins well enough to
criticize him and was not giving him a chance. Yet he caught himself staring at the big white hands that did not look as if they'd ever
done an hour's labor, the fingers soft and freckled as bleached
sausages, the still upturned palms tender and virginal as a baby's.

Huggins fell to talking about himself. He liked this topic of
conversation, figured the rest of the world was afflicted in a like
manner. He had come up from nothing in Arkansas, he told Winer
and his mother, from folks who never had nothing nor wanted
nothing, folks in shotgun shacks with cracks in the floor so you
could keep an eye on the chickens, and he figured if he was ever
going to be anything he had to do it on his own hook. He had
begun by selling fancy overpriced coaloil lamps to the colored folks
in the underside of Little Rock, later taking on a line of Bibles with
negro Jesuses.

Winer sat only halflistening to this oral history. He had worked hard and his shoulders ached from nailing and he kept yawning. Weariness seemed to have crept up from his ankles and he could still hear and feel the rhythmic swing of the hammer in some dreamlike part of his mind. Amber Rose's face drifted unbidden into his thoughts and would not leave. Huggins's car was paid off free and clear, he learned, there was no man in all the world who could claim Huggins owed him a dime. Winer stared across the yard, wishing himself elsewhere. The day was waning, the blue timberline across the field already an indecipherable stain, the sedge washed by broad swaths of failing light.

The trio formed a curious tableau on the porch of the unlit house, teacher and disciples perhaps, the boy pretending to listen, the man preaching softly the arcane gospel of himself, speaking so earnestly he might have been imparting hidden knowledge of the workings of the world or spinning a web to draw them into some dadaistic conspiracy. The woman sat in her chair, still, unrocking, hands momentarily stayed from their darning. Her eyes were downcast to her lap, the yellow lids slick and veined with a delicate blue tracery of capillaries. She seemed rapt, transfixed, and Winer realized that he did not know her, felt a brief and bitter stab of regret that he had never tried to learn her. She was less real to him than the yellowing daguerreotypes of other strangers in her own picturebox.

Hardin had square, boxlike hands with thick fingers and he kept the nails cut straight across almost into the quick. The nails were hornlike and scrupulously clean. He was forever paring them when he spoke with Winer.

"Where did you get that knife?"

"Lord, son, I don't know. I had it I guess ten or twelve year."

"Let me see it a minute."

Hardin handed him the knife handle first.

The grips were bone the color of oxblood. CASE, the trademark said. Winer sat for a time holding it. "This is my father's knife," he said.

"Seems like I did find it somewheres."

A small, irregular W was filed into the base of the blade the way all the tools were marked but Winer would have known it anyway. The knife was an integral part of the memory of his father, the knife and the black slouch hat and the cold, remote way the eyes had of looking at the world. But they had never looked at Winer that way. The knife was wound up with the way his father had glanced at him when he started to town or to the field to plow. Winer the child would be hesitant, uncertain whether he should go or stay. "Well, are you comin or not?" his father would ask. "You know I can't get nothin done without you to supervise."

He smelled the knife.

"What'd you do that for?"

Winer flushed. "I don't know. He always had a plug of tobacco in the same pocket with the knife. The knife always had crumbled-up chewing tobacco inside it and it always smelled just like old Red Ox twist."

"I remember where I got that knife now. I hadn't thought about it in years. It was a holler or two over across your line. Seems like kind of a cedar grove in there, where I reckon he'd been cuttin fence-post. The knife was layin on a sandbar down by a spring in the mouth of the holler. But it was like I said ten or twelve year ago and any smell of chewin tobacco would be long gone."

"I don't know why I did that."

"Your pa lit out, didn't he?"

"I don't know what happened to him. I never did believe he lit out and I don't believe it now."

"Well, folks is funny. I don't care how close you think you know somebody, you don't know what wheels is turnin in their head. Course you don't remember but times was hard for folks back then. Times was tightern a banjo string. Lots of folks was on the road. He might've just throwed up his hands and said fuck it and lit out."

"No."

"Well. I ain't tryin to tell you what to think about your own daddy. But seems to me me and you's a lot alike."

No, Winer thought, still looking at the knife lying open in his hand. I am not like you. I'll never be like you. I'm not like Oliver either but both of you want to tell me what to do. What to think. Both of you are always sayin, I'm not tryin to tell you, but you're tellin me just the same. I am like myself. If I am like anybody then I am like him.

"My own daddy cut out on me in February of the year I was eight year old. This was in Cullman, Alabama. I never will forget it, nor forget Christmas that year. They always told us Santy Claus and me and my sister used to go out and hunt for reindeer tracks. The ground was froze hard as a rock but we use to hunt anyway. Course they never was much, a apple and a orange and a handful of penny candy. A few nuts. But this year they wadnt nothin in our socks. I wondered what the hell it was we'd done. I went out where Pa was standin in the yard. He was lookin off down the road though there wadnt nothin to see. Just what you see when you look down a road. After awhile Pa noticed us and reached in his pocket and handed me and her a quarter. 'Here,' he said. 'Git yins some Santy Claus.' That was when I was eight year old. Before I was nine he was long gone and we was livin with our aunt. She was sleepin with a sectionhand used to take a strop to us just to hear us yell."

Winer didn't say anything.

"Life is hard, Winer. You just got to get hard with it. It's a blackjack game with life dealin and the dealer's always got the edge. You see? You got to get your own edge. Because by God if you don't there'll always be somebody there lyin to you all your life and then handin you a greasy quarter and tellin you to buy some Santy Claus."

"What'll you take for this knife? You found it."

"Hell, take it. You said it belonged to your pa."

"Well, you've had it all these years. Decide what you want for it and hold it out of my pay."

"Hell, no. If it means somethin to ye, take it on. Seems to me it's a damn poor substitute for a pa but such as it is you're welcome to it."

Old woods here and deep. Here the earth was coppercolored with fallen needles and the air had the cool, astringent smell of cedar. An old wagonroad faded out somewhere in the grove then wound away toward home. The piled tops of dead cedars lay bleached and white and indestructible as bone.

He had not been in these woods since he was a child. Time seemed to have stopped here. He halfwaited for the rattle of trace chains, the ring of the axe, the slow turning of wagon wheels against the earth. This used to be an old houseplace, his father had said. The year the tornado came through the storm just picked it up off the foundation rocks and carried it away, no one knew where.

Here an old rusted stovepipe leached from the earth, there the remnants of a washtub. A few old handmade bricks. On a level area of diminished brush the foundation stones themselves, profound, ageless, curious Stonehenge aligned to no known star.

The spring was clotted with leaves. Kneeling there he cleaned them out with his hands, watched the slow swirl of clean water into it, the list of sand and silt. An old one-eyed crayfish pretending invisibility eyed him apprehensively from the clearing water, retreated beneath a stone. A fall wind drove the first leaves from the tree above him, he arose in a drifting storm of them. He drank here, he thought, his eyes scanning the sandbar. Where had the knife been? His father had been fond of the knife, it wasn't like him to lose it, once he had lost it and searched for it for two entire days before it was found and his father had not been one for repeating mistakes.

Winer dried his hands on the seat of his pants, walked on up the hollow. In its mouth he found wreckage he could not account for. Old rusted fifty-five-gallon drums, purposeless shards of mauled metal. A cornucopia of gallon sorghum buckets. Broken glass jugs. He sat on a stump and stared at the refuse. A story resided here could he but decipher it. A jay scolded and then the woods were still and impenetrable again. He arose. He had never accepted before that his father was dead but he accepted it now.

Winer watched his mother at work, her eyes close to the sewing in her lap. Her lids were veined and near lashless, the skin drawn tight and smooth over her cheekbones. She seemed oblivious to him, to anything save the cloth her needle moved in. Her mouth was pursed slightly in the expression of resigned disapproval with which she viewed the world. She is old, he thought suddenly, though he knew she was not. For a moment something in the calm placidity of the face reminded him of the old men in Long's store or Hardin's, the serene face of an old woman looking down at him long ago from the high cab of a cordwood truck and from an Olympus of years, a face quilted and wrinkled by time until it seemed ageless, something found in nature, an old walnut hull found in the woods. Who was she? Aunt, grandmother, surrogate mother? Whoever's she was, she was never mine.

I am your blood, he thought. Half of me is you and yet I know nothing about you. I fed at your breast and yet I draw more memory and knowledge from a lost pocketknife than all your years have showed me. Than all your reproach has taught me.

And you know. Somewhere behind the placid mask you wear

for a face the answer lies. You may not know it but it is there. Somewhere in the vaults of memory, old stacked and yellowing newsprint. There must have been things said I did not hear, did not understand if I did. Or have you known all these years, I've never known your motives or your reasoning. Did you cut his throat while he slept, did a tinker with his pots and pans trouble your dreams even then? Did his forerunner appear to you in a vision long ago, were you just clearing a path for his coming? Or did Pa just walk off down a road, the way you walked off down a road in your head?

"Did Pa ever fool any with whiskey?"

She looked up sharply. "Do what?"

"Did he ever make whiskey? Or sell it?"

"Lord, no. What makes you ask that?"

"I just got to wonderin."

"Well, I'd like to know what got you to wonderin any such as that. Has that lowdown Hardin been feedin you a mess of lies?"

"No."

"Your pa never even drank. I never even knowed him to take a drink of whiskey but one time and that was at a dance before we got married. Your pa was funny turned. He kept to hisself and he never had the patience to put up with a bunch of drunks the way you'd have to do to fool with whiskey."

"You never talked much about him," he said. "Why is that?"

"He said it all when he pulled that door to behind him," she told him.

"Did you ever know my pa to make whiskey?"

"Good God, no. Why? Are you thinkin about settin up and runnin Dallas Hardin out of business?"

"No. I just got to wondering."

"Get you one of these pears," Oliver said. He had his rocker in the shade of the pear tree and was peeling pears into an old blue enamel washpan. Yellow windfall pears lay all about in the sere grass and yellowjackets crawled all over them in an agony of gluttony. The air was rich and winey with the fragrance of the pears.

"I found an old still back in there where the cedar grove is, over by King's Branch. I just wondered who put it there."

"Well, I can't tell you who it was but I can tell you who it wadnt. Not talkin agin your pa but he was downright intolerant about some things. Now, I don't mind bootleggin myself, but whiskeymakin was one of the things he was down on, he was a hard worker and whiskeymakin just looked shiftless to him. Though there's a world of hard work wound up in it as anyone who ever shouldered a hundred-pound sack of sugar through the woods could tell you."

"Whose would you say it was then?"

"Well, when Dallas Hardin first come to this part of the country and didn't have the money to buy the law the way he does now he used to make his own stuff stead of haulin in this here bonded like he does. He had a habit of settin up across Hovington's lines on somebody else in case the revenuers found his rig."

The old man glanced up and something in Winer's expression so startled him that it broke his train of thought and he was momentarily confused. For a second he was seeing the father's eyes in the son's face, cold, sleepylooking eyes.

"No, now, wait a minute," Oliver said bemusedly as if he were talking to himself. "That ain't it atall. My mind's goin in my old age like the rest of me's done gone. Old man Cater Loveless lived back in there and when that tornado come through it just blowed his house away. Now, he made whiskey, Cater did. That was fore your pa bought the land for the taxes on it."

"Then it must've been Loveless's still?"

Oliver looked up. The look was gone from the boy's face. "Likely it was," he agreed. He went back to peeling pears.

The boy stood up. "Where's your bucksaw? I thought I'd cut you up that big poplar the creek washed up."

"Boy, you don't have to do that. Do you have to be doin somethin ever minute?"

"It won't be long till cold weather."

"No, I guess it won't. It never is anymore. Or warm weather either for that matter. Seems like the older you get the faster the wheel rolls."

"Where'd you say the saw was?"

"It's on the crib wall where it always is but I don't see why you can't find nothin to do but cut a old man's wood. When I was your age I was workin twelve hours a day and runnin the women all night. Why ain't you in town doin that?"

Winer started off toward the barn.

"Unless of course you've found somethin a little closer to home."

Winer stopped and turned and Oliver was grinning down into the pan of cutup pears as if something he saw there amused him. Winer went on to the barn.

"You get through we'll sack you up some of these pears to take home," the old man called.

Weekdays were generally slow and nothing Pearl and Wymer couldn't handle and Hardin had lots of unspecified business to take care of. When he left he told no soul where he was going or when he'd be back, just driving off in the Packard or saddling up the Morgan and riding off up the ridge out of sight into the woods. On the days when Hardin was gone Amber Rose would sit outside and watch Winer. There was something curiously tranquil about her. He never saw her read a book or sew or do anything else to occupy her time, she would sit quiet and self-contained and so watchful he came to feel that he could discern the weight of her eyes, could tell the moment her attention fell on him. He remembered her on the schoolbus but she'd never talked then either and she had certainly not looked the way she looked now. He remembered her violet eyes and the coarse black hair but the rest of her had changed. She seemed to have grown up overnight, the way a flower opens up.

He looked up from his homedrawn blueprint and she was standing before him holding a quart jar of peaches in her hands.

"You reckon you can open this? Me nor Mama can't."

Winer laid his pencil aside. "I might can."

She was standing reaching the jar down toward him. When he stood up they were standing very close together and looking down into her face he felt that the air had suddenly become charged with electricity. She met his eyes innocently as if she were unaware of it, perhaps she was. Her hair was parted in the middle so that it fell over both ears and onto her shoulders. Seen closer than he had ever seen it her skin was very clear. He could smell the warm, clean scent of her and the thought of Lipscomb leaning to the sunwashed glass made him dizzy.

"Well, go on and open them if you can. Mama's waitin on me."

He unscrewed the ring and handed her the jar. "You're very strong," she said, an ironic edge to her voice. She took the jar but made no move to leave. "What are you starin at? Is my face on crooked?"

"I just always thought you had the prettiest eyes."

Her hair smelled like soap and he could see the clean line of her scalp where her hair was parted. The sun bright off the white-washed wall fell full on her face and in its light her eyes looked almost drowsy. He could see the dark down along her jawline, the pale, soft fuzz on her upper lip. The lips looked hot and swollen.

"Well, you can talk. I didn't know if you could or not. You ought to try it more often."

"I might if I had someone to talk to," he said. "No need in telling myself things I already know." Above the ringing in his ears all his words sounded dull and clumsy.

"Next time I need a can of peaches opened I reckon you can talk to me," she said. When she smiled her teeth were white and straight. He watched her back through the sun to the house.

In midafternoon she brought out a jar of icewater and then just before quitting time she came out again and set a jar of peaches beside his lunchbox.

"Here," she said. "Don't say I never give you nothin."

Sam Long watched him come up the street from the railroad tracks, a tall young man who seemed heavier through the chest and shoulders every time Long saw him. He passed the window of the grocery store without looking in and went on, a purposeful air of tautness about him as if he were searching for something and knew just where it was hidden. Long went back behind the cash register and took out a ticketbook and studied it and finally laid it aside in a wooden drawer. He lit a short length of cigar stub and waited. A family came in and began to slowly wander the aisles gathering up provisions but Long seemed bemused and abstracted and this time when Winer came by Long went out and stopped him.

Winer waited, a look of friendly curiosity on his face.

"I ain't seen you in the last few weeks. Got to wonderin about you."

"Well, I haven't been getting into town much. I'm working over at Hardin's and staying pretty busy."

"That's what I heard. Hardin payin off by the week, is he?"

"He's paying me well enough. What was it you wanted anyway?"

"I was wonderin when you could do somethin about what you owe me. Your grocer ticket."

"What needs to be done? I've been sending the money in to you on Saturday just like always."

"I'm afraid not."

Winer didn't reply immediately and Long said, "Come on in here a minute and I'll show you the tickets."

"I wouldn't know any more if I looked than I do now. Somethin's not right here. I've been sendin that money in here every week."

"Well, for a long time you did. Ever since you was workin for Weiss. You or your mama'd come in and settle up and get your grocers. You always paid off like a clock tickin. Then about a month or so ago your mama started comin here with that Huggins feller sells them pots and pans. She quit payin but she kept on buyin. I didn't think nothin about it for awhile cause you always been good for it."

Winer didn't say anything for awhile. When he did speak he said, "All right. How much is it?"

"A little over a hundred dollars."

"How little over?"

"A hundred twenty-three is what it is."

"Well, you'll get it, but from now on nobody buys so much as a Co-Cola on my ticket unless I say so. All right?"

"That's fine with me."

Huggins was there the following Friday evening rocking gently in the porch swing, a proprietary air about him, claiming squatter's rights. Winer went on into the house and collected his mirror and razor and soap. He went out the back door and down the path to the spring. He had already bathed and was shaving, kneeling on the bank, when the voice came. He nicked his face with the straight razor when Huggins spoke.

Huggins had made no sound approaching, easing through the brush with a kind of covert stealth, paused standing behind him, framed in the mirror behind Winer's face. Winer watched a scarlet bead of blood well on his jaw, trickle down his face. He wiped it away and lowered the mirror.

"What do you know, good buddy?"

Winer turned. Huggins stood waiting, arms depending at his sides as if Winer had summoned him and he was waiting patiently to see what was required of him. He stood stooped as if he were composed of some strange material slowly turning liquid, a pear-shaped lump of loathsome jelly gravity was slowly drawing misshapen to earth, barely contained by the mismatched clothing he wore, clothing he seemed to have stolen under cover of darkness from random clotheslines.

"What is it? I came up here to take a bath."

"I know ye did. I just needed to talk to ye a minute and wanted to catch ye by yeself."

Have you got a couple of dollars till payday? Winer asked himself.

"Reckon you could loan me about five till Wednesday?"

Winer mentally chided himself for underestimating the reach of Huggins's ambition. He washed the lather off his face and dried it on a towel. He wanted done with Huggins, wanted him gone, he felt constricted and short of breath as if Huggins somehow affected the atmosphere, sucked from it more than his due of oxygen, left it hot and lifeless and barren. He was fumbling out his wallet, thumbing through the money Hardin had paid him. "I guess I can."

His alacrity took Huggins by surprise. He licked his already wet lips, eyeing the money. "Just let me have ten if you can spare it, good buddy. I'll catch ye Wednesday."

Winer paused. "If five'd do a minute ago how did we get up to ten?"

"Well. Five'll do, I reckon. I'll get by on it, I guess."

Winer stood up. He reached Huggins the five-dollar bill, watched him fold it, palm it rapidly, and slide it into his watch-pocket, knew even as he watched that he would see it no more. "You're going to have to get by on it," he said. "I'm paying my own grocery ticket this week."

"Do what?"

"I've been meaning all week to ask you about my grocery ticket out at Long's. I've been sending money out there every week and somehow or other I seem to owe him more money all the time. Do you know how a thing like that could be?"

"Lord, no. I guess you better ask Sam Long. His tickets must be messed up."

"His tickets are all right. Mine are the ones messed up. What are you trying to pull on me?"

"You need to talk to your mama."

"You say talk to Sam Long. Or talk to my mama. I'd about as soon talk to you as anybody I know."

"I ain't no bookkeeper."

"No. You ain't no bookkeeper. There's two or three things I can think of that you are but you ain't no bookkeeper. And I'll tell you something. I work for my pay. And if you think I'm busting my ass every day so you can drink it up at the poolhall or pay for Goddamn pots and pans then you're living in a dreamworld."

"You got a good bit of a mouth on ye for a youngen, ain't ye?"

I'm going to hit him, Winer thought. Then he thought, no, I'd have to touch him.

"Boy, me and you's goin to have to get somethin straight. Now, you work with me and I'll work with ye, you make it hard on me and I'll hand it right back to ye. Your mama thinks a right smart of me and we gettin purty serious. We might be gettin married one of these times, we might just all pick up and go north. Me and you'll be in the same family then and you know as well as I do that a family ain't got but one boss."

"Why, Goddamn you." Winer dropped the razor and mirror, heard the clink of glass breaking on stone. He grasped the collar of Huggins's shirt, twisted, felt the soft tug of thread breaking, the collar button pulling away. He kept the fabric between his fist and the white, hairless flesh of Huggins's throat. "I'll tell you right now," Winer said. "What you and her do is your business. But it'll be a cold day in hell when you boss me around."

Huggins was walking awkwardly backward, trying to get away. He had thought Winer a boy, nothing to contend with, but he had never really looked at him. Now he was seeing the hard brown shoulders, the corded arms, and Winer watched fear rise up in Huggins's eyes like liquid filling a glass, before it his own twinned image, the tiny faces cold and remote and malevolent, leaning into the black little eyes.

He released his grip and Huggins staggered backward, almost fell when a stone turned beneath his foot. He winced and stood massaging his ankle. "You stuckup little prick," he said. "You sorry shitass." He was breathing as if he had run a long way, a harsh, sucking rasp. He buttoned the shirt with what buttons remained and ran a shaking hand through his hair and went shambling back through the brush. When he judged himself safely out of reach he said, "We do get married the first thing I'm doin is puttin your ass on the road." He went on.

Winer gathered his gear again. The mirror lay in triangular shards, each reflecting its own blue sky or baring tree, a shattered glass landscape. He waited awhile until he heard the car start up and drive away before he went to the house. When he got there he saw that wherever Huggins had gone his mother had gone too.

His father had built the house, a man conscientious of the plumbness of corners, the pitch of rafters. All these years had passed and the floorjoists were unsagging, the ceilings level and true. Would that other things had seen fit to endure so well. For the house smelled of waiting, of last year's winter fires, it seemed to have been constructed solely in anticipation of some moment that had not arrived yet, or passed unnoticed long ago.

He drank a cup of coffee on the doorstep and after awhile he went back in and he was surprised that so little time had passed. He turned the radio on. "From WJJD in Chicago," the radio said. "Here's Randy Blake with the Suppertime Frolic." A song began, the scraping of a fiddle. He ascended the ladder into the attic.

When he descended with his toilet articles and a change of clothing in a brown paper bag the radio was singing, "I didn't hear nobody pray, sweet Jesus, I didn't hear nobody pray. Whiskey and blood run together, but I didn't hear nobody pray." Winer stood clutching the bag, staring about the room. He turned the radio off and went out.

He struck out across the field, following in the wake of the sun. The western sky was mottled red as if the town he moved toward lay in flames. Behind him at the wood's edge darkness gathered and pursued him stealthily across the field. At its edge he paused uncertainly, sat for a time on a stone. He did not know for sure where he was going or even why he was going there. He laid the bag between his feet and sat with his hands clasped across his knees, staring back the way he had come. "Hellfire," he said. "It's my house." He thought for a moment he might go back but he did not arise from the stone. A dull weight of anger seemed to hold him where he sat.

Dusk drew on, the dark stain of night seeping across the field. The sky turned a washedout lavender, darkened incrementally, a star came out. Another, pinpricks through the tapestry of night. Against the purple heavens the pinewoods turned oblique and foreign, took on the texture of flocked velvet. A chorus of whippoorwills arose, the steady onenote whirr of dryflies. The world of detail was vanishing, all the world he could see merging color and shape, changing, the horizon of trees dimensionless and dark against paler dark like pinchbeck trees stamped from tin.

He got up. He took up the bag and skirting the field followed an old near-lost wagonpath, came out from under the stoic and eyeless gaze of a scarecrow into a cornfield, passed through the stalks with the blades making dry sibilant whispers against his clothing. Faintly beyond the twisted stalks of corn he could see the blacktop highway like a moving river of ink. His faint shadow appeared like a spectral image. He turned and the moon hung poised over the spiked treeline. It was full and clouds shuttled across its remote face. They shifted constantly in the press of some high wind and against the yellow face they were near translucent so that the moon was an amorphous world in turmoil, seas and continents in perpetual flux, forming and reforming in patterns eternally random. He came through the last of the corn and down an embankment and onto the blacktop. He went on toward town in silence save the hollow slap of his shoes on the pavement.

The wrecked Buick had been there as long as Winer could remember, a casualty of some forgotten accident. It sat below the tieyard slowly vanishing in a riotous sprouting of honeysuckle and kudzu as if the years had altered its chemistry, made it arable so that in summertime fireorange bells of cowitch bloomed from its quarter panels. He opened the front door against the gentle resistance of honeysuckle, threw the sack onto the floorboard. He closed the door soundlessly, peering across the car toward the lights of the shacks bordering the railroad tracks. Temporarylooking, accidental houses hinting some connection with the traintracks, some misbegotten by-products themselves of the trains coming and going. He walked past the dark bulks of stacked tires onto the street and went on toward town. A cur dog on a length of chain suspended from a clothesline followed him to the end of its tether, the chain skirling on its clothesline faintly musical. When the line tautened the dog sat on its haunches and watched him go.

In the Snowwhite Cafe he ate two grilled-cheese sandwiches and drank a large glass of milk. He paid and sat for a time listening to the jukebox and the clanging of the pinball machine, watched past his reflection in the glass the near-dark streets where Friday night's business began to accomplish itself, strolling couples arm in arm, girls bright as justpicked flowers, halfdrunk belligerent men herded homeward by fierce women with bitter, persecuted faces.

"Goddamn if it ain't old Winer," a jovial voice said. Winer turned to see a broad red face grinning down at him, a face he remembered from school. Chessor's name was Wendall but no one remembered it anymore. His father had nicknamed him Buttcut because he was the first son and his father had said he was as tough as the butt cut off a whiteoak log and the name had stuck. Buttcut had conscientiously lived up to his name. He had been a tackle on the football team and though he had been out of school for two years he still wore the black-and-gold school jacket and seemed to be making a career out of being a former athlete.

"Hey, Buttcut. Sit down."

Chessor seated himself in the booth across the red formica table. "Boy, where you been keepin yourself? We figured you was dead or off to the wars one."

"Naw, I'm still around. I've been carpentering down at Mormon Springs. Building Hardin's honkytonk or whatever."

Chessor turned toward the general area of the counter. "Hey, bring us a Co-Cola," he called. He turned back to Winer. "You seen old Shoemaker?" When Winer shook his head Chessor said, "I heard he was lookin for you. Tryin to fix up some way for you to graduate or somethin. He had somethin or another lined up for you and then you didn't come back in the fall. And say you ain't seen him? I heard he went out and talked to your mama."

"I don't know. If he did she never said so."

"Maybe not then. You ought to be there this year though. They're drivin old Toby crazy, the seniors is. Just like we done when I was there. Carryin on the old tradition. Nobody even crackin a book, just fuckin off is all."

A girl in a white lisle uniform set two glasses of Coke and cracked ice on the table. She laid a ticket upside down beside them. "Watch your mouth or you'll be drinkin these on the sidewalks," she said. "It's ladies in here if you didn't but know it."

"If you see one holler at me and I'll tone it down," Chessor told her.

The girl turned and went toward the front of the restaurant, her left leg bent slightly outward at the knee and the tennis shoe she wore on her left foot hissing softly against the slick waxed tile.

"That gimplegged slut," Buttcut said. "I'm goin to have to straighten her ass out." His face cleared, the old jovial look returned. "Old Toby won't never make it till graduation time. That son of a bitch'll be in a asylum long before then. I seen him in the drugstore, you can see it in his eyes. I member when I was in school he had this gray hat he was real proud of. He'd ordered it from somewhere. I got it and cut it up on the bandsaw in woodworkin class. It made the purtiest little gray strips. I took em and hid em in his desk drawer and when he found em he cried like a baby. I swear. I think he's about three-quarters queer anyway."

Buttcut looked all about, leaned farther still toward Winer, and lowered his voice. "This year Ann Barnett, she put a rubber on his desk. Put lotion or somethin in it so it looked like a used one. Old Toby come in and started French class and seen it and turned white as a bedsheet. Set there lookin at it with his nose flared out. You know how scared of germs the son of a bitch is, always scared he's goin to catch somethin. Well. Anyway Ann said everybody was just fallin out of their seats. Toby finally took out his handkerchief and spread it over his hand and picked up his pencil by the point and worried that rubber around till he got that pencil stuck up in it. Then he picked it up and run across the room holdin it way out in front of him and a little off to the side like germs was blowin off of it. He throwed it in the wastebasket and then the pencil and then he throwed in the handkerchief. Never said word one. Went back and set down and went to conjugatin French verbs like nothin ever happened."

Winer sat smiling distractedly and listening, occasionally sipping his Coke. Behind the mask of his eyes he was trying to get a fix on Ann Barnett's face, to single hers from the throng of faces swarming in his mind, but he could not. All he could recall was blond hair and iriscolored eyes. He could see Toby Witherspoon's gentle, beleaguered face but all these things Buttcut was telling him sounded strange and foreign, the obscure rites of some race he'd barely heard of or one he'd forsaken long ago. He felt a cold remove from them, set apart, like a spectator never asked to participate, a face pressed against a window of frozen glass.

Buttcut looked at his watch. "You want to go a dollar partners on the pinball machine? I got a date directly but we still got time."

"I reckon not. All they do is eat my money and leave me broke."

"Hell, son, you got to know how to make em walk and talk. I'll do the playin, all you got to do is set back and watch."

He gave Chessor a dollar and adding one of his own Chessor exchanged them for a roll of nickels. It was an experience to watch Buttcut play pinball. He talked to the machine, cajoled it, swore at it. He caressed it, fondled it, fell upon it with his fists when it did not do his bidding. Leaning across it he coerced the rolling, gleaming balls to the pockets he wanted, his enormous frame thrust across the machine like a lover. Ultimately he beat the machine two hundred forty games and checked them off for twelve dollars. "Walkin and talkin," he said gleefully, counting six ones onto Winer's waiting palm.

"I believe I am part pinball machine," he said. "There's one in the family tree somewhere. I come in and seen one slippin out my mama's back door. Listen, I got to pick Sue up. You want me to drop you somewhere?"

"No. I'm not going anyplace in particular. I just came out here to kill some time."

"Find you a girl. You ought to be able to pick one up after the picture show lets out."

"I may do that."

"I'll see you then."

After Buttcut went out Winer finished his Coke and carried the check to the counter and paid. He went out as well. He stood for a moment uncertainly before the plate glass window of the restaurant and then he went on up the street.

Sam Long was about to close up when Winer got there. The store was bare of customers and even the old men had been rousted from their benches. Winer wondered idly did they have homes, where did they go when the store closed. Long was sweeping about the coalstove with a longhandled broom.

"What can I do you for, Youngblood?"

Winer laid four ten-dollar bills on the counter. "I'll give you the rest of it next week."

Long leaned the broom against the counter and came around behind. He began to fumble through dozens of ticketbooks. "Don't worry about it, boy. I wadnt dunnin you exactly. I just knowed that Huggins feller and I thought it might be somethin you didn't know was goin on." He made the deduction from the books and handed Winer a receipt. "I don't want you feelin hard at me. I always appreciate your business."

"I don't feel hard at you," Winer said. He pocketed the receipt and started toward the door.

"Come back now," Long called.

It grew cloudy and more chill yet and a small cold rain began to fall, wan mist near opaque in the yellow streetlamps. He walked past the darkened storefronts with their CLOSED signs and sat for a time on a bench in the poolroom. He thought he might see someone he knew or wanted to know but he did not. Outside he stood momentarily beneath the dripping awning then went on down the street. Before de Vries's cabstand he stood as if he were waiting for something. The thought of going home depressed him but the thought of not going did not cheer him appreciably. He stared out at the wet street and the ritualistic cruising of the cars. Once he recognized Buttcut Chessor and his girlfriend and he lifted a hand but Buttcut did not see him. After awhile Motormouth's trickedout Chrysler drove by then circled the block and passed again. This time it stopped, the springloaded antenna whiplashing soundlessly in its socket.

"Hey, Winer. Seen any women?"

"Just from a distance."

"What you been doin tonight?"

"Running with the crazy folks," Winer said.

"Hell, let's run with a few more. I've got a sixpack or three in here with me. I'se just fixin to go out and see these women I know. You want to ride out with me?"

Winer considered his options. "Why not," he said. He got into the car. "Drive down by the tieyard. I've got some stuff in that old Buick I need to pick up."

Down fabled roads reverting now to woods Winer felt himself imprisoned by the dark beyond the carlights and by the compulsive timbre of Motormouth's voice, a drone obsessed with spewing out words without regard for truth or even for coherence, as if he must spit out vast quantities of them and rearrange them to his liking, step back, and admire the various patterns he could construct: these old tales of love and betrayal had no truth beyond his retelling of them, for each retelling shaped his past, made him immortal, gave him an infinite number of lives.

They drove through a land in ruin, a sprawling, unkept wood of thousands of acres, land bought by distant companies or folks who'd never seen it. Yet they passed unlit houses and old tilting grocery stories with their rusting gaspumps attendant and it was like driving through a country where civilization had fallen and vanished, where the gods had turned vengeful or perverse so that the denizens had picked up their lives and fled. Old canted oblique shanties built without regard for roads or the uses of them, folks for whom footpaths would serve as well. Dark bulks rising out of the mouths of hollows, trees growing through their outraged roofs. Old stone flues standing blackened and solitary like sentries frozen at their posts waiting for a relief that did not come and did not come. Longdeserted ghostroads, haunts of homeless drunks and haphazard lovers.

"I thought nobody lived here in the Harrikin anymore."

"They don't hardly."

"I can't say I blame them. How far is it to where these women you know live?"

"I don't know. Eight or ten mile. Open us up another one of them beers."

The road worsened until in places Winer only suspected it was a road, faint vestigial imprint of where a road had been, narrowing, choked by the willows lowering upon it and always descending, Hodges riding the brakes and gearing down, until it was a wonder to Winer that folks still survived in so remote an area. They forded nameless shallow streams, wheels spinning on slick limestone, slid lockwheeled on into brackenencroached darkness, darkness multiplied by itself so that you would doubt the ability of light to defray it.

Where the woods fell away the ground leveled out and Winer could see the sky again. The rain had ceased and the clouds had broken up and a weird, otherworldly light from the stars lay on the land. Here buildings clustered together, yet still empty, unlit. They passed great brick furnaces brooding starkly up out of the fields attended by purposeless machinery black and slick with rain, silent. The roads intersected here and the car rattled over a railroad crossing where trains did not cross anymore.

"Right about here," Motormouth was saying to himself. Past a house indistinguishable to Winer from any of the others the car slowed to a crawl, Motormouth peering across Winer toward a lightless building that looked like an old schoolhouse save the yard was cluttered with the deceased bodies of automobiles so dismembered they appeared autopsied. Motormouth blew the horn one short burst but did not stop. They accelerated and drove around the curve past the house.

"We'll go down here to the lake and turn. Time we get back she'll be out by the mailbox and waitin."

"She? I thought there was more than one of them. Women, you said."

"Well, yeah, that's what I meant. Her and her sister."

Winer had long since stopped believing anything Motormouth said but he did not want to get out here. Wherever here was it was miles from anywhere he had ever been and he had not seen a lighted house, a telephone pole. He guessed wherever he was was better than sleeping, these days he had come to feel that life was spinning past him, leaving him helpless. Sleep only accelerated this feeling of impotence. While he slept the world spun on, changed, situations altered and grew more complex, left him more inadequate to deal with them.

Where they stopped by the lake's edge there was a pier extending out into the water. Past it under the still sky the water lay motionless as glass. It was a lake of india ink, the dark water tending away to nothingness where lay no shoreline, no horizon, just the blueblack mist above it where his mind constructed miragelike images that were not there. In the night it seemed to go on forever and this to be the point where everything ceased, land's end, everything beyond this uncharted.

Motormouth lit a cigarette, arced his match into the black expanse of water. "This used to be a good place when I was a kid. Use to be kept up and you could swim in it. Now it's growed up with some kind of damned chokeweed and a man'd have to swim with a stick in one hand to beat the cottonmouths off. You see that bluff down there?" He pointed westward along the waterline to where a shapeless bulk reared against the heavens. Jagged slashes of trees serrated its summit and above them hung a wirethin rind of brass-colored moon. "That's a old quarry, like a big cave. It used to be the whitecaps' headquarters, them nightriders used to meet there fore they'd raid somebody. Now it's a road goes in, and a turnaround. Folks parks in there and screws, or used to, I guess they still do. I used to bring the old lady out here fore we got married. It'd be hot, July or August, we'd swim awhile then go back in there. God, it was dark. Black as the ace of spades." His voice grew rueful, coarsened by the hard edge of the past. "Them was the good old days," he finished. "Whatever luck I ever had just dried up and blowed away."

Winer did not immediately reply. He stood silently staring at the dim outline of the bluff within which the whitecaps had met, in his mind he could hear the horses' hooves click steel on stone, hear the vague, interweaving voices through pillowcase masks. In some curious way he felt pity for Motormouth but at the same time he felt a man was accountable for what he did and he felt a man made his own luck. He thought of Oliver. William Tell Oliver seemed the only person he knew who was at peace with his own past, who was not forever reworking old events, changing them. "You talk like a ninety-year-old man getting ready to die," he told Motormouth. "All you need is some kind of a change."

"Let's change our luck right now," Motormouth said. "Let's ease on back up the road."

He drove a little way past the house and stopped the car. They did not have long to wait. Almost immediately footsteps came up behind the car. Winer turned. In the pale light a heavyset black man was coming alongside the car. He swung a shotgun in his hand as casually as if it were an extension of his arm. "Lord God," Winer said.

"Hey." The black man was at the window. He leaned an arm on the roof, peered in. Motormouth leapt wildly in his seat, then appeared frozen, his right hand on the ignition key, his left on the steering wheel. "Hey there," he said. Winer slid down in his seat and stared down the starlit road, dreaming himself speeding along it, all this forgotten.

"What you whitefolks wantin out here?" Light winked off a gold tooth, the eyes seemed congested with anger. There was no deference in his manner, the hour and the place and sawed-off shotgun seemed to have precluded all need of it.

"We—" Motormouth's mind reeled far ahead, constructing in one quantum leap an entire scenario, characters, dialogue, events. In the instant of its creation it became truth to him, absolved him of all wrongdoing, all evil intentions, and he became confident of his mission.

"We was a bunch of us foxhuntin down here the other night," he said easily. "We was runnin several dogs and one of em ain't come up yet. You ain't seen a strange one around here, have ye?"

"What kind of a dog was it?" The man's face was close to Motormouth's and Winer could smell raw whiskey on his breath. Suddenly the night seemed volatile, unpredictable, events were swirling like liquid, waiting for a pattern to coalesce.

"Big old black-and-tan. Had a tore ear and a collar on it said its name was Ridgerunner."

"I ain't seen no such dog."

"Well. It was right up the road there."

"You sure it wadnt a scrawny old white hound with some yeller up and down its backbone? That's about as strange a one as I've seen tonight."

Motormouth swallowed visibly. "No. It was a black-and-tan." He cranked the car and the black man stepped back. "You ain't seen it I best be gettin on. I'd appreciate it if ye'd keep ye eyes open for it."

"You lookin for a fuckin dogcatcher you in the wrong neighborhood," the black man said.

"Well. We'll see ye."

Winer looked back and the man was standing in the middle of the road watching them go, the gun still slung at his side.

"That uppity black son of a bitch," Motormouth said. "A little more and I'd've had to get out and whup his ass."

"How much more could there be?" Winer wondered aloud.

He spent the next three days and nights at Motormouth's house. Monday morning Hodges drove him to Hardin's and picked him up that afternoon after work. Monday evening they arose from the supper table to see a police cruiser halt in the yard. A deputy got out with a folded white paper in his hand.

"More Goddamned papers," Motormouth said. "Goddamned divorce papers and peace warrants and now here comes some more. I reckon they must've moved her in a desk and chair in that judge's office so she'd be handy when the notion struck her to swear out somethin. She ever gets caught up I reckon that whole courthouse bunch can just lock up and go to the house."

They stood in the cool dusk while Garrison read Motormouth this news. It was that he had been evicted. His wife owned this house and she wanted him out of it. She wanted him out yesterday but perhaps today would serve. "Well, Goddamn," Motormouth kept saying in a put-upon tone. The deputy read on. When he had finished he had Motormouth sign the paper and he handed him a copy and got back in the squad car. "I'll be back in the mornin to make sure you're gone," he warned.

"I never doubted it for a Goddamn minute," Motormouth told him.

The car drove away. Motormouth sat on the edge of the porch in a deep study of his options. They seemed to grow more limited day by day. "I know where there's a good place down by the river," he finally said.

With full dark they went with all they could stuff into or lash onto the Chrysler. Mattresses clotheslined athwart the trunk. A dining table tied atop with legs stiffly extending upward like some arcane beast rigid in death. Trophy of some surrealistic hunt. Refugees. A family of Okies displaced in time as well as location. Like a rolling trashdump they went bumping down a logroad alongside the river to where the spring floodwaters had deposited an almost intact cabin in a grove of trees. The log cabin sat canted against a giant hackberry, its floors perpetually tilted. Damp odors of other times, other folks, who knew who? Doris loves Bobby, the wallpaper said. They set up housekeeping in this crooked house. Luxuries abounded, here were bricks to bring the cots to a semblance of level. That night they could watch the stars through the roof where the shakes were missing. Music from the car radio, old songs of empty beds and thwarted dreams. When the radio was turned off there was just the placating voice of the river.

They were still there Thursday when Bellwether found them. Bellwether came down through the damp beggarlice and blackberry briars with an aggrieved look about him. He stopped by the fire where coffee boiled in a pot and began to pick Spanish nettles from his clothes. His khakis were wet almost to the waist. He hadn't known about the road, he had come up the bank of the river and he was not happy. It was Winer himself he sought.

"You a hard feller to find."

"I didn't know I was lost."

Winer was alone. Fearing more papers or something that required his presence before an oaken bench Motormouth had faded back into the brush. But Bellwether had not even inquired after him.

"Well, you may not be but your mama thinks you are. She asked me to try and find out where you was."

"I haven't broken any laws I know about. And if she wanted to see me I was working right up the road at Hardin's."

"There's nobody accused you of breaking any laws. I told you I was just doin a favor for your mama. She said tell you to come home. She wants to see you about somethin."

"What?"

"Best I can gather her and Leo Huggins is gettin married. He's got promises of a job over in Arkansas and you and your mama's supposed to go with him."

"Who said so?"

"I just said I'd try and get word to you. What you do is your business."

"Well. Thanks for telling me anyway."

"You goin down there I'll run you by. I told her I'd let her know if I saw you."

"I'll just have Motormouth run me down there after awhile."

But he didn't. It was the weekend before he went and that was a day too late. There wasn't anyone there at all.

Winer and the girl were standing in a corner, hidden from the house by the weatherboarded walls.

"Why would I want to do a thing like that?" she asked him. "I'd be liable to get caught." She seemed to be teasing him, everything she said had an ironic quality as if she were reserving the right to take back anything she said.

"So what if you did? What is he to you? It looks to me like anybody could slip out of a honkytonk for a few minutes."

"I can't."

"Can't or won't?"

"Anyway, why should I have to slip out and meet you in the woods? Why can't you get a car like anybody else?"

"Well. I got my eye on one. I just wanted to see you."

"Then I guess that's your reason." She smiled. "Have you got one for me?"

He leaned and twisted her face up to him. She didn't resist. He could feel her hair around his fingers, the delicate bones beneath her ear. She opened her mouth beneath his. Her breath was clean and sweet. She leaned against him. "You know I want to."

"I'll know you want to when I see you coming," he said. His throat and chest felt tight and constricted. He felt as if he were drowning.

"I'll try," she said.

He lay on a tabled shelf of limestone and watched the slow, majestic roll of the fall constellations. He realized with something akin to regret that he had no names to affix to them though he'd known them all his life. The stars looked bright and close and earlier an orange harvest moon had cradled up out of the pines so huge he felt he could reach up and touch it. By its light the Mormon Springs branch was frozen motionless and it gleamed like silver, the woods deep and still. It seemed strange to lie here and listen to the sounds of the jukebox filtered up out of the darkness, windbrought and maudlin plaints, but no less real for being maudlin. Once or twice cries of anger or exultation arose and he thought he might go see what prompted them but he did not. He just lay with his coat rolled beneath his head for a pillow and listened to all the sounds of the night, ears attuned for her footfalls.

He wondered what time it was, felt it must be past midnight. The night wore on and he did not hear the jukebox for long periods of time, nor the cries of drunks, and the occasional car he heard seemed to be leaving rather than arriving. A while longer, he thought. He was keyed up and tense as if expecting something to happen in the next few minutes that would alter his life forever.

An owl on the wing shuttled across the moon and after awhile he heard it or its brother calling from out of the fabled dark of Mormon Springs. Where dwelt the ghosts of murdered Mormons and their convert wives and some of the men who had come down this hillside so long ago, the slayers slain. He wondered had the face of the country changed, perhaps they passed this upheaval of the earth. Had folks learned from history, from the shifting of the seasons?

She is not coming, he was thinking. At length he rose. It had turned colder and time seemed to be slowing, to be gearing down for the long haul to dawn. He put the jacket on and buttoned it and picked his way through the stark and silver woods. He crossed the stream at its narrowest point and ascended through ironwood and willow until he came out in the field. In the fierce moonlight the field was profoundly still and his squat shadow the only thing in motion, a stygian and perverse version of himself that ran ahead distorting and miming his movements.

He angled around the hill until he could see the house. He sat on a stone hugging himself against the chill and watched like a thief awaiting an opportunity to steal. After an hour or so a bitter core of anger rose in him and he got up to go but then a figure came out of the house and moved almost instantly into the shadows the woods threw and he could barely watch its progress toward the spring.

Winer changed course and moved as silently as he could into the thickening brush. Anticipation intense as prayer seized him. Tree to tree stealthily to the edge of the embankment and after a moment he heard a voice that appeared to be in conversation with itself. A stone rolled beneath his feet and splashed into the water and he was looking down at a soldier urinating into the stream. The soldier looked up blearyeyed toward the source of this disturbance and leapt backward fumbling with his clothing. Moonlight winked off his upturned glasses and he looked pale and frightened as if some younger variation of the grim reaper had been visited upon him or a revenant from some old violence played here long ago.

When Winer did not vanish or leap upon him the soldier steadied himself and staggered back down to the stream. He adjusted his campaign cap. "What outfit you from?" he called to Winer. Winer spat into the listing stream and made no reply save departure.

She came once at midmorning and spoke to him but he was cool and distant and disinclined to conversation. "Be mad then," she told him. She left but he hardly missed her. Winer's head hurt from lack of sleep and his arms and legs felt heavy and sluggish and were loath to do his bidding.

He made it through the long morning and when he broke for lunch she came back. He hadn't brought any lunch but he had a jar of coffee and he was drinking that when she stepped up onto the subflooring.

"I can't stay but a minute and if you're goin to fight I'll just go back in."

"I never sent for you."

"You sent for me last night, whether you know it or not."

"Yeah. For what good it did."

"I wasn't goin to tell you this but the reason I couldn't come was he made me set with a man."

"Who did?"

"Hardin. Dallas."

"He made you, did he. He hold a gun on you?"

"No."

"I don't guess he had to."

"Just shut up. You don't know anything about anything."

"I know I sat up all night in the mouth of that holler like a fool holding the sack on a snipehunt. That's all I know."

"Well. I couldn't help it."

"Sure, you couldn't. I bet you couldn't help telling every soldier in there about it too. Well, you better enjoy it because it's the last laugh you'll get on me."

"Nathan, I really wanted to. I swear to God I did. His eyes were on me every minute."

"How come he made you sit with a man? Who was it anyway?"

"I don't know who he was. Some fat farmer. He'd just come back from sellin his cows or somethin. He was wavin his money around and Dallas made me set with him till his money was all gone. I thought he never was goin to pass out."

"How'd he make you?"

"I don't know. He just told me I had to."

"What would he do if you didn't?"

"I don't know." She fell silent.

When she had been a little girl she had tried to think of Hardin as her father. A father was strong and Hardin looked as remorseless and implacable as an Old Testament God, there was no give to him. The man whose blood she'd sprung from was flimsy as a paperdoll father you'd cut from a catalog, a father who when the light was behind him looked curiously transparent. No light shone through Hardin and in a moment of insight she thought she had seen a similar core of stubbornness in Winer. Somehow you knew without shoving him that there was no give to him either.

"You don't know. How could you not know?"

She was quiet for a time. She remembered the way Hardin had been looking at her for the last year or so, as though he were deciding what to do with her.

"Do you always do what people order you to? What if I'd ordered you to meet me? What would you have done then?"

"Don't go so fast," she said. She gave him just a trace of a smile and shrugged. "You're not quite Dallas Hardin," she said.

"Have you ever wondered what he'd do?"

Whatever it took, she thought, thinking of Hardin as bottomless.

"All this is easy for you to say," she told him. "You put up your tools every night and go home. I'm already at home. There's nowhere else for me to go. You don't know him."

"I believe I know him about as well as I need to."

He'd been looking into her eyes and for just an instant something flickered there that was older than he, older than anybody, some knowledge that couldn't be measured in years.

"You know him better," she said.

"I know him well enough to know he's not paying me to shoot the breeze with you. I've got to get to work. This has been a long day anyhow."

"I might could get out on a Sunday. There's nobody much around here then and Dallas don't pay me much mind."

"I'm once a fool," Winer said. "Twice don't interest me."

"I'll meet you anywhere you say."

She was studying him and something in her face seemed to alter slightly even as she watched him, somehow giving him the feeling that she had divined some quality in him that he wasn't even aware of.

He tried to think. His mind was murky and slow, it seemed to be grinding toward an ultimate halt. "All right," he finally said. "The only place I can think of where nobody can see us is where Weiss used to live. Meet me there Sunday evening."

Paying his debt to Motormouth, Winer had invited him to stay until he found a permanent residence but Motormouth seemed to have passed beyond the need for shelter and he stayed only three days. He found the walls too confining, the house too stationary to suit him. He was too well acclimated to the motion of wheels, the random and accessible distances of the riverbank, the precarious existence that shuttled him from Hardin's to the river, from de Vries's cabstand to the highway. Some creature of the night half-domesticated reverting back to wildness, staying out for longer and longer periods then just not coming back at all.

Then Winer was alone. He put up the winter's wood and stacked the porch with it. On these first cool evenings he'd build himself a fire and sit before it. He quit worrying and wondering about the future and decided to just let it roll. By lamplight he'd read before the flickering fire and he found the silence not hard to take. He was working hard now trying to beat winter. In bed he would sometimes lie in a halfstupor of weariness before sleep came but he felt that somehow a fair exchange had been made, someone paid him money to endure this exhaustion. I am a carpenter, he thought. He was something, somebody, there was a name he could affix to himself. And there was a routine and an order to these days that endeared them to him, they were long, slow days he would remember in times to come when order and symmetry were things more dreamt than experienced. I am paying my way, he thought, carrying my own weight, and on these last late fall days he found something that had always eluded him, a cold and solitary peace.

Having finally gotten her alone, Winer was at some loss as to how to proceed. All the clever conversation he had thought of fled, and such shards as he remembered no longer seemed applicable. Her clean profile roiled his mind and he felt opportunity sliding away while he sat with dry mouth and sweaty palms. "How come you quit school?" he finally fell back on asking.

"I just got tired of it. Why did you?"

"I didn't. I'm goin back next year."

"I'm not. I wouldn't set foot inside that schoolhouse for a thousand-dollar bill."

Below them a car appeared on the winding roadway. She fell silent and watched its passage, studied it until it was lost from sight near Oliver's house. She turned to Winer. "Did you know that car?"

"Not to speak to," Winer said

She arose, smoothed her skirt. "We're goin to have to go in the house. If anybody sees me up here they'll tell Dallas."

"For somebody who can hustle a drunk out of his cattle money and never bat an eye you're awfully concerned with appearances," Winer said. But he instantly regretted saying it and arose and held the storm door for her and they passed into the semigloom of the living room. They stood uncertainly looking about then Winer suddenly felt uncomfortable in the abandoned house and he caught her arm and led her through a sliding glass door onto a concrete patio.

"There's nothin to sit on here," she complained.

"We can get a blanket or something out of the house if you want to."

"Why don't we just stay in there?"

"I just don't feel right. It's still Weiss's house, even if it is up for sale. Besides, it seems like I can hear that old woman breathin in there."

"That's silly."

"I guess so."

They sat side by side on the edge of the concrete porch with their feet in the uncut grass. Below the long, dark line of the chickenhouses the afternoon sun hung in a sky devoid of clouds.

"This is a real nice place. I guess Mr. Weiss must've been rich."

"I doubt if he was rich. I suppose they lived all right though."

"It's the nicest house I was ever in."

"I got a cousin lives in Ackerman's Field," Winer said. "Lives in a house you wouldn't believe. There's velvet wallpaper on the walls and all these fancy chandeliers hanging everywhere. And both of them crazy as bessie bugs."

She sat leaning forward with her arms crossed atop her round knees and imbued with the composed air he had become accustomed to. Studying the pristine lines of her profile he was suddenly struck with a sense of inadequacy, he could not imagine what had brought her here to meet him. She could have had her pick of all of them. Yet there was something of inevitability about it, as if it all had been ordained long ago, when he was a child, when she was a child. There seemed to be nothing to say, nor any need for it. She felt it too, for when he touched her she turned toward him as if the touch were something she had been waiting for.

He drew her to him with a kind of constrained urgency until her cheek rested against his shoulder. She remained so for a moment then turned her face up toward him. Her teeth were white against her tanned face. Her eyes looked violet. She closed them when he kissed her, her left hand was a cool and scarcely perceptible weight on the base of his neck, her right hand lay against his stomach.

When he went for the blanket he got a bottle of Weiss's homemade strawberry wine from beneath the counter and two glasses and before he remembered the power was off turned on the faucet to rinse them. He settled for wiping the dust off with a towel and canting them against the sun through the window. They looked clean. He found blankets stacked in a bedroom closet. Passing a mirror he fetched up startled for a moment by his reflection, he and his mirror image were face to face conspiratorially like cothiefs ransacking a house, their arms caught up with plunder. Both their thin faces looked feral and furtive, harried.

Amber Rose lay on his left arm, her dress girdled about her waist. Their eyes were closed and he could feel the red weight of the sun through his eyelids. His right hand lay on her abdomen. The flesh of her stomach was cool and soft. He slid his fingers under the elastic of her panties and downward and when she made no objection downward further until he cupped the mound between her legs, the hair there crisp and curled, laid the weight of a finger where her flesh was cleft when she opened her legs. When he kissed her her mouth tasted like the wine and when he opened his eyes she was watching him. She seemed drained of volition, her face looked vacuous and stricken in the sun. Her dress was unbuttoned to the waist and her brassiere unhooked and against the brown skin of her belly her breasts looked white and fragile, flowers unused to the sun. She reached a hand down and placed it over his own, guiding him, her hips a gently increasing pressure against the heel of his hand. Then she moved the hand away and he felt it at his zipper. She took his erect penis in her hand and began to masturbate him gently. Even as she did so a part of him that stood observing all this wondered at her dexterity but did not dwell on it at any length. She slid her other hand down and clasped him with both hands. Then without saying anything she released him and hooked her thumbs in the waistband of her underwear and slid it down over her hips. He watched as she raised her hips from the blanket and slid the panties off one leg, then the other. She unbuttoned his pants and pulled them down until he arose and shucked out of them, feeling clumsy and absurd standing here in the heat of the day in his shirttail with her watching and he felt that the woods were full of folks crouched laughing behind bushes but he couldn't have stopped if they had been. If Hardin had leapt upon him with a hawkbill knife. He pulled the T-shirt off and when he laid it aside she was reaching up toward him.

"Pull off your dress."

"Do it for me if you want to."

She raised her arms and he pulled the dress awkwardly over her head and started to fold it but she said, "No, let it go, it don't matter." He lay on her balancing his weight on his elbows. "You won't break me," she said. "I'm not made of glass." He could feel her breasts pooled against his chest, the hot length of his sex where their flesh lay as if fused.

It seemed to him there ought to be something to say but if there was he didn't know what. For a crazy moment it occurred to him to ask her if she'd rather wait until they were married for in the last quarter hour or so he'd commenced thinking in just such a fashion. But her breath on his throat forestalled him. "Go on," she said. "I want you to." He reached down fumbling between them but after a moment she said, "Here. Let me." He raised enough to permit her hand and she guided him into her.

She was hot and wet and tight and entry was harder than he'd expected and he hesitated, unmoving, glancing down to see if he was hurting her, but her eyes were clenched tightly closed and her hands were tightening on his arms.

"I don't want to hurt you."

"It's all right," she said. "Go on, I want you to."

In the slow, breathless moment of penetration he felt that he had wounded her beyond any restitution he had the power to make and he felt that he had thrown his lot with her forevermore, had in some manner inextricably tied their fates. Whether she wanted it so or not.

She made ready to go. They had stayed longer than she meant to and the sun was already burning away the timbered horizon in the west and the first bullbats were dropping plumb and sheer as if they moved in fixed isobars or were in some manner gyroscoped.

"You thought I was a whore, didn't you?" Her voice through the fabric of her dress was muffled. She pulled the dress down and was arranging her hair, smoothing it backward with both hands.

"No. I never thought that."

"But you thought I'd done it before."

"I figured you had."

"I guess I've heard them talk about everything two people can do to each other but I never did any of it. Mama always watched me like a hawk and Dallas, he's even worse." She pulled her panties on, her skirt caught up in them and she freed it. He was staring bemusedly at the hair crinkled against the cloth. "Quit lookin like that," she said. "You know I've got to go." She arose. "I always used to have the idea that Dallas was goin to sell me off, you know, like to the highest bidder. A auction. Sacrificin a virgin." She smiled ruefully. "I guess this is the one time he got beat."

After she had gone he dressed and sat on the edge of the porch with the blanket across his shoulders, for the day had grown chill. Blue dusk lay pooled about the fields. He thought to finish the wine but it had gone flat and treacly. He corked it and set it aside wondering how he had ever tasted summer in it. Without her the world seemed bland and empty. In the silence he imagined he could still hear her voice, some obsession with detail caused him to seek meanings where there were only words. He felt curiously alive, everything before this seemed gray and ambiguous, everything he'd heard garbled and indistinct.

He knew he should be going but here it still seemed to be happening, it was all around him, and some instinct of apprehension told him it might never happen again. It couldn't be wasted. Every nuance, sensation, had to be absorbed. Dusk drew on and the horizon blurred with the failed sun and at last he arose to go, loath still to leave here for the dark house with its ringing emptiness and the gabled attic with its stacked books wherein he'd mistakenly believed all of life was told. He went down the highway past the FOR SALE sign and climbed the locked gate and so into the road. He went on listening to the sounds of night as if he had never heard them before. He passed Oliver's unlit house but the old man was not about and all he heard of life was the goats' bells tinkling off in the restive dark.

In the last days of Indian summer the light had a hazy look of blue distances to it like a world peered at through smoked glass. It was windy that fall and the air was full of leaves. The wind blew out of the west and they used to take blankets below the chickenhouses where there was a line of cedars for a windbreak and lie beneath a yellow poplar there in the sun. Yellow leaves drifted, clashed gently in a muted world. Sad time of dying, change in the air, who knew what kind. There seemed little permanence to this world, what he saw of it came drifting down through baring limbs and the branches left limned against the blue void looked skeletal and brittle as bone.

Amber Rose would lie drowsing in the sun, an arm thrown across her face. He studied her body almost covertly, the symmetry of her nipples, the dark, enigmatic juncture of her thighs. Parting the kinked black hair with his fingers he leaned and kissed her there, she stirred drowsily against his face. Faint taste of salt, of distant seas. Some other taste, something elemental, primal, shorn of custom. His tongue delineated the complexities of her sex, he raised his face to study the enigma he found there. She seemed fragile and vulnerable, wounded by life at the moment of conception with the ultimate weapon, the means to be wounded again and again, cleft there with the force of a blow.

When she could she would meet him at night. He cached blankets in the hollow at Mormon Springs and wrapped in them he would lie in the lee of the limestone rocks and await her. Dry leaves shoaled in the hollow and he could hear a long way off. It would be warm in the blankets and the night imbued Winer and the girl with a desperate sense of immediacy, of urgency, they lay tired but not sated for they were learning that there were hungers that did not abate.

Laughing, she slid down the length of his body and took him into her mouth. The blanket slid away and he could see her dark head at the Y of his body like some spectral succubus feasting while beyond them the trees reared and tossed in the wind and the throb of the jukebox and the cries of the stricken and the drunk came faint and dreamlike like cries from a madhouse in a haunted wood. His hands knotted in her hair and pulling her atop him he could feel her heart hammering against him through her naked breast.

"You used to drive Lipscomb crazy," he told her once. "He used to find excuses to see up your dress."

"I know it. I wanted you to look though."

"Why?"

"I don't know. I just wanted to make you hard, all right?"

"It's all right with me," he said.

Her face was pale and composed in the moonlight. Black curls tousled as if she slept in perpetual storm. His finger traced the delicate line of her jaw.

"Briar Rose," he said.

"What?"

"I think I'll call you Briar Rose. I like it better than Amber Rose and besides I like briar roses. They're sweet and I like the way they smell. And you do look like somebody out of a fairy tale."

"Like somebody's wicked stepsister or something?"

"You can be the princess in mine."

A new, soft world of the senses here she ushered him into. A world of infinite variety he had but heard rumored. On these sweet urgent nights he came to feel he was indeed living out an erotic fairytale, the dark prince who'd stolen the princess from the evil king. And like the protagonists of a fairytale they played out their games in a country of intrigues and secret corners and fierce inclement weather where nothing was what it seemed.

"You look like a man pickin cotton," Motormouth told him. "Cept you grabbin trouble with both hands and stuffin it in a sack and never once lookin over your shoulder."

"What are you talking about, Motormouth?"

"Listen at ye. You may not be as slick hardly as you think you are."

Motormouth sat in Winer's living room. He crouched on the edge of the sofa with a glass of 7 Up and bootleg whiskey in his hand. The drink had the smoky, oily quality of nitroglycerin and he held it carefully as if dropping it might annihilate them both.

"I never was one for parables and hard sayings," Winer told him. "You got anything I need to hear just say so straight out."

"You think you're in tight with him. But when he finds out, and he damn sure will, he will kill your ass and hide you or rig it up so it looks like he killed you in self-defense."

"I'm still kindly left in the dark."

"A little bird flew down and lit on my shoulder and whispered in my ear. It said, 'You better warn little Nathan. He's buyin trouble by the pound and he's got about all he can go with.'"

"That little bird, did it have a name?"

"You seen one of these lit old birds you seen em all."

Winer didn't say anything.

"Hardin wanted her hisself," Motormouth said.

"You did too," Winer said. "But you never got her."

Motormouth arose and stretched. He looked about the room. There was an air of time about it, as if folks had grown old and died here. I BELIEVE IN THE POWER OF THE LIVING GOD, a glittercard above the fireplace said. "I got to get on," Motormouth said. "Hell. I'm goin to Chicago or Detroit or somewhere. Some place got some size about it. I'm about burnt out on this damn place anyway."

That was what he said but the only place he quit this night was Winer's front room.

"This is nothing but trouble," Winer told her. She lay against him beneath the blanket. "I've got to get a car somehow. A way of getting around so we can get away from him."

Her hair was a soft black cloud against his cheek. She was warm in his arms, he could feel the delicate bones beneath her flesh. She was like some small beast he'd caught in the woods, held too roughly, felt jerking with hammering rabbit's heart in his hands. He was afraid if he held on to her he'd hurt her but there was no way now he could let her go.

"This is all right," she said against his throat. "You take everything too serious."

"It's better than all right but we've still got to get a car. If we had one we could drive into town anytime we wanted."

She seemed to be thinking over the idea of a car. Then she said, "Or anyplace else we wanted to go."

"It seems like I have to be with you all the time. When I'm not it's like I'm drunk or on dope or somethin. I just drag through the day waitin for night to come. Everything else just seems dead."

She didn't reply. Everything seemed to be moving her closer to the line she didn't want to get to. She guessed sooner or later everyone was going to have to know but she'd just as soon it was later. Slipping out would be easier than openly defying Dallas Hardin. Experience had taught her that. Defying Dallas Hardin was something best done from as great a distance as possible.

Then he went one night and the blankets were gone from the stumphole, the leaves kicked aside. He sat on the stone anyway waiting and the night crept by like something crippled almost past motion until the rind of moon set behind the blurred trees. The jukebox played on and approaching cautiously he could see the oblique yellow light falling through the trees and hear the sounds of merriment but she never came. He sat crouched in the darkness until his mind began to play tricks on him. He could hear her feet kicking through the dry leaves, her soft laugh, see her face, conspirator's finger to her lips. He grew apprehensive and felt something was watching him out of the dark with yellow goat's eyes but if it was it never said so.

That was on a Sunday night and all the next week he wondered at her composure, at the duplicity flesh seemed capable of. Watching her move serenely across the yard he hardly knew her as the girl who lay against him in the dark, who cried out his name and clung to him as if she were drowning, being sucked downward into a maelstrom of turbulent water. Who whispered nighttime endearments the daylight always stole away from him.

When Hardin paid him off on Friday he said, "Winer, me and you got a pretty good business arrangement goin. You work to suit me and I pay to suit you. And I got other plans for us too, plans got some real money tied up in em."

Winer didn't ask what plans or in fact say anything. He had been waiting all week for this and he recognized Hardin's speech as mere preamble.

"I don't want to make you mad. But you kindly steppin on my toes here slippin around with that girl and I'm goin to have to put a stop to it. I thought you'd do me straighter than that."

Winer folded the money and slid it into the pocket of his jeans. "You? I don't see that it's got anything to do with you."

"Say you don't? I told you I had plans. Son, I got plans workin in my head ever minute and they don't all concern you. I got plans for her too."

"What kind of plans?"

"What they are ain't nothin to you. I'm just tellin you we got to keep things on a business footin here and leave all this personal shit out of it."

"What kind of plans?"

"Well, I told you it ain't none of your business. But have you ever really looked at her? I been around a long time and I ain't seen many that looks like that. And let me tell you, I been around long enough to know they don't look like that long. Like a peach hangin there on a tree. It's July and it's hot and you're standin there tryin to decide whether to pick it or not. One day it ain't hardly right and then there's a minute when it is and then it's rotten and the yeller-jackets is eatin it. You see? I been waitin for this minute and the time's right now. There's a world of money to be made and I can't have anybody muddyin the water. Even you."

He paused, offering Winer an opportunity to reply. When he did not Hardin said, "Let's just leave it at that. Let's just say I'm concerned about her welfare. Hell, I raised her. I knowed her when she was a kid runnin around the yard naked. She's like a daughter to me. All I'm askin you to do is give me your word you'll leave her alone. Hell, she ain't nothin but a kid. You sweettalk her and turn her head and no tellin what's liable to happen."

In that moment Winer realized it was impossible to promise anything. Each succeeding moment seemed shaped by the one preceding it. Everything was volatile, in flux, and there was nothing anywhere he could count on. "Don't hand me that shit," he said. "You don't seem to be considering what she thinks. Are you?"

"Do what?"

"You heard me. Don't hand me that daughter shit, save it for somebody that believes it."

"Nobody talks to me that way anymore, Winer. I done growed out of puttin up with it. Now me and you . . . here, you wait a minute."

Winer was gone. He'd only turned and walked a step or two but he was gone just the same.

There was a chill to the weather that night and after early dark fell Winer laid cedar kindling and built a fire. He made himself a pot of coffee and sat before the fire drinking it and soaking up the heat. He'd put the last of the roofing on that day and his shoulders ached from hauling the rolls of roofing up with a rope. He was half-asleep when Hardin came.

Hardin had been drinking. He was not drunk but Winer could smell whiskey on his breath and his face had a flushed and reckless look.

"Get in here where it's warm a minute. I need to talk to you."

Winer got in on the passenger side and closed the door with its expensive muted click and leaned his head on the rich upholstery. There was a warm, leathery smell of money about the car.

"Winer, I don't want me and you to have a fallin out. I think maybe we got off on the wrong foot back there and I think we ort to work it out."

"I don't guess there's anything left to work out. You want me to do something I can't do and I guess that's all there is to it."

"Well, you kind of got me backed into a corner on this thing and you ortnt fuck with a man backed in a corner."

"If you're in a corner then it's a corner you picked yourself. You act like I'm going to mistreat her. I wouldn't hurt her for the world."

"Goddamn it, Winer." By the yellow domelight Hardin's face looked almost pained. "You're goin to have to make up your mind. Just what is it you want? Pussy? Winder curtains? A little white house somers with roses climbin on it? I know what you're thinkin, boy, but believe me, it ain't like that. And never was. All in God's world it is is a split. All it is is a hole and over half the people in the world's got em. And nary a one of em worth dyin over. You shut your eyes or put a sack over their face and you can't tell one from the other. You believe that?"

"No," Winer said.

"And on top of that you don't even know her. I do. I've knowed her from the time she was five year old and you wouldn't know her if you slept with her the rest of your life. You see her but you don't know her."

"I know her well enough. You paid me off tonight and we're even now. Let's stay that way. You find somebody else to finish your building and I'll find another place to work."

"You dipshit fool. You think I couldn't have found a dozen carpenters better than you? You think for what I been payin you I couldn't find somebody to build a fuckin honkytonk? Wake up, Winer, you been livin in a dream world."

Winer turned to study Hardin's asymmetrical face. "Then why did you hire me?"

For a millisecond the eyes were perplexed. "Damned if I know. I reckon deep down I was just fuckin with you."

"What do you mean?"

"Just let it be. It ain't got nothin to do with this."

Winer got out. Before he closed the car door he said, "I aim to see her. There's nothing you can do to stop me."

"Hell, you done been stopped. You was stopped the minute I kicked them comestained blankets out of the stumphole. You was stopped and never even knowed it."

Deputy Cooper stood at the edge of the porch waiting while Hardin read the paper. Amber Rose was sitting against a porch stanchion with her dress high on her brown thighs. Cooper kept trying not to look. "Pull your dress down," Hardin said without looking up from the paper. When he had finished it he handed it back to Cooper. "All right. I see what it says. All this whereas and wherefore bullshit. Now, what does it mean?"

"Well. All it is is a summons. It means you got to go to court. There's goin to be a hearin. He got it up at Franklin. Blalock did. He tried to get Judge Humphries to issue one and course he wouldn't, he told Blalock he'd just have to work this deal about the horses out with you. Blalock he throwed a regular fit they said nearly foamin at the mouth and went to Franklin and seen a circuit judge up there and he wrote one up. It come down this mornin and I brought it on out."

"I reckon you didn't have no selection. You doin all right, Cooper, and Bellwether ain't goin to be sheriff always. We might fool around and run you next election they hold."

"You know I always tried to work with you, Mr. Hardin."

"Shore you did. But that Bellwether, now . . . he's aimin to wake up one of these times out of a job. Or just not wake up at all."

Hardin sat down in a canebottom rocker, leaned back, closed his eyes. "What'd happen if I just don't show up at this hearin or whatever?"

"If one of you don't go then the othern gets a judgment agin him. Like if you don't show, the judge'll automatically find for Blalock. He gets them horses back and you don't get nothin."

"Goddamn him."

"I can't help it. That's just the way it works."

"I know you can't. But he ain't gettin them fuckin horses. If he does it'll be when I'm dead and gone. All these sons of bitches startin to shove me around, Cooper, and I don't aim to have it."

"I don't blame you about that, Mr. Hardin." Cooper was turning his cap over and over in his hands, eyeing the door. The girl hadn't pulled her dress down but Cooper was looking everywhere but at her.

On a cold, bright day in late November Winer and Motormouth set out toward Clifton seeking gainful employment. The prospect of working regularly again and the idea of starting a day with a clear purpose and working toward it cheered Winer and he rode along listening bemusedly to the fantasies Motormouth spun for him.

"We'll get us a little place down here when we get to makin good," he said. "Buy us some slick clothes. Boy, they got some honkytonks down here so rough you kindly peep in first then sidle through the door real quick. And women? I'se in one down here one time and this old gal, just as I come in the door she come up and grabbed me by the pecker and just led me off."

Winer said something noncommittal and stared off across the river. The highway was running parallel with the water now and beyond the border of cypress and willow the water was cold and metalliclooking, choppy in the windy sun. Far and away to his right what looked like an island and rising from it some enormous circular structure of gray stone like a silo or lighthouse and past this farther still three great pillars brooding in the mist like pylons for a bridge no longer there. He did not inquire the purpose of any of this lest Motormouth be inspired toward further fabrication, for no one had ever heard Motormouth admit the existence of anything he did not know and he always had an answer for everything even if he had to make it up. Winer watched them vanish like something unknown on a foreign coast and they drove on past used-car lots with their sad pennants fluttering on guywires and past old tilting groceries and barns with their tin roofs advertising Bruton Snuff and Popcola and Groves' Chill Tonic like fading hieroglyphs scribed by some prior race.

"Some of these old riverrats," Motormouth mused. "These old boys work the barges and stay out a week or two at a time. You think they ain't ready when they hit port? They'd as soon cut ye throat with a rusty pocketknife as look at ye. They make Hardin look like a home-ec teacher. You have to be careful you walk soft," he cautioned Winer. "A boy like you ain't never been out of the county could get in a lot of trouble around here."

Coming into Clifton they stopped for breakfast and directions at a place called Mother Leona's. Winer judged himself safe in any place named Mother Leona's but he didn't see her about after all and his eggs and homefries were dished up by a surlylooking man in dirty whites and a chef's hat cocked on the back of his head.

"We down here lookin for work," Motormouth volunteered.

"I ain't hirin today," the man said.

"No, we lookin for where they load the ties. We heard they was hirin."

"That'd be down by the docks."

"I guess so. We ain't never done it but we'll shore give her a whirl. We hard workers."

"You don't have to sell me," the man said, lowering a basket of sliced potatoes into popping grease. "I don't do the hirin for that neither."

Winer broke a biscuit open and paused suddenly with his butterladen knife. A perfectly intact candlefly, wings spread for flight, was seized in the snowy dough like an artifact from broken stone. He sat for a time studying it like an archaeologist pondering its significance or how it came to be there so halt in flight and at length he laid bread and knife aside.

Motormouth pushed his empty plate back, chewed, and swallowed. He drank coffee. "Where's these here docks at?" he asked.

The counterman turned from the spitting grill as if he might inspect these outlanders more closely. "They generally always down by the river," he said at length.

A mountain of crossties guided them to where the work progressed. Men were unjamming the ties with tiepicks and dragging them to where other workers loaded them onto a system of chutes that slid them to yet another crew in the hull of a barge. They stood for a time watching the men work, admiring the smooth efficiency with which the workers hefted the ties from the dock, the riverward giving his end of the tie a small, neat spin just so onto the chute and the near one pushing with the same force each time and the tie gliding smoothly down the oiled chute to slam against the bulkhead of the barge. "Hell, they ain't nothin to it," Motormouth said. "Look at the way them fellers goes about it. Reckon who you ask?"

Winer didn't reply. He was studying the ties. They were nine-by-twelve green oak he judged to be ten or twelve feet long and they had a distinctly heavy look about them despite the deceptive ease with which they were slung onto the chutes.

They approached the river. The barge rocked in the cold gray water, a wind out of the north behind them blew scraps of paper past them and aloft over the river like dirty stringless kites. Nameless birds foraged the choppy waters and beyond them the river's farther shore looked blurred and unreal and no less bleak and drear than this one.

The barge was secured by hawsers tied to bits on the dock and it rocked against its cushion of old cartires strung together. Two men in the aft of the boat took the ties as they came off the chute and aligned them in stacks. The chutes seemed always to have a tie coming off, a tie sliding, another one being loaded on. An almost hypnotic ritual of economic motion. The workers were big men, heavily muscled, even in this cold wind off the river they worked in their shirtsleeves.

"There's a feller now we can ask," Motormouth said.

A man wearing a yellow hardhat and carrying a clipboard was striding toward them across the pier. He had opened his mouth to speak when a cry from the barge gave him pause and he turned to see who had called out.

Winer had seen it. A tie cocked sideways and jammed the chute and a huge black man reached an expert hand to free it just as the next tie slammed into it with a loud thock. He stared for a moment in amazement at his hand from which the four fingers were severed at the second joint. Blood welled then ran down his arm into his sleeve and he sat down heavily in the water sloshing in the hull of the barge. "Goddamn it," the man in the yellow hat said. He laid the clipboard on the dock and his hardhat atop to hold the papers in the wind and swung down a rope ladder into the barge. The black man was leaning up against the bulkhead with his hand clutched between his knees. His eyes were closed and his face ashen and it wore an expression of stoic forbearance.

Winer and Motormouth stood uncertainly for a moment. The two men on the upper end of the chutes had ceased loading and now they hunkered and took out tobacco and began rolling cigarettes. "Course we don't have to rush into nothin," Motormouth said. He had taken a tentative step or two away from the river and toward the stores and cafes of town. "I guess we could study about it awhile."

"Yeah, we could," Winer said. "We could study about it a good long while."

He'd sleep cold now and in the mornings find on the glass and metal of the Chrysler a rimpled rime of frost. Lying on his back Motormouth would stare upward a time into the ratty upholstery and then unfold himself, his distorted reflection in rustpocked chrome mocking him, a jerky caricature. The wind along the river these chill mornings would clash softly in the sere stalks of weeds, he'd hear it gently scuttling dislodged leaves against the car. Through the frosted glass there was little of the world he could see yet more of it than he wanted. He was peering into a world locked in the soft cold seize of ice.

Such mornings as these brought the bitter memories of winters past and he fell to thinking of walls and ceilings and flues. Of a porch ricked with seasoned wood and the smell of smoke sucked along the ridges. Of the soft length of her laid against him on December mornings. The way her hair looked in the morning, tousled as if she'd fallen asleep in a storm.

He drove past the house. It looked still and empty and he had no expectation of seeing her yet there she was, standing before the smokehouse door peering in, a sweater pulled about her shoulders. He slowed, looked all about. He could see no one else. No car or sign of one. He stopped. A core of something near fear lay in the pit of his stomach, anticipation and dread ran in his veins like oil and water.

It was cold in the front room as well, colder than in the spare light of the sun, a musty chill of unused rooms and closed doors. A jumble of stovepipes littered the floor, a film of soot and ashes dusted the linoleum. He sighted up the flue, saw only the gunmetal sameness of the sky, half a bird's nest perched precariously on a loosened brick. He was standing in the middle of the floor rubbing his hands together and looking about when she came through the kitchen door. She paused on the threshold and stood watching him.

"You get out of here. You got no business here."

"Just checkin ye out," he said. "Come back, have ye?"

"Yes, I've come back but not to you. It's my house, you know. Daddy give it to me."

"Daddy's welcome to it," Motormouth said. He took out a cigarette and lit it. He stood shifting his weight from one to the other of his thin legs as if torn between going and staying whether she wanted him to or not. The wind off the stretch of field rippled the tin of the roof and sang softly across the flue. A loose pane of glass tinkled in its sash like a chime. "Turnin cold, ain't it?"

"It does most ever year about this time."

"I look for a bad winter this year."

"I never knowed of a good one. You still ain't said what you're doin here. You know I got papers says you ain't allowed here."

"I don't want much of nothin. I was just drivin by and I happened to think of all them carparts I got in the smokehouse. I wouldn't want nothin to happen to em."

"Then get em and go."

"I will in a minute. Say, are you thinkin about movin back in here sure enough?"

"What's it to you?"

"Just makin conversation."

"Make it another place, with somebody else."

"Are you movin back in here?"

"What if I am?"

"Nothin." He paused. "By yourself?"

"No."

"Oh, Blalock too, huh. Is there not enough room in that big old house of his?"

"I told you what we do is our business."

"You're still married to me."

"I won't be in a few days."

He thought he might fare better if he changed the subject. "What was you doin peepin in the smokehouse?"

"I was fixin to put up the stove. It's cold."

"Lord, you can't move that heavy old thing. It's castiron. Why don't Blalock put it up for ye? That ain't no woman's job."

"He ain't here. He took off a load of cattle to Memphis or somewheres."

"Get Clyde to do it then."

"Him and Cecil got into it. That's why we're comin up here. They got into it over me."

"Well, ain't you the belle of the ball."

She didn't say anything.

"And say Cecil ain't here?"

"Didn't I just get through sayin so?"

He crossed the room and balanced himself on the arm of the sofa, glanced about for an ashtray and finding none tipped off ashes into the cuff of his trousers. She had not moved, stood watching him reflectively from the door. "Don't make yourself at home," she told him. "You won't be here long enough for that." But there was no vehemence or urgency to her voice, she sounded almost abstracted, as if other things occupied her mind. She crossed her arms, shook back her long hair from her forehead, he watched the smooth, milky flesh of her throat. "Maybe we could try it again," he said. His voice sounded strange to him, a dry croak.

She just shook her head. "There is no way in hell," she told him. "I aim to have Cecil and there won't nothin stand in my way."

"Cecil's rollin towards Memphis," he said. His mouth felt as though it had dust in it. The wing of red hair fell across her brow again, she blew it away in a curious gesture he had seen a thousand times. The past twisted in him like a knife, sharp as broken glass. Old words of endearment he need not have said tasted bitter and dry as ashes. He thought of Blalock long gone, Memphis seemed thousands of miles away and drifting in the mists of some lost continent. The wind sucked through the cracks by the windows and told him of a world gone vacant, no one left save these two. He thought of his hands on her throat, of his weight bearing down on her, forcing her legs apart with a knee, sliding himself into her. Dark and nameless specters bore their visions through his mind. He thought of her supine in a shallow grave, her green eyes and the sullen pout of her mouth impacted with earth, the cones of her breasts hard and white as ivory, ice crystals frozen in the red hair under her belly. The rains of winter seeping into her flesh, the seeds of springs sprouting in the cavities of her body.

"Why are you lookin at me like that?"

"I ain't."

"You look halfcrazy when you do that. You was always doin that."

The cigarette burned his fingers and he looked at it in wonder. He dropped it, smudged it with a boot into the worn and patternless linoleum. He arose. "Well. I guess I better get on. I just thought I'd see how ye was."

"This is how I am."

Although he had stood up to go he made no further move to do so. She was watching him. "That thing weighs nigh two hundred pounds," he said. "I wish you luck with it."

"There was anything to you you'd help me put it up. It's settin right out there where you put it last spring."

"Yeah," he said, trying to get a focus on last spring, a definition of it. Spring seemed years ago.

"You help me get it in the back door and I'll get it the rest of the way in myself."

"I bet it'll be cold tonight. I may need it myself." For a fey moment he thought of the heater set up by the riverbank, himself housed only by the walls of the world, the elements. "A few minutes ago you called me crazy," he told her. "I may be but I ain't crazy enough yet to put up a heatin stove for some other son of a bitch to warm by."

"It wouldn't hurt you to help me. It wouldn't cost you a dime."

"I made you my best deal. You come back to me and we'll go to town and get some grocers and I'll put it up and build us a big fire in it."

"Forget it. Cecil can put it up when he gets back."

He took a deep breath. "All right then. I'll tell you what I will do. You give me a little and I'll put the damned thing up for you."

"You are crazy."

"What could it hurt? Ain't Cecil in Memphis? Ain't we married?"

"Just in name only."

"That's close enough for me," Motormouth said. He crossed the room, stood beside her. The top of her head did not even reach his shoulder. She did not move away. He knew suddenly with a shock of exultation that she was going to do it.

She undressed at the foot of the bed. He kicked his boots off, shucked out of his slacks and lay watching her. She unhooked her brassiere. A strap secured by a safety pin made her more vulnerable, less remote. She slid out of her skirt, it pooled at her feet. She began to roll down her panties, looked up, and saw him watching her. She flounced her hair back from her forehead and pushed her underwear down defiantly, her eyes hard and fierce. "Get your eyes full," she told him. He stared at the cool, mounded flesh of her belly, the snarled rustcolored pubic hair. In the cold air gooseflesh crept up the ivory of her thighs, her nipples hardened and elongated.

When he inserted himself into her her face did not change, nor when he began to move inside her. He labored above her as if inch by inch he would force his entire body into her, merge with her, become her, he sweated in the juncture of her body while she lay abstracted, lost in the pattern of the ceiling wallpaper, and he knew she had defeated him once again. Her pale flesh looked pristine, unused. He thought of the countless times he had lain in her arms, that Blalock had lain inside her, that she had lain down with faceless names that were just taunts she had flung at him. Yet none of them had hurt or marked or even touched her. She was unused.

"Why did you quit? Are you done?"

He hadn't known he had. "I was just thinkin," he said. He commenced again halfheartedly.

She laughed deep in her throat. "You never could think and do this at the same time," she said.

She had dragged it almost to the smokehouse door, its legs leaving skidded indentations in the rough flooring. He stood looking down at it. It looked ungodly heavy. She watched him from the kitchen door, buttoning her blouse. He squatted in the earth by the door, studying it. Figuring the easiest way to move it. He could not remember how he had gotten it there in the first place.

He looked up. The sun was nearing its zenith but the light had a thin, faraway quality to it, the red orb stingy and remote, and it seemed to him that it was speeding away from him, the earth settling incrementally into some age seized in ice. Baring branches rustled softly, told sweet ageold secrets he'd never know. He was thinking about Blalock. He could see him opening the door of the stove, throwing a stick of wood in, stirring the roiling coals with a poker. Settling back in the armchair, sighing, feet cocked aloft to the warmth of the heater, now opening his farm magazine.

"Piss on you," he told the stove.

He started toward his car.

"You dirty son of a bitch," she shrieked at the immutability of his back. He had heard it all before and he went on. He wheeled the Chrysler back into the yard and then it leapt forward, spun smoking across the ditch and onto the gravel road. He sped off toward town.

Winer went down the embankment through a cold gray drizzle. The bracken was already wet and by the time he reached the car he was soaked to the thighs and angry. Motormouth had a fire built in the stone grill constructed for campers and a pan set atop it but the fire was guttering in the rain and smoking and heavy smoke bellied bluely away down the riverbank. Winer could hear the soft hiss of rain falling in the river.

He opened the car door and got in. Motormouth sat behind the wheel. He was staring out the rainwashed windshield toward the blurred river as if at some landscape he was hurtling fulltilt toward. Winer slammed the door. "You're a hell of a lot of trouble," he said. "You moved. You could have told me where you were movin to."

"I didn't know myself. It come on me sudden."

"All this stuff coming on you sudden is going to put you in the pen or under the ground," Winer said. "Rape comes on you sudden. Living like a crazyman in an automobile parked in the bushes comes on you sudden. You move but you don't move good enough.

All I had to do was ask at the grocery store. I guess it come on you sudden to tell Patton, just in case anybody wondered where you were or had any warrants to serve or anything."

"Yeah. Well, hell. I told him to just tell you."

"Well, you're a trusting soul. The power of a ten-dollar bill may be lost on you, but it's not on Blalock or Patton."

"Is Blalock huntin me sure enough?"

"That's why I come down here. He's told it all over town what he's going to do when he catches you. He says you raped her and beat her and he says he swore out a warrant against you. Likely he's just blowing about the warrant, but he's told so many folks he's going to whip your ass he's just about bound to do it whether he wants to or not."

"Do you think he can do it?"

"Has a cat got an ass? Of course he can do it. Hell, he'd make two of you and enough left over to referee."

"No, I mean that rape stuff. Can he make that stick? You can't rape your own wife, can ye?"

"I don't know."

"I don't mind gettin a asswhippin, he wouldn't get no cherry, but thinkin about hard time up at Brushy gives me a chill."

"I'd have to ask somebody. How about cranking this thing up and turning the heater on? I'm cold all the way to the bone."

Motormouth cranked the car and it sat idling, vibrating rhythmically. Winer turned the heater on, shuddered at the onrush of cold air, turned it back off. "Does this thing not work?"

"It has to warm up. Ask who?"

"Somebody that knows something about the law. A lawyer, a judge, you know."

"I know you best keep away from them kind of folks. You'll have us both in the pen. Anyway, I never raped her and I damn sure never laid a hand on her. I know exactly what's the matter with him. He's mad because he had to put up that Goddamned heatin stove by hisself."

"Maybe. Anyway, he's hunting you."

192

"I'm fixin to leave as soon as I get a stake. I'm burnt out on this place anyhow. I'm sick of it. The only place I ever want to see this place is in a rearview mirror."

He fell into a ruminative silence. Winer turned the heater on, held his hands cupped to the warming air. "I'm goin north," Motormouth said. "Chicago. That's a place for a feller like me. I could make it big in a place like Chitown. There ain't no angles to play in a dump like this. There's a world of angles in a town that size. That's what I need."

"What you need is a keeper," Winer said. "And about thirty feet of heavy-gauge chain to hold you back by."

A wan and sourceless light guided his steps off the road and into Oliver's yard. He had the paper under his coat, for the air was full of moisture, a cold mizzling past mist and not yet rain. It was just past daybreak though there was no sun or promise of one. He passed through a dull leaden dripping from the trees. Three bedraggled cocks already risen had taken shelter beneath an old white cooktable in Oliver's frontyard. They watched him by disconsolately with eyes like bits of colored glass.

Yellow light flared through a window. Smoke rolled from the old man's flue and Winer knew he was just up, for the smoke had a blue, greasy look to it and smelled of kerosene. He crossed the porch and knocked on the door and waited, tucking his shoulders in and hugging himself with his arms.

"It ain't locked," a voice called.

He opened the door and went into the front room. It was almost as cold inside as out. The old man was crouched before the open stove door cramming newspapers into the orange-red maw of its throat. He turned a harried face up toward Winer. The room reeked of kerosene.

"Boy, I'm about froze to death and I think this thing has gone on a sitdown strike or somethin." Oliver began to feed the fire long, curled shavings of yellow pine.

"It just turned cold in the night. I went to sleep warm and woke up about four o'clock freezin to death."

"I looked for a bad winter."

"I think you found one," Winer said. He spread his hands for the feeble warmth radiating upward from the heater.

"Is it snowin yet?"

"I believe it's too cold to snow."

"We'll make us some coffee here directly this thing ever decides to burn." Oliver blew out the lamp and they sat silently in the flickering light of the stove and the spectral gray dawn at the window. The fire caught and the area immediately surrounding the stove began to warm though cold held to the room and it was impossible to sit where the old man's couch was. Oliver filled a pan with ice and water and set it on to boil. He looked halffrozen. His face looked gray and bloodless and he stamped about trying to get the circulation going in his feet, rubbing his hands together briskly.

"What're you doin out so early anyway? You ain't workin in this mess are you?"

"No. I don't work there anymore."

"Say you don't? How come?"

"I quit. I just thought I might go out to town today. I was just waiting to see how it's going to be."

"I know how it's goin to be," Oliver said bleakly. "By God cold just like it is now clear on through till spring of the year."

"It'll warm up again. This is just a cold snap."

"I don't look for it to."

"You got plenty of wood?"

Oliver poured crushed coffeebeans into the boiling water. "I got a world of it but it's all on the stump," he said.

"If it don't get too rough I'll come over after awhile and cut you a load."

"Ah, no need in that. I can buy me a little jag. I guess you got your own to worry about."

"I cut some back in the summer when I wasn't doing anything. Anyway, what I came to see you about was signing this paper for me." As he spoke Winer was withdrawing the typed note from beneath his jacket and proffering it toward the old man.

Oliver shook his head. "You'll have to read it to me. What is it?"

"It's a note to borrow some money. I found a car I wanted down at Kittrel's carlot and they sent me over to the bank, they have to have a cosigner and the man there said they'd let me have the money if you'll sign the note." Winer paused. "You were the only one I could think of who might sign it."

"Well, well," the old man said. He took the paper and studied it at arm's length, peering at the typed hieroglyphs he couldn't read. He seemed imbued with a curious sense of pride and as the room filled with the fragrance of boiled coffee and the heat from the stove dissipated the chill he grew expansive. He laid the note with care atop the table and taking the pan from the stove filled two earthenware mugs with coffee.

"I hope it ain't like the paper I signed for Hodges one time," Oliver said, grinning to himself. He handed Winer a cup of coffee. "There for a few years I kindly took a interest in that boy. I had a idy I might help him a little here and there, kindly straighten him out, but I doubt you could do that with a block and tackle. He come down here one time with a paper he wanted me to sign. He'd answered a advertisement in one of these here farm papers and he was goin to be a salesman, I made my X and two or three weeks later we went out town to pick up this stuff that come in. Lord God. You never seen the like of junk. It come in on a boxcar at the depot. It was boxes and boxes of stuff, looked like stock for a grocer store. Pie fillin and flavorin and horse liniment and you wouldn't believe the bottles of sweetsmellin stuff. He had to hire a truck to haul it home in and I don't reckon he ever sold any of it. They dunned me about it a long time and I used to get letters from this lawyer in Chicago and I finally scraped around and paid it. I don't know what Hodges finally done with it, I believe he used all that brilliantine himself and he smelled purty high for a year or two and then it all died out."

"I'll pay the note off."

"I know you will. I was just thinkin about how Hodges looked when he saw all that stuff. All them boxes and him without even a bicycle to haul it on."

Weather accomplished what Blalock nor anyone else had been able to do. It got Motormouth in motion. He turned up around noon at Winer's, complaining.

"Goddamn, I'm about froze to death," he told Winer. "You talk about cold. Last night I near about shook myself to death and woke up with the river froze over and the weather says just more of the same. The radio said the windshield factor was ten below zero."

"The what?"

"It said the windshield factor was ten below zero and bearable winds."

"I think it said variable."

"Varable or bearable, it's a cold son of a bitch. Are you about ready?"

"Ready? Ready for what?"

"Hellfire. To leave. To go to Chicago like we said."

"Good God, no. I'm as far north as I'll be this winter."

"Well, I'm goin. I was goin to sell the Chrysler to Kittrel but I'll give you first shot at it. You want it?"

They went out into the yard and stood looking at it. A cold drizzle fell and the car gleamed dully. Winer studied it from all angles, imagining what it looked like beneath the array of antennas and lights and coontails.

"I'll take eighty-five dollars cash money and if it ain't worth two hundred I'll kiss ye ass. I give twenty dollars for them foglights by theirselves."

"I guess you know what you want to do."

"The hell of it is I don't know whether I do or not. I bet that's a big place up there. I wanted you to go with me but I reckon you got stars in your eyes."

Winer took out his wallet. "I'll give you eighty-five for it if you'll show me how to drive it. I never drove anything except Weiss's tractor."

"Why hell yes, slide your ass in here, son. You'll be learnin from a master."

Late in the day they drove into town and parked by the bus station and Motormouth went in and got his ticket. He returned with it and they sat awaiting the bus and staring out across the rainwet streets and an unaccustomed silence settled upon Motormouth, a vague depression befell him as dusk drew on. At last the bus came and he got out with his cardboard box lashed with staging and strode purposefully toward it and mounted the steps. He turned and raised a hand. The bus door closed behind him with a soft pneumatic hiss. Winer watched the bus out of sight.

Oliver must have already been abed, for he was in his long underwear when he cracked the door and peered out. Winer handed him the banknote.

"You can tear this up. I don't reckon I need it after all."

"Well. I heard of a good credit risk but you about the beat of any I ever seen."

"I never even used it. I bought Motormouth's car and it was a lot cheaper than the one Kittrel had."

"Well, where's Hodges gone off to?"

"His bus ticket said Chicago."

"Chicago," Oliver repeated in an awed voice. "Lord God."

She must have been watching from a window, for as soon as he parked the car the front door opened and she came out onto the porch. Grinning, she came down the steps and approached the car.

"What are you doin with Motormouth Hodges's car?" she asked.

"It's mine, I bought it," he said. He got out and let the door fall to, walked all around the car pointing out its virtues. She wasn't really looking at the car, stood grinning at him in a curiously maternal way.

"Okay, okay," she said. "You don't have to sell it to me."

"You want to go for a ride?"

"I don't know. How'd you learn to drive so fast?"

"Motormouth showed me."

She was laughing. "Oh Lord. I reckon I'll just wait then."

"He said I was learning from a master."

"Well. Maybe in that case. I never rode with a master before."

Mormon Springs fell away and on the way to town he was seized by a feeling of elation, the colors and sounds of this bleak winter day seemed heightened and he was possessed by a rockhard assurance that things were going right. Turning momentarily from the road he glanced at her bright profile against the dreary, rolling countryside and he didn't see how things could go wrong for anyone who had a girl who looked as pretty as she did: there was a juststruck perfection, she looked new and unused to him, nothing had quite touched her.

"You know what I'd like to do?"

"No, but you can do whatever you want to."

"I want to eat at the Daridip. I never did that before."

"Where's Hardin at?"

"I don't know and I don't care. He can't stop me if I'm already with you, can he?"

"What'd he say to you about those blankets?"

"Nothin."

Winer looked at her. He didn't believe her but he didn't say so.

"Then I want to go down on Brushy where they buried Daddy. I ain't been down there since the funeral and I been wantin to go. You reckon we could?"

"I don't care. I said we'd do whatever you wanted to."

The grave was an oval of red earth. Wire flowers tilted and twisted askew by fall winds. Cliched sentiments gone weather-beaten and forgotten, cheap celluloid flowers blatant in their artifice. There was no headstone and a metal marker driven into the earth certified who was there in watermarked type. THOMAS HOVINGTON, she read. It was like being famous, she thought, seeing your name in cold print like that. She'd never seen it before.

She knelt and pulled her skirt down over her knees and arranged the tacky remnants of flowers to some semblance of order she carried in her head. Hands gentle to rotted crepepaper leached colorless and limp.

"He never helped me much, but he might've if he hadn't been so sick. I was a kid when they put him in the ground," she said. "It was just this year but I ain't a kid no more. I seen the hearse come all new and shiny and they took him out in that box and drove away. 'Goin back after another one,' I thought. I had never thought about folks doin that for a livin. I get a little boy I never want him to be one of them."

An old man and woman were passing among the gravestones. Old gray man in a black suitcoat. Winer watched him. Prospective tenants perhaps, folks just visiting their neighbors. He wanted gone.

She arose. She was crying brokenly. She clung to his arm. "They had to break his back," she said. "They ought never to have done that."

He put his arms around her and drew her wet face into the hollow of his throat. He couldn't think of anything to say.

"You got any money?"

"Sure I got money. Why?"

"Stop up here." She pointed.

He pulled into the empty parking lot. It was the Cozy Court Motel. They sat for a time, his finger awkwardly drumming on the steering wheel, she with a calm serenity, staring out across the cold-looking pavement toward the numbered doors.

"We'll play like we're somebody else," she said. "Somebody real nice."

He didn't say anything. He got out and closed the door and went across the asphalt to where blue neon said the office was.

Later they lay in bed, her back to him, the length of her body against him. The sun was lowering itself in the west and threw the window yellowlit and oblique on the eastern wall. Past her rounded shoulder he watched it slide slowly across the limegreen plaster and he wished there was some way to halt it but there was not.

He stopped the car on the last curve before Hardin's and cut the switch off and drew her against him.

"We ought not to have drove back here at all. We should have just kept on goin."

"Goin where?"

"I don't know."

"Will he hurt you?"

"He never has really."

"Tell me if he does."

She looked at him wryly. "Why? What will you do? Kill him? Defend my honor? It's easy for you. All you have to do is drive out of sight and it's over for you."

They sat in silence. He thought of the curious progression of things, the way the ragged edges of one event dovetailed into another like the pieces of a puzzle, no single piece independent of the whole.

"It ought not to have been like this," he said suddenly.

"What?"

"If any one thing had been different then the rest would have too. We might be married. We might be a thousand miles away."

She smiled. "We might be dead," she said.

"We may be yet," he told her.

"You want to see everything at once, Nathan. You want it every bit in front of you where you can look at it, make choices. I ain't like that. I never had a choice to make. I just do what there is to do and then I don't worry over it. It's done."

"All I want right now is for you to never get out that door," he said.

She leaned and kissed his cheek. Then she got out anyway.

She traced the outline of her lips with a pink lipstick, pressed her lips together to smooth it. She studied her face speculatively in the mirror. Her eyes opened startled when Hardin's reflection appeared behind hers.

"Think you're goin somewheres?"

"Nathan Winer's takin me to the show."

"No he's not."

"Yes he is. Mama's done said I could go."

"Mama don't call the shots around here and ain't never if memory serves."

"Well, she calls them with me. You're not my daddy."

"I damn sure ain't," he said. "And never claimed to be." He came up behind her until their bodies touched and took the mirror from her hand and laid it aside. He embraced her from behind, a hand cupping each breast.

"Quit," she said, twisting away, but his arms tightened and finally she stood without moving, slack in his arms. His touch appeared to drain her of any will of her own, as if she were absorbing some slowmoving but deadly poison from his body to hers. She was quite still, like some marvelous representation of human flesh lacking any spark to animate. They stood so for a long time.

"Mama's crazy. She'll kill you one of these days."

"I'm like a cat," Hardin said. "I take a lot of killin." He kept on massaging her breasts gently.

"I'm a grown woman, Dallas. I can pick up and leave here anytime I want to. And if I'm of a mind to go with Nathan Winer or anybody else I want to, you can't stop me."

"I just did," Hardin said. "And it didn't hurt a bit, did it?" He turned her toward him but she twisted her face away. "Quit," she said. "Quit it, Dallas."

"You think I don't know you? You think I'm goin to let you throw yourself away on some redneck with dirty fingernails and no idy at all what he's got? Sure I am. The hell I am."

He released her. He lit a cigarette and stood studying her.

"Throw you a change of clothes in a suitcase," he told her. "Long as you're already dressed up we might as well go somewhere."

"Go where?"

"You'll see when we get there."

"You think I'm goin anywhere at all with you you're badly mistaken."

"Get it packed or you'll by God go without it." Hardin turned on his heel and went through the long front room just as Pearl came through the door. She stepped aside to let him pass and then stood there watching Amber Rose and Amber Rose watching her, but neither of them spoke.

Winer smelled strongly of Old Spice and he had something on his hair that plastered it gleaming to the contours of his skull and he had on a new white shirt. One long room of the honkytonk had been sheetrocked though not yet plastered or painted. A bar was aligned against the narrow end of the room and tables and chairs were spaced about the floor. Winer passed through the doorway and into the sounds of Saturday-night merriment as though he were accustomed to it and seated himself at one of the bright new stools at the bar.

"Lord God, Winer," Wymer said. "You smell like you broke a twenty-dollar bill in the barbershop and had to take the change out in trade."

Winer gave him a small, tight smile and sat absentmindedly tapping a halfdollar on the bar. "Let me have a Coke, Wymer."

Wymer set up the bottle but refused the coin. "Pearl's givin it away tonight," he said wryly. "Everthing's on the house."

"Do what?"

"Hell, yeah. She's pissed at Hardin about somethin and she's already give away enough beer and whiskey to give the whole county a hangover."

"What's she mad at Hardin about?"

"You'd have to ask them. They don't tell me their business." He stood unsteadily, arranged his thin hair with his fingers to cover his bald spot. His small eyes flitted drunkenly about the room as if Hardin might be crouched behind a table watching. "They got me right in the middle," he complained. "He's gone off God knows where and all I know for certain is he's goin to have a shitfit when he does get back. I just may be somewhere's else when it happens too. . . . He keeps talkin bout this Mexcan feller he's bringin up from Memphis. I guess I'm out of a job anyway."

Winer drank Coke. "How come you to go along with her? I thought you were workin for Hardin."

"I don't know who in hell I work for. Right now I'm workin for that 30-06 she throwed on me awhile ago."

"I see," Winer said though he didn't. He arose with his bottle. "I'll see you."

"You better drink up while it's free. You won't never see this again in your lifetime."

"I got to get on."

He crossed onto the porch and knocked on the door, the screen rattling loosely on its hinges.

"Who's there? Get away from that damned door."

"It's Nathan Winer. Can I see you a minute?"

"What do you want?"

"I just need to see you a minute."

After a time he heard her get up heavily and he heard her mumbling to herself or another. The door opened and she stood leaning heavily against the jamb. He could smell the raw-whiskey smell of her and her sweat and the curious volatile smell of her anger.

"What is it?"

"I just wanted Amber Rose," he said. "We were supposed to go to the show in Ackerman's Field."

"Well, she ain't here, Nathan. She's gone off to Columbia or somewheres with Dallas."

"We were supposed to go to the show. She said she wanted to."

"Dallas didn't say for sure where they were goin or when they'd be back." She drank from an upturned bottle. Lowered it and reached it toward Winer. "Get you a little drink there."

"I wouldn't care for any."

"Here." She took the Coke bottle from him and filled it to overflowing from the bottle she held. "Come in and set awhile with me. We'll wait on em together."

"No, I may wait out in the car awhile. I got me a car."

"Say you have? That's real nice, Nathan."

"We were going to the show in it."

"Well, I don't know where she is."

"If you were guessing what time would you guess they'd be back?"

She pondered a moment. "I'd guess when I seen them comin," she said.

Sometime in the small hours of the night he sat on Weiss's couch drinking strawberry wine. He sat in the silence with the thin crystal goblet balanced on his knee.

The silence seemed distilled, pure, silence augmenting itself. The walls were listening, the room hushed and waiting. In this silence he seemed receptive to all the world of experience, sensation multiplied by sensation rushed to him as if he were attuned to a vast stream of data bombarding him from every side. He drank from the wineglass and he could taste the musky heat of the berries, feel the weight of the sun, detect the difference between sunshine and shade, smell the strawberries and their leaves and the earth, see the dry fissured texture of last year's earth, the serried grasses, the minute but vast life that flourished there. Laughter, conversations he was too weary to listen to funneled into his ears. He had heard all the words anyway, only the progressions had changed. He could hear Hodges's voice, its halfcocky whine torn between bullying and wheedling, he could hear Amber Rose's soft ironic voice and smell the clean soap smell of her, hear the rustle of her clothing. He could hear Weiss's clipped and scornful cadence. The dark oppressed him. This dark house of stopped clocks and forfeit lives and seized machinery. Here in the weary telluric dark past and present intersected seamlessly and he saw how there was no true beginning or end and all things once done were done forever and went spreading outward faint and fainter and that the face of a young girl carried at once within it a bitter worn harridan and past that the satinpillowed death's head of the grave. He rested his head on the couch arm and he could hear Weiss and his wife talking, hear all their lives flow past him like a highway he could enter and depart at will. He heard her asthmatic wheeze and the shuffle of her bedroom slippers and the click of the little dog's claws on the tile and he got up. He drained the glass and set it by the couch. He went out into the cold night without looking back.

Cold dreary days now of winter in earnest and every day it seemed to rain. A cold, spiritless rain out of a leaden sky and he used to sit and watch out the weeping glass but there was nothing to see save brittle weeds and the coldlooking dripping woods. Water freezing on the clothesline, a gleaming strand of suspended ice.

There seemed to be nowhere he wanted to go and no soul in all the world he wanted to talk to. He'd sit by the fire and try to read but the words skittered off the page like playful mice and he thought he'd never seen grayer or longer days.

On this gray, chill Sunday there was an air almost pastoral about Mormon Springs, an air of pause as if time must be given to ponder the events of Saturday night. Or respite to gear up for the week ahead. There was a hush here, a silence that seemed to gather about the pit. Winer kicking through beerbottles and cigarette packs and the random debris of Saturday night seemed somehow resolute, calm, he seemed to have broached some line he'd never expected to and made a decision he was at peace with.

Sleepy Sunday windows, no one about save a drunk dozing in the backseat of a parked car. No smoke from the flue of Hovington's house. Winer went on past it and past the bundled bricks and to the unpainted boardwalled honkytonk and went in.

A trio of silent men sat before the hushed jukebox like worshipers at some fallen or discredited shrine and they glanced up as Winer passed and approached the bar and then they looked away. They had the strangely attentive attitude of men listening to music no one else can hear.

Hardin sat on a stool at the bar. An enormous dark man sat on the next stool over and neither of them seemed aware of Winer. Winer stood awkwardly awaiting acknowledgment and he felt dazed and sleeprobbed and he could smell his own nervous sweat. Hardin was drinking some dark liquid from a glass with icecubes in it and when he drained the glass he set it atop the bar with a small liquid rattle of ice and sat staring into its depths as if he read the configurations of his future or someone else's there and they did not please him.

"What do you want, Winer?"

"I want to talk to you a minute by yourself."

"Anything you got to say to me can be said right here. I don't believe you know this feller here. Winer, this is Jiminiz. I brought him up from Memphis to help with my light work. Jiminiz used to bust heads in the meanest whorehouse on Beale Street and I reckon this place is goin to seem like a vacation to him."

Jiminiz turned a dark, moonshaped face toward Winer but made no further overture and there was no look at all in his eyes. His white shirt was open to the waist and his chest and belly were laced with a scrollwork of old scars. His smooth black hair was shiny with brilliantine. Winer noticed that the collar of the white shirt was soiled. There was an air of violence constrained about him, he was mantled with a flimsy and makeshift indolence.

"Winer used to be a pretty good feller till he got him a little pussy," Hardin told Jiminiz. "Then he just flew all to pieces. Don't know who his friends are anymore. Just can't keep off that old thin ice."

Jiminiz seemed not to have heard but after a time he said, "Pussy warps a man's head worse than codeine ever did." His voice was mellifluous and touched with a soft Spanish lilt. "I guess next to gettin caught pussy has caused me more trouble than anything else."

"I want to see you outside," Winer told Hardin.

"I look just the same in here." Hardin poured Jack Daniels into a glass, sat turning it on the formica, studying the series of interlocking rings the bottom of the cold glass made. "All this old shit keeps buildin up," he said. "One thing after another. Seems like ever which way I turn I got folks snappin at my heels and worryin me. Well, I ain't never been one to put things off. I believe if somethin's botherin you cut it out right at the start. Be done with it and get on to somethin else. Now, me and Jiminiz aims to set some folks straight. So why don't you just ease out of here?"

"I'm goin to see her."

"Goddamn it, Winer. Does it have to be spoonfed to you a word at a time? I've got money tied up here. I've bought her clothes and fed her and by God raised her and now you think you'll get her off somewheres and get her to thinkin about dishes and baby buggies and such shit and it all goes out the winder. Like hell it does. Folks around here beginnin to think they can shove me this way and that and I reckon I'm goin to have to bang some more heads together. They think I'm mellerin down or somethin. But we'll see. Now, pick up that long face and that draggy ass and get out of my place. I'm sick of it, do you hear me? You and your money ain't no good in here."

"I'll tell you what, Hardin. Why don't you put me out?"

"No, you won't tell me what. You won't tell me jackshit. I'll tell you what. I don't have to put you out. I told you Jiminiz does my light work. He'll have you out of here so fast all you'll remember about it is how bad it hurt."

Winer was watching Jiminiz. The man sat cupping a tiny shot-glass of bourbon in his hand. He seemed unaware that he was under discussion. But Winer wasn't really seeing him, he was seeing the long, slow days of Indian summer, days of dreamy peace, the rafters going up in the heat of the sun, the feel of the icy fruitjar against his face. The ebony fall of her hair against the whitewashed wall. The way his arms were thickening day by day with the raising of the heavy oak timbers and the smell of the hot green wood curing in the sun. I can do it, he was thinking. The tenseness left him, he stood loose against the bar, light and arrogant on the balls of his feet.

"Take me out, Jiminiz," he said.

Jiminiz smiled a small, onesided smile. "I don't work for you," he said. "The man pays me off on a Friday gives my orders."

Hardin stood watching Winer and something in the boy's posture or in his face was evocative and recalled to him another who had snapped at his heels long ago. He knew by the way he was standing what was on his mind and he could see the imprint of the knife through denim and he thought in wonder, The same knife. For a millisecond the past seemed about to engulf him as if old deeds were never done and over with and there were things that must be done in perpetuity. As if he must go on forever taking this selfsame knife away from folks.

"He'll have a knife," he said tiredly.

"He won't use it," Jiminiz said offhandedly. "I've seen a thousand of him."

"Then take him out," Hardin said.

Jiminiz drained his shotglass and set it aside. "Easy money," he said.

Winer waited. When Jiminiz approached him he swung as hard as he could at the calm, dark face. Jiminiz ducked and Winer felt his fist glance off the slick black hair and his momentum carried him sideways. Jiminiz straightened and positioned his feet and though his fist seemed to travel only six or eight inches before it struck Winer's ribcage Winer felt his lungs empty in a sharp explosion of pain and he went reeling backward.

The covey of drunks flushed like startled quail when Winer struck the table. It overturned and he fell in a cascade of playing cards and falling glass and the drunks erupted from toppled chairs and developed a simultaneous interest in what lay beyond the door. Winer got up on all fours slowly shaking his head from side to side like a bear set upon by dogs. He was trying to breathe. His breath whistled eerily in his throat and the room seemed to have tilted to a forty-five-degree angle and poised there, Winer waiting for the furniture to slide sideways and pile up on the left periphery of his vision. Marvelously defying gravity and tilted as well, Jiminiz was crossing the room toward him, his fists cocked. Behind him a tilted Hardin watched as if this were all beyond his interest.

Winer got up clutching a chair and when he threw it Jiminiz just grinned and fended it away onehanded and kept coming. Winer stiffened and hit Jiminiz in the belly with his right and crossed with his left and a slight shudder ran through Jiminiz and then he hit Winer full in the face.

Lights flickered in Winer's head and he hit the floor limber-necked with his head slapping the hardwood flooring and they flickered again. Perhaps he dozed for a moment for when he came to himself Jiminiz was standing over him with a look of infinite patience on his face. Winer was lying on his back and he rose to his elbows and lay staring out across his prone body. Nothing seemed to have changed. The chairs were still scattered and the table capsized and Hardin still sat on a stool drinking. Winer had fallen in broken glass and his arms were bleeding.

Then Hardin spoke. Winer could hear him though there was a roaring in his ears like far-off water. "Mark him up a little," Hardin said. "Mess them smooth jaws up. Ever time he looks in a shavin mirror I want him to remember how sweet that pussy was."

"Then let him get up," Jiminiz said. "I don't like hittin a man already down and I don't like hittin a man already out on his feet and don't know when he's whipped."

"He'll get up," Hardin said contemptuously. "You couldn't keep him down with a fuckin logchain. He ain't got sense enough to lay down and quit."

Winer was trying. It hurt him to move and it hurt to breathe and it hurt to talk. "You better make him kill me," he said. "Because if I live you won't. You're a dead man."

"I know the words to that old song," Hardin said. "I've heard it often enough."

"You gettin up or stayin down?" Jiminiz asked.

The price he paid was dear but Winer got up. There was blood welling in his mouth and his eyes had a slick, shiny look like glass. For a few moments he managed to evade Jiminiz but the Mexican moved like a boxer, graceful despite his size, feinting, jabbing through Winer's flimsy guard at will. Winer sat down hard with his vision darkening and the last thing he saw was the dark bulk of Jiminiz coming on and Jiminiz hit him some more but he had stopped feeling it.

The water had turned red. Winer squeezed the washrag out in it and went back to cleaning his face with the pink cloth, studying his cuts in the mirror.

"Who was it done it? Hardin?" Oliver sat straddling a ladder-back chair, his dead pipe clutched in his teeth.

"He subcontracted it out to some Mexican."

"Mexcan?"

"Some bouncer or something he brought up here from Memphis."

"Big feller?"

Winer was gingerly daubing his face with alcohol. "I hope I never see one bigger," he said. "But it wouldn't have mattered anyway. I had some idea I was tougher than I turned out to be."

"I seen you come by the house right slow drivin like a drunk man. I knowed you wouldn't be drunk so I figured I might ort to step up here and see would you live. Do you reckon you will?"

"I expect so."

"You shore ain't goin to be much in the purty department for a good long while."

"I never was anyway."

"Looks like you may have ye a scar or two to remember that Mexcan by. What'd he whup you with? A stick of stovewood? Or a choppin axe?"

"I think he had a ring on and he sort of twisted his fist when he hit me."

"Boy, I just don't know what to say. Goddamn it, there just ain't nothin to say. You ort to go to the high sheriff. Bellwether's a fair man, what I hear."

"Hardin'd just swear I started it. Which I did. He gave me every out there was and I just wouldn't take them, I had Pa's old knife and I was going to cut one or both of them. Then he chopped me right good in the ribs and all my intentions just flew away."

"You think you'll be all right?"

"I hurt too much to think. It must have stove in my ribs or something."

"Let's get in ye car and try to make it in to see Ratcliff."

"I'll be all right in the morning."

"Lord God, boy. Now ain't nothin to the way you'll feel in the mornin. I remember one time I got locked up in Nashville for a public drunk and a pair of them blueboys played around with me for awhile. I went to bed feelin purty good and when I got up next day I fell right flat on my face. I hurt in places I didn't even know I had. . . . Say, what did yins have ye fallin out about anyway?"

"We just got into it."

"Well, whatever it was you ought to swear out a warrant and have him locked up anyway."

"No. I've got an idea or two of my own."

He made his way through the slack Monday-morning commerce, a felthatted old man in a gray suitcoat too big through the shoulders and chest carrying a shoebox tucked tightly under his arm as though he conveyed something of unreckonable value. Whatever his business was it drew him down North Main and left at the General Cafe and across toward where the courthouse sat on its carpet of winter brown. A flag on a flagpole set in concrete fluttered and snapped in the bitter wind.

Old courthouse sounds and smells and the way his footfalls echoed hollowly in the sepulchral silence brought back other days so strongly he fancied he felt guiding hands on an elbow, steel chafing his wrists, heard other harsher footsteps that echoed his own. Days when the wildness lay on him and he bought time by the second and paid for it by the year. "I said I'd never darken these doors," he told himself. "And I wouldn't if it wadnt for the boy, if there was any way in God's world around it."

He went down the stairs to the basement level and past the library to where the high sheriff's office was. The door was locked. There was a sign on it. BACK IN FIVE MINUTES, the sign said. There was a bench in the hall by the door and the old man seated himself there with the box in his lap and waited. He waited with the patient forbearance of the old, through some acquired knowledge that sooner or later all things come to pass. Past the concrete stairs that ascended to the level of the courthouse yard he could see a gray square of winter light and the bare branches of trees. He sat idly watching foraging birds flit from tree to tree as if he had never seen such a thing before.

It was an hour before Bellwether came and when he did he had Cooper in tow. He nodded to Oliver and unlocked the door.

"How you makin it, Mr. Oliver?"

"I'm tolerable, I reckon. You need to set your watch."

"I expect I do. But if I did it'd be the only thing workin right around here and just foul everything else up. Did you need to see me about somethin?"

"I wanted to talk to you a few minutes."

"Come on in here and get you a seat."

Oliver took off his hat and seated himself in a straightback chair. He crossed his legs and hung his hat on a spindly knee and sat cradling the shoebox in his lap. Bellwether glanced at the shoe-box a time or two but he didn't say anything. He poured himself a cup of cold coffee from the unplugged coffeepot and drank and shuddered and sat waiting for Oliver to speak.

At length Oliver cleared his throat. "What I had to say was just for you," he said. "Not this young feller here."

Bellwether looked up sharply. "Well, he's a deputy sheriff in this county. I reckon whatever you had to talk to me about had to do with law enforcement."

"Yeah, it did," Oliver said. "That's why I'd just as lief this feller here didn't know nothin about it."

"Anything that pertains to law enforcement in this county is my business," Cooper said. "Like he told you, I'm a deputy sheriff."

Oliver arose, put on his hat. "I'll be gettin on if that's the way of it," he said. "Yins may hear it but you won't hear it from me."

"Wait a minute, now," Bellwether said. "Sit down there, Mr. Oliver." He looked from the old man's flinty face to Cooper's and back again. "Is there somethin goin on here I don't know about or what?"

Cooper shrugged. "If it is it's news to me."

"What about it, Mr. Oliver?"

"I've said my piece."

Cooper favored Oliver with a look of perplexed innocence. "What have you got against me, Mr. Oliver? I don't reckon I ever stepped on your toes, did I? Hell, I don't even hardly know you."

"Cooper, you go on over to the General and drink you a cup of coffee. Bring me one when you come back."

"Why, hellfire. I ain't done nothin, ain't actin like I have. If he knows somethin on me let him say so or shut the hell up."

"Mr. Oliver?"

"It ain't nothin to me what he does, he don't work for me. But the man I come to see you about totes this feller in his pocket like a handkerchief. He's bought and paid for and I don't like where the money come from."

"Why, hellfire. A string of Goddamn lies."

"I seen you drivin out to Hardin's place last spring. I seen him hand you money and you slip it down in your britches pocket and you and him had a regular get-together. The brotherly love was just drippin off yins both. After awhile you left and they flew to totin out whiskey like the house was afire. Time the rest of the laws got there that place was as bare of whiskey as a Baptist footwashin."

"You Goddamned lyin troublemaker," Cooper said, rising, his face fiery with rage. "Sheriff, he—"

"Go get that coffee, Cooper."

Cooper crossed to the door. He opened it and stood for a moment as if undecided what to do. He turned back toward the room. "Damn it, Sheriff," he said. Then he walked through the doorway and slammed the door behind him.

"If that story's true you ought to told me long before this, Mr. Oliver."

"It wadnt nothin to me. That's yins lookout. I just come about Hardin and if I'd wanted him to know my business I'd just cut out the middleman and deal with him direct."

Bellwether didn't say anything. He took out a pack of Luckies, tipped one out and smelled it reflectively, sat turning it in his fingers studying it as if he'd never come across another quite like it before.

"This other thing though, I ort to have come about it." Oliver was silent a moment and when he spoke his voice was charged with vehemence. "I knowed yins would work it around and blame it on me or I would've done brought it in. God knows I never wanted it on me. But I didn't want no more time and I didn't want that boy thinkin it was me killed his pa. I reckon I'd've brought it anyway if I hadn't knowed he'd kill Hardin and throw his own life away."

Bellwether had arisen. "Here, slow down a little," he said. He touched the old man's shoulder. "I can't follow just whatever it is we're talkin about here."

"Course I didn't care for him killin Hardin cept for messin his ownself up. I think a right smart of that boy."

"Who are we talkin about here, Mr. Oliver?"

"Hardin, Hardin," the old man said impatiently, he seemed to think Bellwether bereft of his senses. "What do you think? Somethin's got to be done about him. Somebody's goin to have to waste a cartridge on him and I wish I'd done it myself a long time ago. He's just usin up air other folks could put to good use."

"Mr. Oliver, have you got somethin I can use against Dallas Hardin or is this just some kind of general complaint?"

Oliver set the shoebox on Bellwether's desk. Bellwether crossed behind the desk and reseated himself in the chair and drew the box toward him, a hand on either end of it. He sat for a moment without opening it.

"There he is," the old man said. "He's yourn. I've done with it, I wash my hands of it. I'll let yins worry about it for awhile."

Bellwether opened the shoebox and folded the crinkly tissue aside. He sat staring down at all there was of Nathan Winer. His face didn't change. He folded the paper gently back over the skull and took up the cigarette he'd laid aside and lit it. He leaned back in the chair and laced his fingers across his stomach.

"Tell me a story, Mr. Oliver," he said.

"I don't mind buyin a pig in a poke," Hardin told Cooper. "If I figure I might ever have a use for the poke. But hell, you don't even know what sort of a poke it is you got."

"Well. It's more a feelin than anythin else. I know he told Bellwether somethin about you and I know it was somethin purty serious. He give Bellwether somethin he brought in a shoebox too but I don't know what it was."

"Say he did?"

"Yeah. And he wanted me out from there, got right feisty about it and got Bellwether down on my neck. He seen me and you together back in the spring and he seen me take money."

"Seen it or heard about it?"

"He says he seen it."

"Yeah. I guess he did at that. I wish I'd a killed that old son of a bitch long ago when I had the chance."

"Well, what are we goin to do?"

"Do? Hellfire. How do I know what to do if I don't even know what it is you're tellin me? All I know is my path and his has wound up a little close to suit me and I believe they're goin to cross a little later down the line."

*　　*　　*

Motormouth took a taxicab from Ackerman's Field to Winer's. Through the cab window he studied the cold silver fields and wondered what he'd tell Winer about Chicago. But he didn't guess it mattered. Chicago had been different than he'd expected, fastmoving folks who were caught up in their own lives and had no time for you. All the time he was there instead of becoming a memory the thought of the wife who had quit him grew stronger. The last week in Chicago while he waited for his last paycheck he stayed in his room and drank and he forgot to eat and finally he began to hear voices. Footsteps approached his door and a fist knocked, but when he opened the door there was no one there. He was sitting on the sofa when his mother said quite clearly, "Clifford." He did not even open his eyes. His mother was long dead and he knew it could not be her.

On the bus back he had dreamed of his wife but when he awoke he could not call the dream back any easier than he had been able to call the wife. Snowy little towns in Indiana and Missouri had rolled past and he thought he might get off at any one of them and the rest of his life would be different but he had not.

It was the middle of the night when he got there but he woke Winer anyway. He wanted to borrow the Chrysler. He said he only wanted it for a couple of hours. He told Winer that he had a good job in Chicago and that they had given him a paid vacation. Winer didn't believe paid vacations came that easily even in Chicago but he was halfasleep and for some reason he lent Hodges the car anyway. Perhaps it was because he had never come to think of it as his own, it had always been Motormouth's. More likely it was because of the curious aura Motormouth projected that Winer did not know what to make of. Watching Motormouth drive away Winer at the attic window was already having second thoughts but the taillights grew faint down the Mormon Springs road and were gone.

Motormouth drove to the house where his wife and Blalock lived but there was no one home. He thought he might drive off down to Hardin's and drink a beer while he waited but he was there three days before Hardin decided what to do with him.

These were days when Hardin felt set upon from every side and Motormouth's arrival did nothing to cheer him, it was just one more trial to bear, and he felt before this winter was through he would be either gone or as hard and wiry as the ironwoods that clung precariously on the bluffs above the pit.

A state prosecutor had appointed a man to evaluate such properties of Hardin's as had been destroyed by the Morgans and he had arrived and gone, a necktied man from Nashville wearing a blue suit and totting up figures in a notebook that he consigned to a briefcase. It didn't look promising to Hardin. The accountant had stood with his head cocked sideways studying the garden, or lack of one, then looked all about, uncertain of the spot, and just shook his head. The man hadn't seemed impressed with Hardin's claim or with Hardin either for that matter, Hardin guessed the man figured Nashville was far enough out of reach or that he planned to die home in bed.

Hardin went out to the pen and watched the stallion lope toward him to nuzzle the sugar cubes he palmed from his coat pocket and something old and unnameable stirred in him, almost an intimation of destiny: he felt an intense nostalgia for himself as he had surely been, he felt that if he could magically be back on Flint Creek where he had grown up, just him and the stallion, then he could attain a measure of peace. Suddenly he felt like an old man reeling down the years of his life and all he saw worth holding on to was the horse: in his vision he saw himself and the Morgan moving like phantoms through the unalterable geography of his youth and he could smell the brittle air of childhood winters, feel the hot weight of the sun, smell the sharecropped cotton holding back the sack he dragged across the sandy red earth. His father's voice bespoke him out of a dead time and to dispel it he drank from an uptilted halfpint then pocketed it and went back into the house to the fire.

When he went that afternoon to the honkytonk Motormouth was still there. He had been drinking steadily for all the time he'd been here and perhaps before and he seemed to have arrived at some bleak outpost of drunkenness, a strange, ravaged sobriety, and

Hardin thought he'd never seen a man so close to death, his own or somebody else's.

"You want him gone?" Jiminiz asked.

"No," Hardin said.

"He gets on my nerves. He slept in here again last night too, at that back booth. He was here when I came in this mornin."

"I know it."

"Well, I guess you know what you want. You're the man with the hairy balls."

"Yes I am," Hardin agreed.

With his mug of coffee he crossed to the table where Motormouth sat and seated himself across from him. He set the mug on the formica and lit a cigarette with the gold lighter and breathed out a shifting haze of smoke and watched Motormouth through it.

"I'm goin to give you some advice," he said after a time. "I'm goin to tell you one time and then I'll let you be, you can drink yourself to death or put a pistol to your head or just whatever suits you."

"Hell, I'm all right. I aim to drive off over to the old lady's here directly and talk to her."

"No you don't. You aim to set here and drink till your liver or pocketbook or my patience just gives completely out. That's what you aim to do."

"I'm goin to quit this old drinkin soon as I figure out what to do about my wife."

"You know what your trouble is, Hodges? You let people run over you. You don't stand up for yourself. Hell, no wonder Blalock's fuckin your old woman. I guess he figures it's all right with you. You ain't never had it out with him, have you?"

"Well, we ain't never talked about it right out."

"Talkin don't settle nothin. You got to let him know where you stand. You just lettin him railroad you, you supportin her all this time and him fuckin her and layin back laughin about it. Tellin it all over the poolhall you raped her."

"Yeah, he done that all right."

"And you let him. Where I come from we do things a little different. What it boils down to is the edge. You let him get a foot in the door and never said a word and let him get a edge over you. You got to get one of your own. You get a edge over him and you can lead him around like a lapdog."

Motormouth was looking more and more skeptical. "Hell, you know Blalock. How overbearin he is."

"Nobody ain't goin to just hand you a edge. Like everthing else in this world you got to take it. You take a feller sets hisself up like Blalock you got to kick the stilts out from under him. You'd be surprised how humble he gets. Back home we'd take a feller like that to see Patsy."

"You'd do what?"

"Take him to see Patsy, that's a thing we had back where I come from. You take a feller with his hatsize growed a size or two too big and tell him Patsy wants to see him real bad. Patsy's a gal got the hots for him, some gal he don't know but that's been eyein him. It ain't no trouble to get him to believe it, I never seen a feller yet wouldn't believe some gal had the hots for him.

"Then what we'd do is take him out to someplace don't nobody live and tell him to go to the door and Patsy'd be in there waitin on him. He'd be all primed and ready to go, he'd go struttin up to the door like a bantyrooster and we'd have a feller in there with a shotgun waitin on him. He'd jump out hollerin about folks leavin his daughter alone and cut down on him with that scattergun, course we'd have the shell doctored, all the shot out of it and nothin left but powder and cap, but the feller all set for Patsy didn't know that. He'd get right lightfooted. I've seen these old rawboned sawmill hands piss theirselves and run over halfgrown saplins and whatever else got in their way. Eyes rolled back in their heads. That gun wouldn't hurt em but I've sure seen em hurt theirselves.

"And you know what? They wasn't ever the same after that. They'd lost their edge. They couldn't go that extra fraction of a inch no more. Oh, they'd fly off ever now and then and act like they was goin to get rough but just when they started to push they'd look at you and know you was seein em runnin through the bushes with their hands throwed up. They just didn't have it no more."

He laid on the table before Motormouth a waxed shotgun shell. It was a deep burgundy red, its end shorn cleanly with a knife. He turned it toward Hodges to show that it was empty. Nothing in it save darkness. "I got a plan for you," he said. "You want my advice or not?"

Hodges didn't say anything.

Hardin arose. "Come on," he said. "I got a thing to show you in the office and I got a plan to lay out for you. I've had it workin in my head for awhile and I want to see what you think of it."

Motormouth got up and stood swaying unsteadily a moment, then he followed Hardin across the hardwood flooring toward the back room Hardin referred to as his office.

"Go on and I'll be in in a minute," Hardin said. He turned to the bar. Jiminiz was watching him with a face devoid of curiosity.

"See if you can get Blalock on the telephone," Hardin said. "Tell him I said come get his horses."

Jiminiz took a thin phonebook from beneath the bar and began to leaf through it, ceased, his forefinger tracing down the list of names.

"When he comes if I ain't in here you go out with Hodges and take four or five of these highbinders with you. Hodges got a trick he aims to play on Blalock."

Jiminiz nodded, he had the phone off the hook, dialing.

"What I like about you is you never ask me why," Hardin said. "Why is that, Jiminiz?"

"I'm afraid you'd tell me," Jiminiz said.

Bright in the winter sun the Morgan came up from the copse of trees when Hardin approached the wire. It paused a few feet from the wire fence and watched him, halfarrogant, halfinquisitive. Its breath steamed in the cold air. "You want to ride around awhile or see us a show here directly?" he asked the horse. He lit a cigarette and returned the lighter to his pocket, feeling as he did so the empty cartridge he had palmed. He withdrew the shell and studied it a moment, wondering where he had heard the story he had told Hodges or even if he had heard it at all, if it was just some tale his mind had told them both. He tossed the shell into the sere weeds and stood leaning against the gate smoking. "All right, we'll ride then," he said. "We'll go in a minute. We waitin on a truck right now."

There was less time than he expected between the cessation of the truck motor and the shot. There was a man's voice and a shout and he was swinging into the saddle when the explosion came. When it did a tremor coursed through the horse's withers and its steel shoes did a quick little dance on the frozen ground. He kicked its ribs and they went through the gate toward the branch. They crossed the stream and went up the steep slope, the horse laboring on the unsure limestone footing, faster then through the stony sedgefield.

He did not look back until they were on the ridge and when he did he could see the tableau of men gathered about the truck and the winding chert road with the Chrysler fleeing down it in silence. He watched it out of sight. The men looked like animated miniatures, unreal, against the muted winter landscape they milled and moved without purpose about one of their number who had fallen and lay unmoving, a puppet unstrung perhaps, or one who had fled at last the exhortations of a mad puppeteer.

The bentlegged waitress watched Winer across the tall vase of celluloid flowers, across the worn tile of the Snowwhite Cafe, where he sat near the plateglass window watching the street, occasionally sipping from his coffeecup, a menu face up but unread before him. There was a curious air of indecision about her but after a time she seemed to make up her mind. She took up her cigarette from the ashtray and crossed the room.

"What on earth happened to your face? You don't even look like yourself."

Winer looked up at her approach then back toward where the street tended away into darkness near the railroad tracks. "I got in a fight," he said. "Have you seen Buttcut Chessor around?"

"No I ain't and I ain't likely to. He's barred from here. He come in here the other night and started a fight and they like to tore the place apart. I had him barred."

"What was the fight about?"

"Oh, he was just mad. Ollie Simmons fired him from the sawmill. He'd been cuttin logs and he got into it with the sawyer over somethin. Then he cut a beetree and it was solid at the top and the bottom, the log was, and he plugged the hole in it and carried it to the mill with the other logs. When the sawyer sawed it open they said the bees just boiled out and they like to stung him to death. They fired him."

"I guess he's down at the poolhall then."

"I wouldn't know. He beat up Ollie and two that tried to stop it and I called the law. They locked him up but I think he's out. Why you want to waste your time on a crazy thing like him?"

"I just wondered where he was."

"Wherever he is he ain't worth botherin about. That other buddy of yours is long gone, ain't he? Motormouth?"

"So they say."

"Reckon he really killed that Blalock feller? I heard Hardin had it done."

"I don't know. All I know is Blalock's dead and Motormouth's gone in my car."

"You look lonesome tonight."

"I don't reckon."

"Say you don't reckon? Well, are you lonesome or ain't you?"

"I'm not lonesome," Winer said.

"You may be later on," she said enigmatically.

Buttcut studied Winer's face by the harsh white glare of the poolroom. "Lord God, son," he said. "Somebody sure took a strong dislike to your face."

"That's what they keep telling me. I got into it with that Mexican that started working down at Hardin's."

"Did he whip you?"

"Right down to the ground and then into it."

"How big is he?"

Winer studied him. "About your size," he said.

"Well, it ain't no matter for you then. You ought to know better. I heard there was a killin down there."

"I reckon. Motormouth was supposed to have shot Blalock, but I don't know. He came by my house like a bat out of hell and I had a sinking feeling when my car went by. I got a good look at his face and he didn't look like a man who planned on coming back."

"He's crazy but I didn't think he had the nerve to kill nobody."

Winer drank from his Coke and studied the pool game in progress. Roy Pace had found a sucker. Roy was paralyzed from the waist down and went in a wheelchair. His head was oversized and pumpkinshaped and there was a peculiar mongoloid cast to his face but he had won a small fortune off traveling salesmen who put great stock in appearances. As Winer watched he wheeled the chair smoothly to the end of the table. He shot from an awkwardlooking open bridge and the tip of his cue trembled with histrionic nervousness but he ran all the small balls then the eight and shook his huge head as if wonderstruck at such beginner's luck. The sucker shook his head too. "Rack," he called.

"I don't no more believe he killed Blalock than nothing. I believe they set him up somehow."

"I don't know. He was crazy about his old lady and she was livin with Blalock."

"Hey, you want to go over to the General awhile?"

"I don't think so."

Buttcut gestured with his head toward the restroom. "I got a bottle in there. You want a little drink of who shot John?"

"I reckon not."

"Hell, you don't want to do nothin. You about as much fun as a Pentecostal preacher. What are you even doin in here?"

"To tell the truth I just couldn't stay around the house any longer. The walls had started talking to me. I figured I'd leave before I started answering them back."

They stood for a time before the Strand Theater, waiting for the show to let out, Buttcut's car parked at the curb should there be ladies needing escorts home or elsewhere. Such ladies seemed few and far between. Overalled farmers with stoic broadshouldered wives. Stairstep children with stunnedlooking eyes still dreamy with Technicolor visions. Country boys fresh off the farm with manure on their brogans and placid, oxenlike looks on their faces.

"Goddamn it," Buttcut said. "I never seen such a crop of hairyankled men in my life. You'd think with a war bein fought a man might stumble up on a little stray pussy just ever now and then. But hell no."

Two or three people turned to stare at him but his size and his stance stayed them from comment. Winer grasped his arm.

"Hell, let's go. We'll find some women somewhere else."

"Do you still not want to go to the General?"

"No." Winer grinned. "We might go down to the Snowwhite."

"I can't go down there. They barred me. Said they'd get a peace warrant and lock me up if I went back."

"I heard you cut a beetree."

"That lopsided cunt had to call the law. She's pissed cause I won't go with her. She's the same as sicced Ollie Simmons on me. Played up to him and he was goin to kick my ass. That's the last time that'll cross his mind. I had him down and he was goin, 'Let me up, I've had enough.' I said, 'The hell you say. I'm doin this asswhippin. I'll let you know when you've had enough.'"

"I guess we could go back to the poolhall."

"We won't find no women there. Let's go down to Hardin's."

"I'm a slow study but I do learn."

They got back in the car. "I need a drink anyway," Buttcut said. "I hide my bottle in the restroom. That way if they pick me up they won't find no bottle on me. They can get me for a public drunk but they can't prove possession."

"What's the difference?"

"About forty dollars."

The long black Packard sat parked before the poolhall like a waiting limousine. Winer halted a moment looking at it then after a moment followed Buttcut into the glare of light. There were three of them: the girl demure in a white dress sitting at a scarred red table with a fat man in a blue gabardine suit. He was drinking whiskey from a bottle in a brown paper bag and chasing it with beer and the girl was taking delicate sips of Coke through a straw. When she saw Winer her eyes for a moment widened in shock, then she lowered them and fell into a study of her blurred reflection in the worn formica. Winer looked away and studied the fat man's back, the shape of the wallet outlined through trousers too tight across the hips.

Jiminiz was shooting nineball with Roy Pace. He glanced once at Winer with the corners of his eyes widening, then the eyes flicked away. There was no recognition in his face. He chalked his cue and leaned to the green felt to shoot.

"Let's get out of here."

"Hell, no. Ain't this a public place? That's him, ain't it?"

"That's him. How'd you know?"

"Well, I didn't expect two Mexicans that size in Ackerman's Field. I thought you said he was big. That son of a bitch is enormous. Was you fightin over Rose there?"

"That's what it started about."

Buttcut studied her serene profile across the length of the bar. "I can't say I blame you. She batted them long eyelashes a time or two at me I'd go a round myself. Who's that Goddamn salesman or whatever with her?"

"I don't know."

"I seen her a time or two in here with different fellers. Hardin was usually with her. Say, you look kindly down in the mouth, son. How about a little drink?"

"Why not. I guess I might as well."

"I'll go in first and get me one and leave it settin out for you."

Buttcut was only in the restroom for a moment. He kicked the door open and it slammed against the block wall. He came out gagging and spitting and wiping his mouth on a sleeve. Nobody seemed to notice save Winer. Buttcut picked up Roy Pace's beer and turned it up and drank and rinsed his mouth and spat. He stood studying such latenight inhabitants as the poolroom held with a black and malignant eye.

"Who's the son of a bitch that drunk my whiskey and then pissed in the bottle?"

No one answered. Jiminiz leaned and shot gently, the cueball kissing off the three and sinking the four in the corner pocket. He chalked his cue and walked around the table to where the cueball had come to rest near the wall.

"Did you piss in my whiskey?"

Jiminiz studied him with a cold and distant contempt. "No, I didn't," he said.

"Leave this man alone, Chessor," Pace said. "Let him play pool. I'm winnin me a Florida vacation."

"You done it, Goddamn you," Chessor told Pace. "You stillborn chickenfucker. It's just the childish kind of meanness you'd think was funny. If I knowed for sure it was you I'd slap you even sillier than you look."

"It wasn't me, Buttcut, honest." Pace was all bland innocence.

"Well, it was somebody," Buttcut said. "And me and him is goin around and around just here in a minute."

"You hold it down back there," the barkeep called. "Any goin around in here and I'm goin to be on that phone to the law."

Buttcut paused momentarily. "Somebody pissed in my whiskey," he said sullenly.

"Well, it wasn't me," the barkeep said. "It's against the law to even have whiskey in here if you didn't but know it."

"Tell that to the feller with the paper sack," Buttcut said. "But I guess he got permission from Hardin."

The fat man looked up at Buttcut briefly then quickly away. The girl seemed not to have heard but Jiminiz froze in midstroke for a second. Then he completed his shot.

Buttcut ordered a beer and sat on the bench beside Winer. They sat silently watching the game progress. Buttcut sipped from the beer then gave it to Winer and ordered another. He seemed possessed by a dull, malevolent anger. Winer finished the beer and drank another, studying the fat man across the length of the room. Every time the man looked up Winer would be watching, and he glanced up often as if he could feel the weight of Winer's eyes. Roy Pace and Jiminiz seemed almost drunk. Jiminiz was still losing. The fat man looked at his wristwatch a time or two and then he came and said something to Jiminiz but Jiminiz didn't reply or acknowledge his voice.

Finally Buttcut spoke. "You ain't got a hair on your ass if you don't go talk to her," he said. "You got to take up for yourself. You let these sons of bitches run over you and it'll be somebody runnin over you all your life."

"I tried that. It didn't work so well."

"Hellfire. You talked to Hardin. Hardin ain't even here. Don't worry about his guard dog. I got him covered."

"It's my fight, Buttcut, not yours."

Buttcut shrugged. "I aim to try him sooner or later anyway. You might as well get a little somethin out of it."

Winer went with his amber bottle to her table. "Hello, Briar Rose," he said.

"Do you know this young man?" the fat man asked. When she made no reply he turned to Winer. "All these other tables are un-occupied," he said. "Perhaps you'd care to sit somewheres else."

Winer drank beer. The bitter taste of hops at the back of his mouth. "No," he said. "I like it here all right."

The fat man had a hand on Rose's arm. "Well, we'll leave it to you," he said.

"I've got to talk to you," Winer told her.

She was shaking her head. "I don't want to move," she told the man. She looked as if she might cry.

The fat man was studying her with calm, level eyes. "What's goin on here?" he asked. "Is my money not good enough for you or what?"

She was watching Winer but Winer was lost in the deep waters of her eyes, struggling against the seaweed strangling him. "Go away, Nathan," she said.

"Then you go with me."

"I can't. You know I can't."

"It's easy. All you have to do is put one foot in front of the other."

"I can't." She leaned and touched his face. Her forefinger traced the length of a cut. She was crying.

The man turned to Winer in disgust. "I've paid her good money," he said. "Or paid it to Hardin. And I aim to get the benefit of it. Now, I don't know who you are or what your status is but I suggest you get your ass out of here."

Buttcut had come up silent as a cat. He leaned across the table. "Are you havin words with this young feller here?" His breath was fiery with splo whiskey.

The man turned. "None that concern you."

"Funny. I was settin way back on that bench over there and I thought I heard you say somethin about him gettin his ass out of here. I reckon you got the deed to this place ridin in your shirt pocket?"

The man didn't say anything.

"Did I hear that or not?"

"I don't see how it concerns you."

"I'll tell you how it concerns me. You got the look about you of somebody that would drink a man's whiskey then piss in the bottle and put the lid back on and go off somewheres and snigger about it."

The fat man just rolled his eyes upward toward the watermarked ceiling as if he'd fallen among fools and looked resigned.

"Ain't you?" Buttcut persisted.

"I don't know," the fat man finally said.

"You keep studyin on it. You keep wonderin if you and that Mexican there can do it but you better walk mighty soft around me. You try me and you'll go up like a celluloid cat in hell."

Winer arose. "It's not worth fightin about," he said. "If she wants him she can have him. We'll go somewhere else."

"Goddamn it, there's not anywhere else. And nobody's runnin me anywhere."

"Then you all can have it," Winer said. He turned toward Rose's pale face. "I'm leavin. Are you goin with me or stayin with these folks?"

The girl arose, took her purse from the table. "I'm sorry," she told the fat man.

The fat man grasped her arm. "The hell you are. I got a forty-acre farm tied up in you already."

The man in the blue suit was sitting glaring into the girl's face and Winer was standing over them. Without even knowing he was going to Winer hit the man in the face as hard as he could. The man grunted and a mist of blood sprayed down his shirtfront and he went over backward clawing the air. Winer turned rubbing his knuckles to see the green swinging door explode inward and Jiminiz come through it with his poolcue poised like a baseball bat and to see Buttcut fell man and cuestick with a chair. "They Lord God," the barkeep cried. Jiminiz bounced off the dopebox and lit rolling and fetched up against the barchairs routing scrambling drinkers and then he was on his knees trying to get his fingers into his brass knuckles. He had them almost on when Buttcut kicked him in the head. The knucks rattled on the dirty tile. Buttcut kicked them away viciously and stood waiting with his fist cocked. "You hell on boys," he said. "Let's see how you do with a man."

Jiminiz was lying against the bar. His mouth was shattered and bleeding. If he had any breath he didn't waste it. He got up warily ducking outside the perimeter of Buttcut's arms and flicked his long black hair out of his eyes with an abrupt and arrogant movement of his head. He raised his left fist for a guard and came back in. His eyes were expressionless as black glass. He came boring into

Buttcut's clumsy, flatfooted stance with his head ducked and he swatted away Buttcut's right and knocked him into the pinball machine. Buttcut wouldn't fall. He just shook his head in a mildly annoyed sort of way as if flies were bothering him and took a halfstep forward and hit Jiminiz in the face.

The fat man was on his hands and knees trying to get his handkerchief out. Winer was standing over him to see if he tried to help Jiminiz but this was an idea that seemed not to have occurred to him. "A doctor," he said, looking at his bloody hands. "A doctor."

There wasn't any doctor. There was just the frantic barkeep on the phone and a door that looked miles away and the jukebox singing, I have no one to love me except the sailor on the deep blue sea.

When the sirens began Winer was trying to haul Buttcut off Jiminiz. Buttcut was hitting him in the face. "The law's coming," Winer said.

"I'll learn you," Buttcut said. "Now beg me to quit." Jiminiz wouldn't beg.

Jiminiz said, "Fuck you," through broken teeth.

The law came through the door and didn't waste any time. Cooper hit Buttcut alongside the head with a slapstick and a pair of highway patrolmen hauled Winer up between them and started for the door. The girl would stay with him. She swung onto his arm. A young hatchetfaced patrolman named Steele turned from Winer momentarily to disengage her, his face turned in profile to Winer was red and freckled, a sharp, intent face. The expression was that of someone immersed in his work, a surgeon perhaps, removing some unwanted growth. It was a curious electric moment Winer would always remember, the peculiar birdlike feel of her hand clutching his arm and Steele peeling back one talon at a time, the grip finally lessening. When he struck Steele in the jaw the other patrolman blackjacked Winer and he dropped as if his knees had turned to water.

He sat groggily on the floor. The world darkened then lightened. Intercut with still photographs of the girl's pale face were random images like sequences in a film improperly spliced: Buttcut holding Cooper aloft by the ankles and upside down and Cooper flailing wildly with the slapstick and cursing Buttcut's knees. Then Buttcut dropped him and kicked him in the side and stepped across his body into the waiting arms of the highway patrolmen and Winer could hear their labored breathing and after awhile Steele say, "He says he'll come peaceable if we let him ride in the front."

"Let the big motherfucker drive for all of me," Cooper said. "I believe he's tore somethin aloose inside of me."

The cold air of black night, cold frost on the chrome doortrim. The Packard waiting like a hearse. A hard hand in his back and his cheek on the icy concrete, stars spinning out faint and fainter above the flaring streetlamps. So far, so far.

Then Buttcut's legs drawing back, Winer's eyes watching just that, fascinated, the knees coming up in slow motion, the denim tightening over them until you thought it would split, Cooper half-turning, his mouth opening, big brogans kicking out and the windshield exploding in a slow drift of safety glass and the onrush of icy air and the steering wheel clocking as the car slewed against the curb.

Bellwether bore the sad tidings to Oliver and sat with his feet cocked on the hearth while the old man digested them in silence save the loud tick of a clock measuring out the moments.

"I asked him was there anybody he wanted let know," Bellwether said. "He first said no, then he named you."

"What's he charged with?"

"Disorderly conduct and assault."

"What about that Chessor boy?"

"Them two plus public drunkenness. Resistin arrest and assault with intent to commit murder. Destruction of private property, destruction of city property."

"They Lord God."

"There may be a few more by now. The returns are still comin in."

"And you say he whupped that Mexcan feller?"

"I'd say so. He had to have his jaw wired together and he's got a mouthful of busted-up teeth. He just got generally stove up."

"What do you reckon Chessor'll get out of it?"

"He's good for a eleven-twenty-nine anyway."

The old man arose, turned his back to the heat from the stove. "I'll tell you what I'm goin to do," he said. "When his bond is set I aim to go it. I aim to stand good for it, then I'm goin to tell him to ease hisself across the stateline and be gone. What do you think of that?"

"I think you'll be out some money."

"In my time I've spent more and got less out of it." Oliver opened the stovelid and spat into the fire. Flickering flames lacquered his brown face with orange. "You ever get anything back on that skeleton?"

"Skull," Bellwether said. "I was comin to that. Well. It was Winer all right."

"We knowed that. Have you told that boy yet?"

"No. I've got to though. It's not somethin I'm lookin forward to."

"I wish you'd hold up a day or two. He'll kill Dallas Hardin and turn twenty-one in Brushy Mountain state pen."

"No, he won't. There's no proof Hardin even shot him, Mr. Oliver."

"Why, shitfire. You know as well as I'm settin here that Hardin shot him."

"Knowin ain't provin. I can know all day long but what a jury's goin to want to know is how I know."

"Young Winer ain't that picky," Oliver said.

After Bellwether had gone Oliver went to bed but he could not sleep. He lay in the darkness staring at the unseen ceiling. Over the past few days a plan had presented itself for his consideration, little by little, like an image forming on a photographic plate. If I got to do it then this is the only time, he thought. The boy don't know yet and he's out of the way in jail. I won't get this kind of a shot at it again. God knows somebody's got to do it. And it looks like it's goin to have to be me.

William Tell Oliver went three times to the sheriff's office before he caught Cooper there with Bellwether. He pushed the door open a little way and Bellwether was arranging papers in a drawer and Cooper was turning at the noise the door made opening with a cup of coffee in his hand. Cooper looked ill used. His face was battered and swollen and he moved with the caution of a man aware of the fragility of each internal organ.

"Lord God," Oliver said. "What happened to you?"

Cooper just turned away, a sneer deepening further the asymmetry of his discolored face.

Oliver addressed Bellwether. "I paid that boy's fine," he said. "But the judge is keepin him till tomorrow mornin anyhow. They ain't even set bond. They still studyin about it."

"Well. That's between you and the judge, Mr. Oliver. I don't have anything to do with that end of it."

"I know. That ain't what I come about." He leaned on the desk, his hands cupping the rim and supporting his weight. The hands looked dark and gnarled and bewenned and they looked like something carved with infinite patience from knotty walnut.

"I figured when I brought that thing in yins would scout around a little and maybe find somethin out about it. But I reckon not. Yins send it off to Nashville and let em take pictures of it or whatever and doctors look at it through microscopes. And it ten year out of the ground it ort to've been in and no words said over it and no end in sight. Well, I wanted to stay out of it all I could but I see I can't. If yins can't find the straight of it then, I'll have to tell you the rest of it."

Bellwether's eyes were halfclosed and he wore a patient, bemused look. He rested a jaw on a cupped palm. "All right, Mr. Oliver," he said. "Pull you up a chair and drop the other shoe. You been settin with it drawed back long enough."

They sat in the squadcar. Small, cold wind out of the north, a rattle of frozen trees. All was dark save the random orange pulse of Cooper's cigarette, then Hardin's gold lighter flared, his broken profile twinned by the glass beyond it, then darkness again and the sudden rasp of his voice.

"What then?"

"Then he said about dark both of you got into a Diamond-T truck. Said his goats was out and he was huntin em up that branchrun and kindly keepin out of sight in the brush, listening for their bells. Said he was lookin right at that truck when all at once the inside of it just lit up yeller and he heard a boom and directly you got out draggin Winer toward where that big old pit of a thing is."

Cooper could see Hardin's vague dark outline. When Hardin grinned he could see his teeth. "That old son of a bitch," he said. "That sweet old son of a bitch." There was something akin to admiration in his voice as if upon coming across his own traits encoded idiosyncratically in others he could not help but feel kindly toward their possessors. "Course you know it's all a pack of lies."

"Course," Cooper said automatically.

"You think that old man's been settin on a piece of information like that for ten years? The shit he has. He'd a done had me in the pen or a pauper, one or the other. Either that or the worms would've finished up with him a long time ago."

"Well, I knowed all along he was lyin."

"Did you? Somehow I doubt it, Cooper. What you know is what you heard last. When you hear Oliver you know that and then when I talk that's what you know."

Cooper didn't say anything for a moment as if he were marshalling his forces. "I know one thing," he said. "I know Bellwether'll be after Humphries till he issues a warrant first thing Monday mornin and he'll be on your doorstep before the ink's good dry on it."

"Say it comes to trial, Cooper. Just supposin I wasn't able to prove I was innocent and it all boiled down to my word agin his. What do you think would happen?"

"Well." Cooper seemed flattered that his judgment was sought, paused to give it added weight. "I'll tell you just what I think. That old man has lived here in this county all his life and you won't find a man he lied to. He's been rough in his day and had his ups and downs but he'd have to have a awful good reason to come up with a tale like that."

"He's got it too. That Goddamn Winer boy smartin off right and left. Whoever did kill old man Winer ort to've got to him before he went to seed." He fell silent, studying the contents of his wallet. "I thought Jiminiz could teach him a lesson but I see I misplaced my trust. Next time it'll be just me and him one on each end of a gunbarrel and he won't get off so light."

"What do you want me to do?"

"Get me Dr. Sulhaney. Go down to Clifton tonight and tell him I got to see him tomorrow. Not no telephone, tell him I said come. I'll put that old son of a bitch so far back in the crazyhouse he'll wish he'd a stuck to goats and ginseng."

"Sulhaney won't come cheap."

"He never did. Doctors ain't cheap, just deputy sheriffs. Get me that old whiteheaded lawyer Hull too. He looks like a damn senator or a preacher or somethin."

Cooper was watching the pocketbook with the hypnotic eye of a serpent studying a bird. "Hull ain't cheap neither," he said. "It'll cost you a arm and a leg."

"I can always grow another one," Hardin said expansively. "I've done it before."

Bitter cold and timber frozen to the heart kept Simmons's log crew from the woods and drove them to the warmth of Sam Long's coalstove, clustered before the hearth amongst ancient Coke-crate idlers. Beyond the redlettered LONG's on the fogged windows the wind sang hard pellets of hominy snow along the sidewalks, harried children from their dimestore visions, Christmas enshrined out of reach beneath plateglass.

As it was wont to do, the conversation of these malingerers had started with Dallas Hardin and it had remained there.

"All right, say he done it," Sam Long said. "I don't know if he did or he didn't but say he did. You think he'll get day one out of it? Why, hell no. They can't prove he had a thing in the world to do with it."

"Who told it?"

"Hell, everbody's tellin it. You think you can keep a thing like that quiet? The only way's to find it and squirrel it away the way they say old man Oliver did. I don't know who told it first. Teed Niten's wife works in the registrar's office and she said that whole courthouse bunch is talkin about it."

"Well, you're right about one thing," Simmons said. "He won't do no time. But reckon it's Winer sure enough?"

"That's what the government dentist records said. He was World War I. It was Winer all right. Winer with a hole in his skull the size of a number three washtub."

"You remember when Hardin was supposed to've shot old man Wildman? Shot him in the road the way you would a dog and claimed self-defense. Wildman's mama, she seen it but Lord, she was old, must've been ninety if she was a day. Fore it was over Hardin got a doctor to swear she was crazy and had drawed it all up in her head. Hardin got her committed to Boliver and I believe she died there in 1935."

"Yeah," a man named Pope said. "Hardin went to Ratcliff and tried to get him to sign some papers but Ratcliff just laughed at him. Charged him five dollars for a consultation and told him to go to hell. Two or three mornins later Ratcliff went up the steps to open his office and here was a big brown poke with the top rolled down. He thought at first it was okry or stringbeans or somethin of that sort, it was summer and folks used to pay him with garden stuff or just whatever they had. Then that poke moved. Ratcliff hit it with his walkin stick and out come this big old velvettail rattlesnake. He said he like to had a stroke right there. That's what he said but he was able to kill it with his stick and drive to Mormon Springs and throw it on Hardin's porch. That's what got me about it. Why didn't Hardin kill him or burn him out? Less he just always knowed who he had his bluff in with and who he didn't."

"Bluff, hell," Long said. "Ask Nathan Winer about his bluff. Senior or junior."

"That boy's peculiar," Simmons said. "Acts like he's about half-smart."

"That boy's all right," Long said. "If I was Hardin I'd be dreadin him worse than anybody else. Hardin'll have to kill him to stop him."

Amidst the longforsaken oddments of scrapiron Oliver found a thin length of steel with two screwholes that when he hacksawed it aligned themselves with the jambs of the front door. He drove nails through the holes across the closed door and then went into the kitchen.

Figuring Hardin for a backdoor man, he set the leatherbottomed ladderback perpendicular to and about six feet inside the kitchen door. He backed off a time or two and eyed it from different angles, repositioned it slightly to his liking. He toenailed the chair to the kitchen floor with eightpenny nails and lashed the Browning shotgun to the back of the chair with baling wire, twisting out the slack with pliers and clipping the excess neatly and feeling to see was the gun tied securely. He looped a slipknot of staging around the trigger and down through the rungs of the chair and across the worn linoleum to the door and he stood for a time studying it. It presented a complication. The door opened inward. He thought about it then pushed the door all the way inward and tied the staging to the screen door. He opened the door, closed it, took up slack in his line, and reknotted the staging. This time there was a dry click when the door was halfopen. Oliver closed the door and recocked the gun and stood studying it. He packed his pipe and lit it with a kitchen match and went outside and came through the kitchen door.

He had thought so. When the hammer fell he was standing aside to come through the opening the way a man comes through a door and the blast might have torn an arm off but Oliver was not hunting arms this night. He went back and retightened the staging once more and this time the click came when the door was open only an inch or so and a man would be fully in front of it. He nodded thoughtfully to himself. It was a neat, workmanlike job.

Oliver was a man of many cautions so he toenailed each window save one to the ledge so that the kitchen door would be the only access. He had an old hammerless Smith and Wesson revolver and he checked the load and slid it down into a jumper pocket and filled a quart fruitjar with coffee. He took down a cardboard box emblazoned with faded flying ducks and took out one of the waxed red cylinders and loaded the gun and cocked it. He raised the kitchen window and set out the hammer and the nails and coffee and as an afterthought a folded blanket and with some difficulty maneuvered himself outside. He nailed the window closed and took up the coffee and blanket and went on to the barn.

Dark was falling and a cold wind out of the north arose but it was warm wrapped in the blanket and bundled down into the hay. He was hoping for a light night, for he'd have to keep watch on the door. The only visitor he expected was Hardin, for he had seen to it that Winer was still in jail, but still he wanted a good view of the back door and plenty of time to warn folks wandering toward his kitchen.

It grew darker still and the world blurred and vanished in blue murk, then a cold December moon cradled up out of the apple orchard and hung like a corpse candle over a haunted wood.

It'll have to be tonight, he thought. Tonight is all we've got, me and Hardin. Still, I'll be here till two or three o'clock in the mornin.

Infrequent cars passed, then about eight or nine o'clock the traffic picked up and he lay watching the Saturday-night revelers and sipping the now cold coffee and wondering what these folks would think if they knew they were calling on a dead man. He stared at the dark rectangle of screendoor in the cold white moonlight and it held for him a peculiar fascination. It looked like the back door to hell.

The curious altered time of three o'clock in the morning. Pearl sat watching Hardin and the girl. Hardin was as near drunk as he ever seemed to get and he kept feeding the girl whiskey and Coke from his glass. She was watching with a sense of apprehension, a sense of things slipping away from her. Hardin leaned to the girl's ear and whispered something low and then he laughed softly to himself and cupped her breast with a palm. The girl shook her head from side to side. She was tugging at Hardin's hand. "Quit it," she said. Hardin released her breast. He put both elbows on the scarred tabletop and studied the girl's face with an almost clinical detachment. Her eyes looked drowsy and vague, her face had a slack, sleeprobbed look.

Finally Pearl said, "That girl ain't used to drinkin."

"Then it's high time she learned."

"What else you been teachin her? To be a whore?"

"From what I hear she ort to be givin me lessons."

"I won't have you messin her up no worse than what you already have."

"Say you won't? Live half your life with your legs spread and come on to me like a preacher? Shit. What you want and what you get don't always make a set," Hardin said. "But it's late and I had a hard night and more of one still to go and I don't need you yammerin at me like a Goddamned watchdog. And you a fine one to talk about drinkin. Stumblin around like a fat sow on sourmash."

There was a strange anticipatory air about Hardin, a mood she had come to recognize down through the years, though she had never understood or articulated it, as if he dwelt from time to time in some world where everything was heightened, the sounds clearer, the colors brighter and richer, as if he moved briefly through a world of hallucinatory marvels. As if he were never fully alive save when he was nearing the edge.

A moment of insight touched her. "You aim to kill old man Oliver and burn him out, don't you? I heard some of what that law said."

"You hear ever damn thing that ain't nothin to you," Hardin said. "Slippin and spyin around. I think by God you're goin crazy, and I just may have to put you away too. You gettin a little loose at the lip to suit me. Sullin up and poutin around like your little feelins is hurt. Givin away enough whiskey to float a Goddamn motorboat. If you'd just get your ass in bed it'd suit me fine."

He turned abruptly toward the girl, seeming by the mere motion of his head to deny Pearl's very existence. He put his hand on the girl's left breast.

"You wantin to kill him. You look forward to it."

Hardin didn't reply. His yellow eyes were halfclosed. He stroked Amber Rose's breast, massaged it gently with a slow, circular motion of his palm. She raised her eyes to his but she didn't resist. Hardin's motions were slow and deliberate, like motions seen underwater. Her face looked young and very pretty and suddenly Hardin saw past the young woman's face to the features of the child he had seen long ago throwing rocks at Thomas Hovington's chickens and he thought for a moment on the curious circuitry of things but he did not dwell on it.

"What's the matter with her? What did you give her?"

"I ain't give her nothin yet but I may here in a minute if I can get your fat ass out of the room long enough."

"You can get it further than that," Pearl said. "I've stood all I can stand. It's took me long enough but I've got a bait of you. I'm buyin me a bus ticket as long as my arm and I'm ridin till it's used up and that's where I'm gettin off. And I'm takin Rose with me."

"The hell you are."

"She's my daughter and I'm takin her."

"Daughter, hell. Sows don't have daughters. They have pigs and them pigs grow up to be other sows."

"I always done what you said no matter how dirty you done me. All I ever asked was you to leave Rose alone. You promised me you would."

"Then I guess I lied," Hardin said. He arose, stood for a moment leaning unsteadily against the table. He looked at the gold wristwatch. "But I reckon she'll keep. I got things to do."

He crossed the room and went through the bedroom door. When he came back he was carrying the rifle slung under his arm and he went out into the night.

About what he guessed was four o'clock in the morning Oliver saw the Packard go up the road toward town and he arose in confusion. He'd expected Hardin on foot, but there was no mistaking the Packard's taillights. He was waiting for it to stop but it did not stop. He was still watching the fleeing taillights when the shotgun fired and he leapt and spilled cold coffee down his shirtfront but he didn't feel it. He felt a surging of adrenaline sing in his blood and there was a metallic taste like canker in the back of his mouth. He went scrambling awkwardly down the ladder.

Oliver came up the steps to the back porch in a sort of stumbling lope. His breath was coming hard and ragged. There was an enormous hole in the screendoor. The center brace, shotriddled, hung by a shard of screen wire. He looked all about the porch, puzzled. What the hell now, he thought. Could he have made it in before the gun went off? No way in hell, he told himself. He felt a momentary stab of superstitious fear: Was the son of a bitch real, was he flesh and blood? All there was beyond the exploded screen was darkness.

Inside he struck a match on his thumbnail, unglobed the lamp, conscious of the smell of cordite, of other smells, a coarse odor of raw whiskey, an almost animal smell of perspiration, then the room filled up with yellow coaloil-smelling light. At length Oliver turned.

Hardin was hunkered against the far wall. He had the 30-30 cradled between his knees, barrel drawn up against his chest. The yellow goat's eyes were not blank, the old man saw, still holding the lampglobe, but worse than blank, like nothing, like holes poked in a mockup face through which you could catch glimpses of a sere and lifeless yellow landscape.

"I seen that done once before," Hardin said. "All the same you're a slick old bastard. But a man comes up on a house with the front door barred and the windows nailed shut it kindly gives him a peculiar feelin when he sees the back door standin wide open. And a feller goes through another man's door straight on in the middle of the night is tryin to get in good with the undertaker."

"How'd you—"

"I poked it back with a stick and it's a damn good thing I did. What you ort to've done was to've stretched you a string across the door about ankle high and tied it to the trigger. That way I'd've pushed the door back with a stick then eased on in thinkin I had it made and you'd've had kindly an unpleasant surprise for me. As it is you've kindly shit your nest, ain't you?"

Oliver's mouth tasted dry. "What I ort to have done was to laid out in the brush and shot you in the back a long time ago."

Hardin got up. "Well, you didn't," he said. He sounded amused, almost jovial, as if his nearness to death had made him more alive. "You didn't and you won't because your ass is mine now. You tried to kill me and it didn't come off and the way I see it that's the first lick. The next one's mine. That the way it looks to you?"

"The first lick come a long time ago."

"This is between me and you."

"No. The truth is it ain't. At one time it might've been but you can't let well enough alone. You have to try to drag that boy into the same river of shit you swim in and when he won't you hire him halfkilled. You can't even do it yourself."

"Well, you're right about one thing. A man wants somethin done he has to do it hisself. And that's why you see me here in the flesh."

Oliver globed the lamp and the room brightened perceptibly. He could feel the reassuring weight of the pistol dragging down his jumper pocket and he shifted his balance and turned that side slightly away from Hardin toward the window.

"I reckon you get to do the talkin," he said. "You got all the high cards."

"Yes I have," Hardin agreed. "And I'm about to lay out my hand. I been slackin off, easin up, givin all you cocksuckers too much rope. I ort to've killed young Winer instead of tryin to teach him a lesson. But once a fool ain't always a fool. I'll put him where his daddy sleeps when I finish with you."

He turned a wrist toward better light, glanced at the time. "I'm just tryin to figure if I got to do this quick or I got time to play with you a little. You been needlin me pretty steady here lately and I'd like to sort of even the score. But I see I ain't. I reckon I'll have to content myself with this."

He abruptly crossed the floor in two or three strides and hit Oliver savagely alongside the neck with his fist. The old man went sideways in crazy, teetering steps, then his knees unhinged and he fell against the wall and slid down it. Bitter hot bile rose in his throat and he thought for a moment he was going to vomit but he fought it down. He had fallen on the gun and his hip hurt but there was an almost exquisite pleasure to this pain.

Hardin had approached and stood spraddlelegged over him. "You all right?" he asked with mock concern.

"I've done somethin to my hip," the old man said thickly. "I may have broke it."

"Likely you have," Hardin agreed. "A old man's bones is brickle. I'll fix you up with Dr. Feelgood here directly and you won't feel a thing."

Oliver shifted his position and rubbed his hip. He was wondering how good the light was, how drunk Hardin was, how sure he was of himself. He slid his hand into the jumper pocket. When he clasped the cold bone grip of the pistol it was like shaking hands with an old friend.

"Help me up," he said.

"You don't need up. You've wound up what string you had and this is where you was when it played out."

"Help me up so I can lean agin the wall. I don't want to die on my back like a snake you rocked to death."

"All right," Hardin said expansively. "Even if you was a snake I believe I've about pulled your teeth."

He tilted the rifle against the wall and Oliver lifted his left hand toward Hardin and Hardin grasped it. Oliver fired the first shot through the denim and the concussion was enormous in the small room, showering them with splinters and flakes of flourpaste and dead spiders. Even at this range the shot was high and slammed into the loft and he withdrew the piece and fired again. Hardin's face was slack with wonder. He'd thrown up a hand as if he might bat away the bullets with flesh and bone and two fingers disappeared in a pink mist of blood and bonemeal. He was still clasping Oliver's hand. When he finally hit Hardin in the chest Hardin was abruptly jerked from his grip like some soul lost to floodwaters. "Oh let me," he was saying when the fourth bullet struck him but Oliver never found out what he wanted. Hardin got up even with the dark hole charred in his face and then he fell heavily back.

The cold winter constellations spun on, ever paler with the advent of dawn. It was very cold and the night seemed absolutely still. With the passing hours a gray, lusterless light began to suffuse the world. In the east a pale band of paler gray paled further still. Shapes began to accrue form out of shadow and here a star winked out and was no more. Another, the stars were folding. Far in the east the last one burned like a point of white fire and vanished and rose slowly washed the bare blue trees. The world gleamed in its shroud of frost. A mist crept down from the pit and hung there shifting bluely in the wan light.

After a time out of the sound of creaking leather and jangling metal an old stifflegged man appeared leading a horse. The breaths of man and horse plumed in the bitter air like smoke. A rope was knotted into the tracechains and what kept the rope tautened was a man dragged splaylegged across the frozen whorls of earth. The old man did not so much as glance at the house. Man and horse and the curious burden vanished alike in the thick brush shrouding the pit spectral and revenantial and insubstantial as something that might never have been. They were in there for some time, then only the old man and the horse came back out and went back the way they had come.

At length a yellow dog came stealthily up out of the woods and watched the house before approaching it warily. It paced the perimeter of the yard and paused and lay on its belly watching the house as if it expected someone to come out and stone it away. When no one did it arose boldly and crossed to the rear of the house and began to forage in the garbage can by the back stoop. The can tilted, fell, rattled on the frozen ground. After it fed the dog raised its head scenting the air and its hackles rose uneasily and it moved covertly toward the bordering woods and vanished into them.

Early Sunday morning the jailer unlocked the door to the bullpen and motioned for Winer. "The governor called," he said. "Your pardon come through at the last minute."

"What about me?" Chessor wanted to know.

"They just left word to let Winer out. They ain't set your bond yet and I doubt they's a man in the county can go it when they do."

"Well, hellfire."

The town was locked in Sunday quietude, a city under siege. He walked on listening to his footfalls, his discolored reflection pacing him in storefront glass like a maltreated familiar. De Vries's cabstand was the only place open and it was here that Winer heard the news.

"Where did you hear that?"

"Hell, it's all over town. I heard it so much I don't even remember where I heard it first."

"And they know it's Pa?"

"What I heard they ain't no doubt about it and now they sayin old man Oliver seen it done and kept quiet all these years. They say Bellwether's gone after a warrant now. Murder one, and I hope the son of a bitch gets the lectric chair."

"Does Hardin know?"

"If he don't he's the only one. I seen that black Packard go through about daylight. He may be a lost ball in the high weeds."

"Somebody's giving me a runaround."

"Well, it's not me," de Vries said. "I'll tell you anything I can."

"Where's he at then?"

"Who? Bellwether?"

"Hellfire. My pa. What'd they do with him?"

"Well, it was just a skull was all. What I heard they sent it off to them scientists. I guess to see who it was and all. I reckon Bellwether and Oliver was waitin to see for sure it was him before they told you about it."

"Sent it off," Winer said in wonder. He turned and opened the door and went through it.

"Hey, I thought you wanted a cab," de Vries called but Winer had already gone from his sight.

Winer walked down to the Snowwhite and cornered there and went through an alley past the garbagestrewn back doors of merchants and exited by the General Cafe. He seemed unaware of where he was and such Sunday faces as he met he did not acknowledge. He crossed the street against the light and went on across the bare courthouse yard and up the wide steps to the double door. It was locked. He descended the steps and went around to the side. He peered through darkened glass to an invisible interior. He pushed against them but these doors were locked as well. He sat on the concrete stairs to wait. A cold wind sang off the stone coping and bore scraps of dirty paper before it. He had no coat and after a time he began to shiver and he got up. The temperature was falling.

The house when he found it was guarded by two stone lions but theirs was a fallen grandeur. Their whitewashed flesh peeled away in great slashes of plaster and they watched this transgressor with a blind ferocity, their eyes impacted with grime. Winer passed between them down a worn path of faded brick leached into the earth to the wooden doorsteps. The house was a nondescript white frame needing a coat of paint. A knocker mounted in a gargoyle's face hinted the same dubious parentage as the stone lions. He knocked and waited.

He had turned away to go when the door opened.

"Yes?"

He approached the door. He was facing a young woman a few years older than himself. She stood waiting, smoothed a wing of brown hair back from her brow. She had a plain, honest face, her eyes were a soft brown, he thought the way a fawn's eyes must look: there was a curious quality of vulnerability about them, as if they ever sought out the things that would hurt her.

"I was just looking for Sheriff Bellwether."

"I'm sorry, he's not here right now. Is there any way I could help you?"

"Do you know where he is?"

"He left for Franklin early this morning to see Judge Larkin. I'm not sure when he'll be back."

"Well."

"Will you come in? Is it something important you wanted to see him about?"

"I just wanted to see him a minute."

Something he was not aware of in his face touched her, for she stood aside and opened the door wider. "Come on in," she said. "I was just about to have a cup of coffee. Would you care for a cup?"

"I need to be getting on," Winer said but he stepped into the room. She brought him black, steaming coffee in a thin china cup and he drank it sitting awkwardly on the edge of the sofa. He looked about the austere room. There was a makeshift quality about it but it was very clean. A young Bellwether tinted pink watched from a gilt oval frame on the wall, an overseas cap tilted rakishly over his right eyebrow. The woman looked up from her sewing and Winer was watching her.

"Did he say what he wanted to see that Franklin judge about?"

"I'm sorry, he didn't." She smiled. "My husband keeps his business to himself."

He set the halfful cup aside. "Thank you for the coffee," he said. "I'll be getting on."

"He'll be back after awhile. You could leave a message with me. I'll see he gets it."

"No," Winer said, getting up. "I'll leave it somewhere else."

She looked at him strangely with her tremulous brown eyes and he knew she'd misunderstood him. "It's just something I can't talk about," he said. "Thank you for the coffee." He turned and went on out the door. She made to call to him but thought better of it.

He went down the walk to the edge of the street and paused by the blind lions. He rested a moment on a stone shoulder so cold it might have been cast from ice. Displaced beast from climes to the north, strange twilit sunless worlds.

An old grief that should have long ago been allayed by time abruptly twisted in him like a knife. A grief ten years gone, by now the debris of time should have buried it. Ten years. Ten years who knew where and all the words spoken words of denunciation. A bitter redemption touched him, a sense of faith fulfilled, but there was no satisfaction in being right, he would gladly have been proven wrong could events be altered. He turned with blurred vision and went on up the street. She watched from a window. When he was out of sight the curtain fell to.

Along about midmorning a taxicab arrived at Hardin's. It stopped in the yard, idling white puffs of exhaust into the cold air, and Jiminiz got out. He moved stiffly as if his joints did not function properly. His face was swollen and discolored. He slammed the door to and stood studying the unsmoking chimney of the house bemusedly. The driver got out as well. The driver was a wizened, ferretfaced man with quick black eyes that darted uneasily about the yard. He wore a leather changepurse on his belt and he made change for the bill Jiminiz gave him. He got back into the idling car and turned it and went back the way he'd come.

Jiminiz went around back to the long beerjoint and was there only a minute or two before he came back and mounted the porch. He knocked at the front door, waited. He leaned against the door-jamb smoking and when knocking harder brought no response he turned the knob and went in.

Directly he came back out. He went across the yard again to the rear and paused by the litter of papers and cans on the earth study-ing the frozen ground. Something seemed to catch his eye, for he leaned forward hands on knees then straightened and went toward the pit and vanished into the bracken.

He was running awkwardly when he came out of the brush. He ran on to the hardpan of the road and slowed to a fast walk. A hun-dred feet or so down the road he halted and stood still and seemed to be listening to some far-off sound. He looked down the red road. He looked back toward the bleak, still house and studied the slatecolored sky. Nameless winter birds foraged the ruined garden and watched him with hard agate eyes. They took wing and flew patternlessly above him. He went back to the house and went in leaving the door ajar. He came out carrying a nickelplated pistol in his right hand and a cigarbox in his left. He paused a moment on the stoop. He pock-eted the pistol and opened the cigarbox. It was full of money. He began to count it, leafing hurriedly through it, then he gave it up and went back onto the road. This time he didn't look back.

The day drew on. It had not warmed as the day progressed nor had the frost melted. The sun grew more remote and obscure. At its zenith it was no more than an orb of heatless light above the glade. A bank of pale clouds arose in the west and ascended the heavens and beyond them the sky looked dark and threatening. A wind arose. It teased such dead leaves as remained on the trees and sang eerily in the loose tin on the barn. The stallion whinnied from the barnlot and came pacing down the length of barbed-wire fence, its hooves ringing on mire frozen hard as stone. The day grew darker yet. The sun vanished. The wind carried chill on its knife edge and a few pellets of sleet rattled on the tin like birdshot. The sleet fell and lay unmelting in the stony whorls of ice, a wind from the pit blew scraps of paper like dirty snow.

When Winer came he came walking. He came the shortcut across the field and down the branch to the house. He crossed the yard without caution as if he were impervious now to anything the world could do to him. He crossed the porch and pounded on the door and waited. Knocked again. He paused and stood uncertainly. Leaned to a curtained window and shading his eyes peered in, saw only his sepia reflection in opaque glass.

He turned, a gangling figure graceless in the stiff wind. He went down the steps and echoing Jiminiz's movements or moving in patterns preordained he went around the house and through the strewn garbage and pounded on the back door. No one came. He stood before the raw wood honkytonk with its red brick grouped in banded bundles awaiting a mason who'd never come and he tried the door but it was locked. He walked back to where the Packard was always parked and ran a hand through his wild hair like a cartoon figure miming perplexity and leaned to the frozen ground as if he might divine how long the car had been gone and its destination.

He climbed back onto the porch and tried the door. It opened. He peered into the cloistered dark but some old restraint engendered by his upbringing stayed him from trespass and he pulled the door to with a curious air of finality.

He sat on the stoop a time though he did not expect anyone to return. The sleet had not ceased and it had begun to spit snow. He sat wrapping his knees with his arms and it began to snow harder, the snow intensifying first at the border of the far field and obscuring the treeline with a curtain of billowing white. He seemed ill at ease and uncertain as to where he should be and what he should be doing and at length the cold brought him off the steps and into the yard. He went off into the snow turning up his collar against the wind.

At dusk the yellow cur came up from the branch-run and prowled through the garbage without finding anything and it sniffed the air with disquiet and lay down on the earth. The earth was powdered with a thin sheath of white but it was fine, dry snow and it lay in eternally drifting windrows. As dusk drew on the square of yellow light the bedroom window threw deepened and the dog approached and stood in it as if it fostered warmth. It seemed to snow harder where the light fell. At last the dog turned with its tail curled between its legs and followed the scent back to the pit.

Winer had been gone with no luggage save the weight of his father's knife against his leg and no destination save the memory of Amber Rose saying, "Natchez, Mississippi," for six months when William Tell Oliver found the first jar of money.

All that spring he had watched the scavengers arriving, a seemingly unending stream of them prowling Hovington's place, tearing up the floorboards, ripping loose the weatherboarding in splintered shards, prying out the brick beneath the flue until at last it toppled in a rain of mud and broken bricks and soot, all these greedy folk doing more work that spring than they'd ever done before, loath to leave even at night lest another find Hardin's fortune so that at night he could see their lanterns flitting like fireflies about the glade, flashlights in random isobars of yellow light appearing and disappearing like spirit lights in old ghost tales of his youth or warnings prophesying direr events yet to be.

Silhouetted black and motionless against the sun he watched from the ridge like some strange outrider of life, watcher rather than participant, some ungainly prophet from olden times, leaned on his stick watching with bemused arrogance the turmoil of lesser mortals and it came to him one day that old mad Lyle Hodges had been digging not in the wrong place but at the wrong time, through some peculiar quirk in time he had been digging feverishly and obsessively for fruitjars that would not even be buried for another fifty years.

Checking on a patch of twoprong ginseng growing in the shade of an enormous beech he was struck by an aberration of the land

ome subtle difference in country he had known all his life.
ng to where the contour of the slope was altered, he dug with
the point of his handcarved stick, knelt at last to withdraw with
amused contempt a halfgallon jar of Hardin's money, heavy with
coin, the greasy, wadded bills, strange summer provender laid by
for harder times than these.

By the last of August he had found four others. He stored them
at first in the pantry behind old jars of canned goods, ancient cans
of muscadine jelly long gone to burgundy sugar. He grew uneasy
and pried up floorboards in different rooms, scooped out black
loam, consigned the jars to earth once more. He was a man of a
thousand small cautions so he drove a steel stake beside each jar. "If
the house burns and I don't all I'll have to do is kick through the
ashes," he told himself.

For it's young Winer's money, he thought, it is money owed
him for a wrong done long ago.

He waited and the year drew on into a hot, dry summer and the
empty road baked whitely in the sun. The scavengers didn't come
anymore and tales began to arise about Hovington's place. It was
told cursed, haunted, a barren patch of earth forever luckless. One
night a group of boys torched the house and then the honkytonk
and the old man watched the hot red glare, the sparks cascading upward in the updraft from the pit. The next day he walked gingerly
through the hot ashes and the scorched brush to the lip of the
abyss. Felt its cool, fetid breath. Now there was only the pit, timeless, enigmatic, profoundly alien.

Time passed and he began to feel that Winer wasn't coming
back. At last he began to think him dead. He knew that the world
was wide in its turnings and it was fraught with dark alleyways and
pastoral footpaths down which peril lurked with a patience rivaling
that of the very old.

I never needed nobody anyway, he told himself. Nary one of
them, then or now, and at last he was touched with a cold and solitary peace.

For he had the white road baking hot in the noonday sun, the wavering blue treeline, the fierce, sudden violence of summer storms. At night the moon tracked its accustomed course and the timeless whippoorwills tolled from the dark and they might have been the selfsame whippoorwills that called to him in his youth.

That's all that matters, he told himself with a spare and bitter comfort. Those were the things that time did not take away from you. They were the only things that lasted.